COLE GIBSEN

This book is a work of fiction. Names, characters, places, and incidents are the product of the author's imagination or are used fictitiously. Any resemblance to actual events, locales, or persons, living or dead, is coincidental.

Entangled Publishing, LLC
2614 South Timberline Road
Suite 109
Fort Collins, CO 80525
Visit our website at www.entangledpublishing.com.

Embrace is an imprint of Entangled Publishing, LLC.

Edited by Liz Pelletier
Cover design by Louisa Maggio
Cover art from Shutterstock

Manufactured in the United States of America

First Edition July 2015

embrace

Chapter One

Ashlyn

A girl—she can't be more than sixteen—stands on the other side of the counter from me, twirling her long blond hair around her finger. She stares at the ceiling and huffs loudly. "God, can this take any *longer*?" she mutters to the polo-shirt-wearing boy next to her, but I know her words are directed at me.

I snap a clear, plastic lid on her cup and slide it over to her. "There you go!" I force a wide smile even though what I really want is to rip the *obvious* fake extensions off her bitchy, little head. Unfortunately, I need this job too badly to risk doing anything that would get me fired. "Thanks for visiting Live Wire." *Now please go away.*

The girl curls her lip in a sneer. "What is *this*?"

I manage to keep my smile from slipping. "It's a nonfat double shot mocha frappe. Just like you ordered."

"Uh, *no.* It's not *just* like I ordered"—her eyes dart to my nametag—"*Ashlyn.* I specifically asked for *no* whip."

I twist my fingers in my apron to keep from reaching out to strangle her. I make it a point to write a customer's order on the cup exactly as they say it, when they say it. And there's nothing on the damn cup about no whip.

The guy beside her shifts uncomfortably. "Becca, it's not that big a deal."

She glares at him, and even though he's a foot taller than she is, he flinches. "Fine. I'll remember next time to dumb down my order, because obviously doing things right is too hard for some people." She flings a hand in my direction, and her fingers hit the side of the cup. It wobbles, balancing on the bottom rim before tipping over. Mocha frappe and whip cream erupt through the straw hole in the domed lid and all over the counter. She gives me a blank look. "Oops."

I don't know what does it, exactly. Maybe it's the lack of remorse in her eyes, her callous words, or the mocha that continues to gurgle out of the cup, but whatever it is, when I look across the counter, I find she's transformed. My stepdad stands in her place, glaring at me, his lips pursed, ready to spew venom more deadly than that of any viper.

Panic squeezes my ribs in a too-tight embrace. He doesn't have to speak because I already know what he'll say. His voice never stops whispering inside my head. First, he'll call me stupid for screwing up the order. Then he'll tell me how clumsy I am for not catching the drink. And finally, he'll tell me how lazy I am because shouldn't I already have a rag in hand to clean it up?

Right. I need a rag! My pulse thrashes inside my head, drowning out all sound from the coffee shop. I kneel and frantically push aside bundles of napkins and stacks of Styrofoam cups in my search for a rag. I have to clean up this mess. I have minutes, no, seconds before—

A hand clamps down on my shoulder, and I gasp.

"Don't sweat it, Ash," a girl's voice says behind me. "I got this."

I blink several times, and slowly the coffeehouse falls back into place around me. I glance over my shoulder and find Emily—the human equivalent of a tattooed and pierced Tinkerbelle. My coworker slides a freshly made frappe—*sans whip*—beside the fallen drink and leans against the counter, leveling her gaze on the girl. "Have a *great* day," she says, but her tone implies anything but.

The girl's eyes narrow and she opens her mouth to speak, but Emily cuts her off by biting onto her lip ring and softly clicking the metal against her teeth. The girl takes a step backward, and when the guy next to her follows, she elbows him in the ribs and motions to the cup on the counter.

He grabs it, but not before giving Emily a wink. The girl behind him tugs his arm and pulls him out the door.

"What a bitch," Emily mutters and pushes off the counter. "Her parents should be publicly flogged. I mean, good God, you know a girl like that has never heard the word *no* spoken once in her entire life."

"Just one more reason not to have kids," I say before I can stop myself.

"One *more* reason?" She quirks an eyebrow. "You got a problem with kids?"

"Can't stand them," I answer. "All the whining and crying…ugh." I make a face. I actually really like kids. But the lie is so much simpler than explaining that, given my upbringing, I haven't the faintest idea how to raise a child without scarring them for life.

Emily stares at me a moment longer before finally shrugging. "Huh. Well, to each their own."

"Yep." I stand, dust my hands on my apron, and try to appear as though I didn't almost have a panic attack five seconds ago. But then I look at the counter and the mocha still spilled across the laminate. My pulse quickens. "I have to clean that up or else—" I swallow the words before they leave my tongue.

"I got it." Emily glides past me, snatching a towel and spray bottle from a hook on the wall. "If you want, you can take five. Go outside and have a cigarette or something."

"I don't smoke." I shake my head and watch, holding my breath, until she tosses the cup in the trash and wipes up the mess.

"Maybe you should start," Emily says as she returns the rag and cleaner to the wall. She turns to me and folds her arms across her chest. "You look a little…stressed."

Understatement of the year. But it's not like I can afford to tell anyone just how thin the rope is that I'm walking on. I need this job too badly to do anything to jeopardize it with my brand of crazy. Instead I say, "I don't get a lot of sleep."

"Ah, a fellow insomniac." Emily grabs her own iced latte from beneath the counter and raises it in a toast before taking a long draw from the straw.

"Uh, yeah," I agree, because it's much easier than admitting the real reason I don't get much sleep is because of the paper-thin walls of my apartment and the endless stream of men visiting my roommate at all hours of the night. So rather than blast Emily with TMI, I direct my attention to the tattoos decorating her arms. There's so much going on, it's hard to pick out just one image. But among the cluster I spot the hecklers from the Muppet movies, a heart wrapped in barbed wire, and what appears to be an espresso maker. "I like your ink."

"Yeah?" She grins and twists her arms around so I can see them from all angles. "My guy does great work."

"Your guy?"

She relaxes her arms at her side. "My tattoo guy. Not my guy as in my boyfriend or anything because, ew, gross."

I can sympathize. The guy who'd given me my first and only tattoo was bald, about three hundred pounds, and desperately in need of deodorant. *That* was a fun hour.

"So." Emily leans back on the counter and crosses her legs. "How about you? Do you have any ink?"

"Uh… " *Shit.* I remember too late why this isn't a safe topic for discussion. I reflexively hide my arm behind my back, but her eyes widen and I know she's already seen it.

"Oh, no. You *didn't*!" She pushes off the counter and snatches my arm before I can pull away. Once she reads the evidence in the crook of my elbow she groans and throws my arm back at me. "You did. You got inked with a guy's name!" She shakes her head. "Fuck. That's the number one tattoo rule, and you broke it!"

My cheeks burn fire-hot, and I self-consciously clasp my hand over my arm. "I know, I know. It was a stupid thing to do. I just thought—" But the words trail off because I can't bear to admit out loud that I thought a lasting relationship was something that could happen to me. And now I have this guy's name etched on my forearm as a permanent reminder that the only person I can trust not to hurt me is me.

I won't be caught off-guard again.

Emily clucks her tongue. "You can't walk around with some douchebag's brand on your body like a damn cow."

I shrug. "I haven't had the time to get it fixed." Or, more accurately, I haven't had the money. As someone who'd spent several months living out of my '05 Jetta, I have more important things to spend my cash on—like food.

"You have to make time. Look, I don't mean to pry." She puts a hand on my shoulder, and it's all I can do not to back out of her grasp. It's not that she's hurting me, but I'm not used to being touched, much less by someone I hardly know. My skin itches beneath her fingers. "But you seem like you're dealing with...*something*," Emily continues. "It's not my business to ask what that is. All I'm saying is, having some guy's name on your skin, where you see it *every* day, isn't good. Once it's gone, I'm sure you'll feel a whole lot better."

Would I? I look at the elegant, loopy script of Chris's name, and my stomach twists into a knot. Chris insisted it would be the ultimate declaration of my love. And like the fool eighteen-year-old I was then, I believed him. I was scared, and alone, and desperately needed to believe someone cared about me. But now he was gone and I was forced to wear my mistake like a scarlet letter. I rub my palm against the tattoo as if I could smudge it away like Crayola marker. "It would be nice to have it covered. But I haven't had the money—"

"*Psh.*" Emily waves, cutting me off. "Don't worry about the money. I'll take care of it."

My hands fall to my side. "Oh, no, I couldn't."

She gives me a pointed look. "Yes, you could. C'mon,

Ash. Walking around with an ex's name on your arm is bad luck."

I don't believe in bad luck. As far as I know, I'd never walked under a ladder, broken a mirror, spilled salt, or done anything else to bring about the day my mother came home with the man who would become my stepdad. Sometimes shitty things happened whether you deserved them or not, and no crystal, no clover, and no horseshoe would change the fact. I knew this because back then, when I was ten, I'd tried all of those things, only to have them let me down like the frauds they were.

"How about tonight?" Emily asks, breaking through my thoughts. "After work?"

I blink at her, trying to sense her motivations. People don't do something for you without wanting something in return. "But the money… I don't know when I'll be able to pay you back."

She shrugs. "It's not about the money. Besides, if it makes you feel better, I won't actually be *paying*. My guy owes me a favor. So how about it? I'll make the call, and after work, you and I will go to the tattoo parlor where you'll get that covered"—she motions to my tattoo—"and that Chris guy will be nothing but a faded memory. You'll have a fresh start." She smiles at me—a wide, warm smile that displays all of her slightly coffee-stained teeth.

There's something about her. Maybe it's her infectious smile or the hope brimming in her eyes, but I can't turn her down. Besides, it would be nice to pretend my problems extend no further than where to get a tattoo on a Friday night and what party to hit afterward. To be a normal twenty-year-old. For once.

"All right." I laugh. "Let's do it."

"Yay!" She claps her hands together. "You won't regret it. Again, my guy is the best. I'll call him right now."

She reaches for the phone, and my eyes flick to the digital clock above the bags of ground coffee we have for sale on the far wall. At ten until ten, it's nearly closing time, but we'll still be here another forty minutes or so, counting the registers and cleaning equipment. Despite the bright lights in the seating area, darkness creeps around the front windows, seeking to come in. Ten miles away, there's a house shrouded in darkness, where every light is extinguished promptly at ten, and noise is forbidden to the extent that television and phone cords are pulled from the walls, bundled up, and hidden inside locked drawers.

I fight the memory away, and to hide the tremor in my hands, I grab a sleeve of cups from under the counter and stack them on the shelf. "It's probably too late to go tonight," I say. "Don't most tattoo places close at ten?"

Emily nods and punches the numbers on the telephone keypad. "Yeah. But my guy will stay open late for us. Like I said, he owes me."

Must be some favor. Still, I shrug and resume my stacking. Whatever Emily has going on with the tattoo guy to warrant special favors, it's none of my business.

"Hey!" she practically shouts into the receiver. "Don't close up yet. I'm coming by after work because I have a friend who needs a cover up." She's silent as the person on the other end speaks. I can't hear what they're saying, but Emily's mouth twitches into a frown. "Don't be an ass, Lane. You know you owe me." This time, she smiles. "I know. But it's not like you have plans or anything." She waits a second before laughing. "Awesome, you're the best!" She hangs up the phone and turns to me. "We're on!"

I force a smile even though some of my own excitement has faded after listening to her exchange. "Are you sure? I mean, it didn't sound like he was too thrilled about it."

"Lane?" Emily rolls her eyes as she walks to the front door. "He's not excited about anything. God forbid we keep him from watching whatever car show happens to be on cable." She flips over the open sign, locks the deadbolt, and leans against the glass. "Don't worry. He'll get over it. But just to be on the safe side, ignore everything that comes out of his mouth. He can be kind of moody."

A lump wedges in the back of my throat. *Great.* Another Friday night spent with an asshole. And *this* one would have a needle jabbing into my arm. "I don't know, Emily. This is sounding less and less like a good idea. Maybe I can just make an appointment for a time when his shop is open?"

"Don't be ridiculous!" Emily skips behind the counter and hits a button on the register. A second later the cash drawer shoots open and the end-of-shift report spits out. She thumbs through the dollar bills in the drawer. "It's no problem, really. It's not like he has anything better to do. And if he says anything to you, just tell him to shut the fuck up."

"*Right.*"

She shrugs. "That's what I do."

I don't doubt it.

As I gather the dirty ceramic coffee mugs and saucers from the tables and deposit them inside a bus bin, I can't help but wonder what it would be like to be Emily—what her childhood must have been like to have made her so confident and unabashed. I bet she never had rules about what areas she was allowed to occupy when her parents were home. Or that she never had assigned seating in every room. And she certainly didn't have a novel-length list of things she wasn't to touch inside the house.

"You should try it sometime," Emily tells me as I walk past her on my way to the dishwasher.

I pause. "Try what?"

"Telling someone to fuck off. You need to stand up for yourself, Ash."

I rest the bin of dirty dishes against my hip and turn to face her. "I stood up for myself, once," I say, though I don't know why—I've never said anything to anyone before about my time in the house. Maybe it's because I'm out now, and the worst is finally over. Or maybe it's because I feel like I owe Emily an explanation for my earlier breakdown.

"Just once?" Emily quirks an amused eyebrow. "What happened? Did you tell the priest and he made you do a dozen *Hail Mary's*?"

"Not quite," I answer, surprising even myself with the truth. "A busted rib, kicked out of the house, and all of my stuff burned in a bonfire in the backyard—that's what standing up for myself got me."

The pennies Emily is counting slip through her fingers and clatter to the floor like copper raindrops. A few of them roll beneath the edge of the counter, where we'll never reach them, and I cringe. I know our manager will have a fit because the register will be short.

But Emily appears not to notice—or maybe she doesn't care about things as trivial as registers a few cents short. Her lips part, but for the longest time she doesn't move, doesn't say a word, until finally she whispers, "*Jesus,* Ash, I—"

I shake my head, stopping her. I don't want her sympathy; that's not why I told her. And it isn't until this very second, when the ropes of tension ease just a fraction from around my chest, that I realize *why* I told her. I wanted, just for a moment, to spit out the secret that's been sitting on my tongue like a mass of needles.

"That was over a year ago." I readjust my grip on the bus tub. "I'm fine now," I tell her in a way I hope sounds convincing—both to her and myself. I mean, maybe the exact definition of *fine* isn't struggling to pay rent for a shabby two-bedroom apartment that I share with a stripper, but it sure is a hell of a step up from living out of my car like I had been a year ago. And even if I'm not fine, I will be someday, when I have a place of my own and am making my living as a poet. After all, when you're a writer, suffering is just more ink for the page.

The thought pulls the corners of my lips into a smile. I still have hope. It was the one thing that bastard wasn't able to burn to dust in the backyard.

Emily snaps her mouth shut and leans against the counter. "You know, Ash, if you need to work on your self-confidence, you can start by telling *me* to shut the fuck up. It's not like I don't deserve it."

I grin at her. "Shut the fuck up, Emily."

She smiles back. "You know what just happened here? I think we became friends. Now if you'd be so kind to take care of those dishes while I finish counting the drawer, we can head to the tattoo parlor and get you all fixed up."

My smile slips. "Sounds good," I say, even though I know better. It's not that I don't have hope, I just know nothing as simple as a tattoo cover-up is going to *fix* me. But I don't say so, not aloud. Because tonight I want to pretend I'm the kind of girl who could be friends with someone like Emily, a girl who goes out on Friday nights.

A girl whose demons don't run deeper than the ink staining her skin.

Chapter Two

Ashlyn

I follow Emily as she pushes open the wood-framed glass door and walks into the tattoo studio. The door closes behind us with a soft click. Out of habit, I reach back and discreetly turn the knob to make sure it doesn't lock behind me. Only after I've confirmed I haven't been trapped inside do my coiled muscles unwind.

Laminated posters of tattoo designs, everything from butterflies and roses to laughing demons and decaying corpses, fight for space on the cluttered walls. The black and white tile floor gleams, and the room smells like a mix of pizza and antiseptic.

The pizza smell I find odd until I spot the cardboard box sitting on a glass case filled with various barbells and hoops for piercings. My stomach growls, but Emily appears not to notice over the loud rock music blasting from the speakers mounted in the corners of the room. God, how long has it been since I had pizza? My mouth waters. Eating out isn't exactly a luxury I can afford. My meals mainly consist of nutritious dietary staples like instant mac and cheese and peanut butter sandwiches.

Emily walks over to the pizza box, flips the top open, and pulls out a slice. After tearing into a piece of pepperoni, she slides the box in my direction. "Want one?"

Nervously, I glance around. I know I should decline. It's basically stealing to take food without it being offered by the purchaser. But the smell of cheese and crust claws into my empty gut, and I can't refuse. I pull a slice of pepperoni out of the box and nearly die when the warm mozzarella hits my tongue.

"Lane! Hey, dickwad!" Emily calls out despite her full mouth. "We're here!"

Her greeting startles me, and a piece of pizza lodges inside my throat. I sputter and hack to dislodge it. I'm still wheezing when a dark purple curtain covering the doorway behind the counter opens, and a guy steps through.

Suddenly, I can't breathe, and I'm no longer sure it's because of the pizza.

The guy is tall and lean. Colorful tattoos decorate the length of both of his arms. Most of the designs are abstract swirls of color, but amidst the artistic chaos one drawing stands out above the rest: the name Harper written in bright red ink on his collarbone, peeking out from the edge of his white V-neck T-shirt. His dark hair is messy, but in a way that looks intended, and his face has the scruff of someone who's forgotten to shave for several days. His eyes—the color of dark chocolate—narrow when he catches sight of us. He folds his arms and a tendon flexes along his jaw. "Unbelievable, Em. First, you keep me from my bed. Now you're eating my dinner?"

I hold my breath to stop my sputtering and subtly lower the pizza to my side. I feel like a dog that's been caught stealing food off the table.

"Keep your panties on, princess." She slides the pizza box across the counter toward him. "We took *two* pieces. Chill."

His eyes flick to my face, and he frowns before turning to Emily. "Is she choking?"

His question doesn't make sense. I think I would know if I were choking. But then my vision goes a little hazy around the edges, and it dawns on me I haven't taken a breath in some time.

"She's fine," Emily answers. She thumps me on the back, easing the lodged pizza down my throat.

I gasp loudly and take several ragged breaths before I add, "Fine. I'm fine."

"Uh huh." He arches an eyebrow, and my cheeks heat several degrees. Turning away, he snatches a slice of pizza and tears into it. "I'm going to grab a bottle of water," he announces between bites. "You guys want one? I thought I'd ask, even though I know you'll only help yourself."

"Why yes, Lane," Emily says in a singsong voice as she grabs another slice. "I would love a bottle of water. How thoughtful."

I can only nod.

Lane shakes his head and disappears behind the curtain. Once he's gone, I turn to Emily. "You said he was gross," I say, trying my best to sound casual despite the fact my pulse is buzzing like a livewire. "He is *not* gross."

A sly smirk pulls at her lips. "I never said *he* was gross. I said he was not my boyfriend because *that* would be gross—he's my brother."

Her brother? Now that she mentions it, the resemblance is obvious—they both have the same angled chin and sloped nose. "Why didn't you just say that?"

She pulls a pepperoni off her slice of pizza and deposits it on her tongue. "He's the best damn tattoo artist in the state—maybe even the entire Midwest. But people don't tend to believe compliments when given by family members." She pauses, and her smile widens. "Wait. Back up. You think he's *not* gross? What's that supposed to mean?"

I jerk back. "Nothing. I—I didn't mean anything." A blush burns up my neck. I quickly take a bite of pizza large enough to inhibit speaking. I point to my mouth and shrug.

Emily's gaze flicks to the curtain Lane disappeared through. "Listen, Ash, there's something you should know about Lane."

I can't help it. Curiosity pulls at me like marionette stings and I lean forward.

"Earlier you said—" She shakes her head. "No, forget earlier. It doesn't matter." She licks her lips and glances down at her lap. Idly, she pulls another pepperoni from her pizza. "Here's the deal. You're not the first girl to think he's *not gross.* But Lane's an ass. I can say that because I'm his sister and I love him. He's a dickhead. Don't get me wrong—he's had some really bad shit happen to him so, in a way, he's earned the right to be a dick." She shrugs. "So just in case you were getting any ideas, just don't. Steer clear, Ash. You seem like a really sweet girl who's dealing with some stuff.

And Lane will only bring you more pain."

I swallow my bite of pizza, and it feels like a lump of lead sliding down my throat. I'm not sure whether to be offended Emily doesn't think I can take care of myself, or appreciative that she cares enough to warn me. Either way, it wasn't like I was seconds away from jumping on top of him. I mean, I have hormones, but I also have self-control. Besides, I'm not looking for a relationship right now. I'm still trying to walk the tightrope that is my life alone—much less with another person in my balancing act.

"Your brother is an asshole," I say. "Duly noted."

Emily smiles and tosses her pizza crust into the trash can beside the counter. "Good. You'll thank me someday. And, besides, he's technically already involved." She raises her hands and air quotes the word *involved*. I want to ask her what she means when Lane brushes past the curtain carrying the water bottles.

"Here." He hands me a bottle and places another next to Emily. "Since you're keeping me at work late *and* eating my dinner, I really hope this is going to be worth my while."

"Nope." Emily grins as she untwists the cap. "You're going to do this for free."

"What?" His eyes widen, and he slams his unopened bottle against the counter. "Why the hell would I do that?"

"Because of last weekend." She takes a gulp of water and screws the lid back on. "You owe me. And I'd like to transfer my favor to Ashlyn."

He turns his heated gaze on me, and it's all I can do not to shrink against the wall. I want to tell him I didn't put Emily up to this, but the words jumble inside my mouth, hot and thick. Finally, I murmur, "I…I can come back some other time."

"No." Emily slides off the counter. "We're here and you're going to get this done tonight." She presses a finger against her brother's chest. "You're not the only one who's had a rough go of it." His eyes darken, but she appears not to notice. "Ash needs a clean start, and that begins with getting this douchebag's name off her arm. Can you please take the corncob out of your ass long enough to do me this one favor?"

"Fine." Lane sidesteps his sister and walks toward me. "But now you'll owe *me*."

He stalks toward me like a tiger on the hunt. Anger radiates off of him in prickly waves that make my skin itch the closer he gets. I search for an escape, but Lane stands between me and the door. I look at Emily, begging her with my eyes to intervene, but she ignores me, fumbling inside the pizza box for another slice.

Lane stops in front of me and holds out a hand. "Let's have it." Everything about him is hard, from the muscular lines of his chest, which I can see outlined through the thin fabric of his T-shirt, to the frown that appears to have taken permanent residence on his lips. When I make no move to respond, he sighs. "Your tattoo. I need to know what I'm covering up."

Despite the fact that every instinct screams for me to run from the room, I hold up my arm. I don't know why. Maybe it's because I'm so damn used to doing what I'm told, because even though I'm out of the house, I'm still trapped, held hostage by everything I've endured. Disgust washes over me like acid, and it's directed at no one but myself. I should be better now—stronger. But Lane's proven that even after all this time I'm still the same coward as when I was locked inside the house. So damn weak.

He snatches my wrist and pulls me forward so suddenly I gasp. His grip is surprisingly firm and I know even if I tried to break away, I wouldn't be able to. I'm trapped. The thought jumpstarts my heart into a skittering frenzy. He lifts my arm over my head and leans close enough I can smell his cologne—something light with a hint of citrus. He peers at the name etched on my skin and his brow furrows. "You got branded, huh?" He drops my wrist. "Genius move, cupcake."

Something stirs inside me—the warmth of a spark of anger. I cling to it, fanning it like a flame. Anything is better than being afraid. "I have a name," I say. My words are a small triumph, but I'll take it. Maybe deep inside, I have a backbone after all.

"I'm sure you do." His chin lowers, and he meets my eyes. An amused smirk pulls at his lips. "If you're lucky, I might even bother to learn it."

"Lane!" Emily half chokes, half shouts through her mouthful of pizza. "Be nice."

"It's fine, Em," I say before Lane can respond. I'm glad for the anger simmering through me, burning away my fear. I welcome the feeling of my blood boiling over than of wanting to cower and hide. And even though he's a massive jackass, there's something refreshing about his brutal honestly—he's definitely not the type of guy to tell you what you want to hear.

Using my new courage, I push my shoulders back and meet his gaze. "You're one to talk about genius moves—especially when you have a girl's name tattooed on your chest."

Lane crosses his arms. "That's completely different."

"How's that?" I ask, tossing the remainder of my pizza crust in the trash.

He's almost a foot taller than me, and he leans down, closing the distance between us. Miraculously, I don't flinch. "What Harper and I have is special. It's forever."

My throat goes dry but still I hold my ground. "It would have to be special. No normal girl would put up with your superiority complex."

Emily makes a snorting noise before busting out in laughter. "You've got to hand it to the girl. She's known you less than ten minutes and already has you pegged."

Lane doesn't fold under the weight of my insult like I'd hoped. Instead, he has the nerve to smile. "Where'd you find this one, Em? She's feisty."

Emily playfully swats at his shoulder. "Please, Lane. *Please.* Just this once, pretend to be a normal human being. For me? For your little sister who you love so dearly?"

He makes a face before giving an exaggerated sigh. "*Fine.* I won't be a big meanie to your new little friend." He looks at me and extends his hand. His eyes flash with amusement. "Truce?"

I don't move or bother to answer him. He's so damn unreadable, I can't tell if he's being serious or if this is all a big fucking joke to him.

He doesn't wait for me to take his hand and instead snatches my wrist. "Let's do this, shall we?" With a tug, he ushers me to the curtained door behind the counter.

"Have fun you two," Emily sings behind me. "Lane, I'm headed to Peter's party. You should catch up with me when you're done. You, too, Ash. It's going to be a great party, and

I'd love to see your new ink."

"You're leaving?" I try to wrench free from Lane's grip, but his fingers are unrelenting. My confidence crumbles. If Emily ditches me, it will just be Lane and me *alone.* The thought threads across my chest like the laces of a corset.

"Relax, Ash." Emily drops the last of her crust into the trash can and dusts off her hands. "Lane's bark is worse than his bite. Just don't take any of his shit."

Before I can answer Lane drags me behind the curtain, cutting her off from view.

"See ya!" Emily calls out, her voice muffled by the fabric separating us. A second later the front door chimes as it opens and closes.

Lane releases my hand, and I spin around. The floor in this room is the same black and white tile of the first one. The walls are also decorated with posters of tattoo designs, as well as pictures of real tattoos so brilliant and lifelike, I swear the images are about to burst off of the skin they're inked on. These must be examples of his work and, despite his douchebaggery, I can't help but respect his talent.

"Sit," he orders and points to a large padded chair similar to the kind found in dentist offices. Before I can comply, he drops onto a rolling stool and scoots it up to a cabinet with various instruments and jars on top. He opens a drawer and withdraws a plastic packet with a needle sealed inside and lays it out on the counter. Next, he grabs antiseptic, a small bottle of ink, and a box of black latex gloves and sets them in a neat row.

Now's my chance, I think, as I watch him get organized. I can easily make a break for it while he's distracted. As if reading my mind, he pivots on the stool. "Sit," he says again.

Swallowing hard, I walk to the chair, hating myself a little more with each step. I mean, I really do want the tattoo covered, but I hate that the cost is my self-respect. "I'm not a dog," I mumble.

"My apologies," Lane says. He makes an exaggerated sweeping motion with his arm. "Whilst thou, princess, *please* sitteth down? I knowest thou must be accustomed to thrones, but just this once whilst thou make an exception?"

I frown at him as I slide onto the chair. "You know, it would make things a whole lot easier for both of us if you stopped acting like such a dick."

"Sorry, cupcake." He turns back to the counter and resumes organizing his equipment. He pauses long enough to glance at me over his shoulder, his cheek creasing with a wicked smirk. "Who said I liked things easy?"

Chapter Three

Lane

The girl stares at me from the tattoo chair but says nothing. Good. I'm not really in the mood to talk. The sooner I get this tattoo done, the better. With a waiting list for tattoos and cover-ups that exceeds several months, I feel like I live in my shop and the bed in my house is a poor, neglected friend.

I guess it could be worse. Yes, my workload leaves me exhausted, but I'm making insane money. In the end, isn't that all that matters—making sure I can give Harper and myself the best life possible?

I take the girl's wrist and turn it over, exposing the tattoo. The muscles in her forearm go rigid under my touch. She's afraid. But that's not unusual. Most people start to sweat it the second their ass sits in my chair. I lean close and study her ink. The lines are sloppy. I lightly run my finger over the cursive name. She inhales sharply.

I let go of her arm. "You're scarred. Whoever gave you that tattoo dug too deep. Must've hurt like a motherfucker."

She shrugs, and several strands of her dark, wavy hair tumble over her shoulder. "I don't really remember," she says.

I frown. I don't really have patience for bullshitters. Hell, I don't really have patience for anyone, but the people who come into my salon, sit in my chair, and pretend to be immune to pain really torque me, since they're usually the first to pass out or fall to the ground hurling. "Cupcake, this is scarred to hell. It *had* to hurt."

She just stares at me, blinking those insanely large, blue eyes.

"Okay, fine." I wave a hand dismissively. "All I'm saying is the scar tissue is going to make things a bit tricky."

Her face falls. "You can't do it?"

This time, I laugh. "There's no such thing as a tattoo I can't do. I just said it was going to be tricky is all."

"Good." She glances down at the ink on her arm and quickly looks away in disgust. Whoever the hell Chris is, there's certainly no love lost there.

"What am I covering this up with?" I ask.

"Uh… " She bites her lip. "I don't really know."

"You don't– You're fucking kidding me, right?" When she makes no move to answer, I sweep my hand through my hair and pull it at the root, hoping to relieve the tension building inside my head. "Un-fucking-believable," I mutter. "It's one thing to ask me to stay late, but it's another thing entirely to waste my time by coming here not knowing what you want. Could you be a little more inconsiderate?"

The girl shrinks back against the chair. "I…I'm sorry. Your sister planned this so fast, I didn't have time to think about it. Just cover it up with… " She looks around the room before pointing at a display poster. "A butterfly. That will be fine."

Maybe it's the exhaustion of working a twelve-hour shift. Maybe it's because the clock is creeping closer to midnight. Maybe it's because I know my sister is across town raising hell at some party. Whatever the reason, something inside me snaps.

I cross my arms across my chest to keep from reaching for the girl so I can shake her. "First of all, none of my tattoos are just *fine.* Think of me what you will, but I'm an artist and I never settle for *fine.* Secondly, don't be one of those girls. In some countries, tattoos are a rite of passage, something to be earned—not a Spring Break accessory for your bikini. If you want to pick some lame-ass image off a stock poster, one that a thousand other girls already have inked onto their lower backs, then you should turn around and walk right out the door you came in. Do *not* waste my time."

Her eyes widen. "But—"

"*But,*" I repeat, cutting her off, "if you're not here to cover up a mistake with another mistake, if you actually want something that has meaning and says something about who you are, then you may sit in my chair. So what's it going to be, cupcake?"

Her eyes narrow and her slender fingers curl into fists. "I *want* the tattoo."

"Prove it." I wheel my stool beside her. She smells like coffee and apples—a strange combination, but on her it works. "What rite of passage have you completed? What sets you apart from the thousands of co-eds walking through my door looking for a tramp stamp?"

"I… " She falls silent. Her gaze drops to her laced fingers, sitting on her lap. And just when I think my entire night's been a bust, and I'm going to have to drag her from the room, she looks up. "I want to be a poet," she says. "I—I almost have enough poems written for an entire book." She stares at me with an expectant expression, as if waiting for my approval. But that's not what I'm here for. I don't judge anyone's accomplishments, I only tell their stories with ink and blood.

"All right. Now we're getting somewhere." I push back on my stool and glide over to my workstation where I remove a black Sharpie and drawing pad from a sliding drawer. I bite off the cap of the Sharpie and hold it in my teeth. "So a book, maybe?" I start sketching a rough outline. "With drifting pages that circle around— "

"No," she cuts me off.

I spit the Sharpie cap onto my workstation. "No?"

She shakes her head. "I want a typewriter. One of those old-fashioned kinds. My grandma had one when I was a kid, and I used to love playing with it, staining my fingers on the ribbon ink."

Without meaning to, I smile. "Now *that* sounds like a tattoo with some meaning."

She grins back at me, and I can't help notice how her entire face transforms when she does. I mean, she's a pretty girl to begin with, but when she smiles, her face lights up and that mysterious weight that darkens her eyes all but disappears. It's in this moment, when her beauty all but stuns me, that I consider learning her name. I think it's Ashley, or

Ashlyn, or *something.*

But then I think about Harper, and my smile withers. What the fuck am I thinking? Who cares what this girl looks like or how she smiles? Who cares what her name is? *Jesus.* I scribble out my previous drawing of a book and begin to sketch a typewriter. I steal glances of the name etched on her arm, mentally making notes where the lines of the two tattoos will intersect and overlap. I won't be completely sure until I place my drawing on top her old tattoo.

It only takes a minute or so, but I soon I lose myself in my art. My muscles unwind, and the world drops away until there's nothing left but me and my pen.

"That's amazing." Her voice is closer than I expect, and I jolt back. My pen leaves an ugly line from one of the round letter keys, squiggling and inch or so across my drawing. I scowl at it. I know it doesn't really matter that I messed up the stencil, the mistake won't appear on the actual tattoo, but still, I hate making mistakes. The jagged line stares up, mocking me. My fingers curl so tight around the pen my knuckles ache.

"I love it," the girl says. She reaches down to touch the drawing but I pull it from her grasp.

"It's fucked up," I say.

She withdraws her hand back into her lap. "I think it's perfect," she says quietly.

I snort and rip the sketch from the pad. I crumple it up, toss it in the trash, and begin outlining on a fresh sheet.

I glance up at her and nearly fall into her wide, blue eyes. I tighten my grip on my drawing pad, like it's the only thing keeping me from drowning. God, she looks so innocent. Something about her makes me want to wrap my arms around her and shield her from this hell pit that is life. That's crazy, right? I just met her, so why should I care what happens to her? Still, she needs someone. Whoever this Chris fuck was, he was a mistake she didn't see coming. I won't settle for some second-rate tattoo to eradicate him from her life, and I won't let her, either. "I'm the artist, so only my opinion is valid."

Her mouth drops, but the words don't come. A flush burns up her neck. "Why?" she asks finally.

Ignoring her, I grab several colored Sharpies from a cup—I don't like to talk and work. I splay them out on my table and take my time choosing. The red will definitely make the tattoo stand out, but the blue matches her eyes. I grab the blue and twist off the cap.

"Why?" she asks again, louder this time. Apparently, she can't take a hint. "Is it because I ate your pizza without asking? Because I'm keeping you at work late? Or because I'm not paying? Because I'll pay you. You'll have to give me some time, but I'll pay you."

With a sigh, I snap the lid back on the marker and look at her. "What are you talking about?"

Her cheeks burn crimson. "*You!*" She jabs a finger in the air. "Why are you being such an ass?"

"Who says I'm an ass? Maybe *you're* overly sensitive." I pull the cap off a green Sharpie and color in the typewriter's letter keys. The brightness of the green and blue together will be a nice contrast to her dark hair.

She makes a strangled noise and hugs her chest. "You're really something."

"So I've been told. Now, if you're done going on about my many charming attributes, would you mind shutting up?

Please? I can't concentrate with your yammering."

She presses her lips into a tight line. Her eyes take on the shimmery sheen of held back tears.

"Oh, Jesus H. Christ," I mutter. For a millisecond, I sense something inside me twist as an unfamiliar emotion takes hold. Shame? Regret? I can't be sure because the feeling passes as quickly as it came. I pick up my drawing of the typewriter and hold it up, studying it from different angles to make sure it lines up. "Usually people don't start crying until after I bring out the needle."

"I'm *not* crying," she answers, dabbing at her eyes.

"*Right.*"

"I'm not!" She straightens her shoulders. "I wouldn't give you the satisfaction."

"The satisfaction?" I give a harsh bark of a laugh. "Listen up, sweetheart, crying is the last thing in the world to bring me satisfaction. I detest it, I *loathe* it. When someone cries, it makes me grind my teeth together like this until my jaw hurts." I curl my lips back in a snarl, displaying my teeth. "Not a good look for me, cupcake."

Her nostrils flare. "*Ashlyn.*"

I ignore her and turn back to my drawing. *She's not my problem,* I remind myself. Therefore, there's no reason to learn her name. Still, I sneak a look at her and immediately regret it. She looks so small curled up on my chair. She's pulled her knees against her chest and has wrapped her arms around them. Her bottom lip quivers and she quickly bites onto it. God, I want to reach for her, to pull her against me, and…

What the hell is wrong with me? I shake my head, hoping to dislodge my unexpected tenderness toward the girl, before bringing my attention back to my drawing. There's something not quite right with it. I reach for my fine tip Sharpie and add a few more lines. When I'm satisfied, I cap the marker, and set it aside. "All right. Let's see how well this lines up. Arm."

She glares at me without moving.

I'm in no mood for games. She's already fucked with my head enough. "*Arm*," I repeat, and this time I snap my fingers.

With a scowl, she slowly extends her arm. I lay my drawing over the cursive name, repositioning it a few times to make sure the lines of the previous tattoo will be hidden by the new one. "This is going to work nicely," I say.

"At least something in this place will," she mutters.

"*Funny*." I stand and walk to the printer where I copy my drawing onto transfer paper. Before I place it on her skin, I rip open a sanitizing cloth packet and wipe down her arm. Her muscles reflexively tighten each time my hand grazes her skin. It's very annoying. So is her apple-coffee smell. And the softness of her skin. "Can you *try* to sit still?"

"Sorry."

I take the copied image, drop back down on my stool, and line up the stencil over her original tattoo. After I'm done positioning the copy, I take a wet sponge and hold it against the image long enough for the temporary lines to transfer to her skin. I peel the paper from her arm and study my work. "Okay. This is where it's going to be. Now is when you speak up or forever hold your peace."

She looks at the outline of the typewriter on her arm, and her face softens. "It's exactly what I want."

"Good." I glance at the clock and find the time is nearly

midnight. I do not want to be here much longer, especially if Emily is at Peter's party doing God knows what. Sure, at twenty-one, she's *technically* an adult. But it's not like the older brother instinct is something I can turn off. And since Harper is out with her friends, I can't think of a better way to spend my time than making sure my baby sister stays out of trouble. "It's late," I say. "How about we make a deal? I'll draw the outline tonight, and you can come back tomorrow after the shop closes and we'll finish the shading."

Her shoulders slump. "*Another* night with you?"

"I think you meant to say, 'Another night with *you*!'" I open the plastic bag with the needle, slide it out, and fasten it to the tattoo machine.

"*Right.*" She rolls her eyes. "Anyway, I'm fine with coming back tomorrow. I worked a double shift today, so I'm pretty beat. Besides, I can only handle you in short bursts."

I ignore the jab and fill a little cup with ink. "So you're not going to the party with Emily?"

"No." She shakes her head. "I'm going to bed."

Good. One less girl for me to babysit. Again, Ashlyn might be perfectly capable of taking care of herself, but it's that damn older brother instinct. I think it started in third grade when I spotted Jeff Bowlin pulling on my sister's pigtails. I gave him a black eye, and my reputation spread via whispered warnings throughout the school—you do not mess with Lane Garrett's little sister. Later on came the addendum: *or* Emily's friends. Because as I would soon learn, teenage girls are pack animals. They travel together and get into trouble together.

Speaking of girls, I make a mental note to call Harper to see how her night is going, and tell her I love her. I turn on the tattoo machine and the needle pulses. I dip the tip of it into my cup of ink. I look at the girl on my chair. "Are you ready to get started?"

She nods, her eyes never leaving the buzzing needle.

"Good." I roll my stool toward her. "Now sit back and try to relax. This is going to hurt."

Chapter Four

Ashlyn

My arm throbs as I climb out of the car and walk the short distance to my apartment. I can't decide what was the biggest relief: the moment the needle stopped biting into my skin, or the second I climbed off the vinyl chair and got the hell away from Lane.

I glance at the black ink typewriter beneath the plastic wrap taped to my arm. Even though he's a huge asshole, there's no denying Lane's talent. The letter keys overlap the cursive loops of Chris's name, making it all but invisible. When the shading is complete, there'll be nothing left to remind me of my mistake. For that, I'm willing to suffer another night with Lane.

I unlock my apartment door and step inside to the sound of squeals and raucous laughter. Another party—*awesome.* The front door opens into a small kitchen where liquor bottles and fast-food wrappers decorate every inch of space on the short counter. Dirty dishes overflow the sink and the smells of smoke and beer permeate the air.

The urge to cry swells inside my chest like an inflating balloon. Before I'd left for work this morning I'd spent two hours straightening, taking out the trash, washing the dishes, and wiping down all the counters—not to mention scrubbing puke out of the carpet.

I follow the sound of voices, peek around the corner, and find at least a dozen people crammed into the small living room—none of them are my roommate, or even anyone I recognize. A handful of girls are wedged onto the couch. They stare, glassy-eyed, at some reality show on TV. Two guys sit on a loveseat, passing a joint back and forth—the tang of it burns my nostrils.

One of them looks up at me. He smiles, and there's something about it that sends my skin crawling. I shiver and turn away.

"Selena?" I call out for my missing roommate. After she'd begged me to clean up the vomit this morning—she couldn't do it herself because of a *sensitive* stomach—she promised me no more parties.

"Bedroom," one of the girls on the couch mutters. She has platinum blond hair with pink highlights. I realize I *do* recognize her. She's a stripper from the same club Selena works at. Her name is...Diamond? Dazzle? I can't remember, but it's not like it's her real name. One of Selena's friends told me they use stage names to protect their identity. She never said who from—maybe the men at the club, or maybe the girl she's forced to be when she walks on the stage.

Angry tears prick the corner of my eyes as I walk down

the short hall. I should have known she wouldn't keep her word. I'd leave if I could, but finding an apartment with rent this cheap is impossible and I don't exactly relish the idea of going back to living out of my car.

Which is why I've been saving all of my tip money and eating ramen noodles two meals a day. If I keep at my current pace, I should have enough money for a better apartment in about six months. Until then, I'll just have to suck it up.

"Selena?" Her doorway's cracked open. I push it wide, step inside, and immediately recoil in horror. "Oh my God!" I clasp my hands over my mouth as a wash of bile burns up my throat. I know, given Selena's *sensitive stomach*, if I threw up I'll be the one cleaning it up.

Bent over the foot of her bed with her skirt pushed up to her waist, Selena turns to face me as some guy I've never seen before, with his pants around his ankles, continues to thrust against her without breaking his rhythm. "Oh, hey. What's up?" she asks, pushing up on her palms.

With my hands still clasped over my mouth, I shake my head and take a step back, only to bump into the wall. I want to rip my eyes from my skull and drop them in a bucket for scrubbing. Only there's not enough bleach in the world to dissolve the horror burned on them.

With his pelvis still lurching and hands gripping her hips, the guy nods at me with heavy-lidded eyes. "Sup. Who are you?"

I think the sight malfunctioned my brain because my muscles refuse to obey my command to *get the hell out of there.* Instead, I continue to stand and gape at them, like I'm visiting an art gallery and their *performance art* is particularity difficult to interpret.

"That's my new roommate, Ash," Selena answers, as he

continues ramming her from behind. "She's a waitress or something. Right, Ash?"

Oh my God, this is not happening. I am not having a conversation with you while you fuck! I clench my eyes shut and inch toward the door. "I'm leaving. We'll talk later."

"You don't have to go," the guy pants. "Stay. Join in."

"Yeah, Ash," Selena agrees. "It'll be fun!"

No. Nee. Nein. Niet. There aren't enough languages in the world to convey all the ways I want to decline. Instead, I shake my head and feel my way around the doorframe. "I'm going. Now." I slip into the hall, where I finally open my eyes. The mattress springs continue to groan behind me.

"What's her problem?" I hear the guy ask.

"She is *so* uptight," Selena answers. "You have no idea. She was actually up at eight this morning to clean."

"I bet I could loosen her up," the guy answers.

Selena's giggle is the last thing I hear before I stumble down the hallway. The smoke in the living room has grown thicker, burning my lungs and stinging my eyes. I spot a knocked over beer bottle by the edge of the couch. The amber liquid pools on the light beige carpet, but no one seems to notice.

It seems impossible, but I feel as if the mess has multiplied in my brief absence. Towers of cans and dishes appear to grow before my eyes, reaching for the ceiling until I'm sure they'll crash down and bury me alive.

Droplets of sweat prick the back of my neck as I spin around, searching for paper towels, only to find the naked cardboard tube tucked in the sink with the dishes. *Shit.* I pull open the cabinet doors, searching for a dish towel, a rag, *anything* I can use to clean, but there's nothing.

I rake my fingers through my hair. The rational part of

me realizes I no longer live at home with my stepdad. But the damaged part of my brain, the biggest part, screams at me to clean this up or there's going to be hell to pay.

"Hey."

I let my fingers fall and glance up to find Diamond staring at me over the back of the couch. A look of concern is etched across her face. "You okay?" she asks. "You want a drink or something?"

No. I most definitely am not okay. Each breath I take pulls tight across my chest like a rubber band on the verge of snapping. "I...uh...I gotta go." Because I do. I have to get the fuck out of this apartment before I spiral into a panic attack the size of which would surely send me to the ER.

Diamond shrugs and turns her attention back to the television, sinking deeper into the cushion.

With trembling fingers, I reach into my pocket and withdraw my keys. The spasms that shake me make the metal tinkle together like wind chimes.

"Yo, blue eyes," the guy on the loveseat calls. "If you're going out can you pick up some more beer?"

Instead of answering, I push through the front door and slam it behind me. It's late, well past midnight, but I can't stay here. I withdraw my phone from my back pocket. Usually, I wouldn't dream of using my prepaid minutes for anything but an emergency, but in a way, this is. I scroll through the contacts until I find Emily's number.

Are you still at that party? I type.

A few seconds later, she replies. *Sure am. Change your mind about coming out?*

I don't hesitate before writing back, *Text me the address and I'm there.*

"They were having sex?" Emily screeches in that loud way people do when they've had a few to drink. "Right in front of you? And they asked you to join in?"

I nod and Emily howls with laughter, drawing curious glances from those around us. The kitchen is overflowing with people pushing their way to the makeshift bar set up on the island. "Somebody get this girl a beer," she shouts, pointing a finger at me.

As if by magic, a tall, thin guy appears in front of me with a red plastic cup. "Here you go. What's your name?" He practically shoves the cup into my face.

"Her name is *not on your fucking life.*" Emily slaps his hand away, sloshing brown liquid onto his wrist.

"Fuck!" He withdraws the cup and scowls at her. "What the hell?"

"We don't know you," she answers. "That means any drink you give us must have the lid still on or the tab not popped. Who's to say you didn't put something in there?"

I blink at her. I'm a little surprised, as well as impressed, that despite being visibly tipsy, she still has enough sense to think about things like that.

"Like I would want to drug you," the guy says. "Fucking bitch." He turns to leave and Emily holds up both hands with middle fingers extended. He walks up to two guys in the corner of the room. They glare at us.

Nervous knots twist inside my stomach. I grab Emily's hands and pull them to her side. "Em, maybe you could bring it down a notch before we get into trouble?"

She throws her head back and laughs as if I've said the funniest thing in the history of comedy. "*Please.* This is my party and these are my people." She throws her arms wide, accidentally slapping a female passerby across the chest. I mouth an apology to the girl, who sneers as she squeezes past.

Emily reaches around me and plucks a can of beer off the counter. After popping the tab, she thrusts it at me. "Here. Drink this. You've earned it after the night you had."

I start to argue, but between putting up with Lane, coming home to my destroyed apartment, and walking in on my roommate in the middle of—well, whatever the hell it was—I really do want a drink. I take the can from her and swallow the lukewarm liquid in a long draw. When I finish, the can is significantly lighter and my head just fuzzy enough that the memory of that guy's naked, pimpled ass fades a fraction. But not enough, so I finish the can.

Emily laughs, takes the empty can from me and hands me a new one. "That a girl." She takes a drink from her own beer. "I'm so glad you decided to come out tonight. I figured you'd need a drink after spending time with Lane, but I had no idea your night was only going to get worse. Speaking of—" She grabs my wrist. "How did the tattoo turn out?"

Still holding the can, I push my shirtsleeve past my elbow, exposing the plastic wrap beneath. "It's only an outline until tomorrow when I go back for the shading. You weren't joking when you said your brother is good. When this is done, it'll be like the other tattoo never existed."

She grins and drops my wrist. "I *told* you he's the best around. It's going to look amazing."

"Yeah, well, thanks." I slowly roll my sleeve back into place. Once Chris' name is covered up, I'll be able to wear short-sleeved shirts again without being reminded of one of my biggest mistakes. "With the way my money situation is, I don't know when I would have been able to do this."

Emily waves my words away. "Don't mention it. I'm happy to help out a friend."

Friend. The word sinks through my body like an anchor. I quickly swallow another gulp of beer. I haven't had any real friends since middle school, when my mom remarried and we moved a hundred miles away. Sure, there were girls I was friendly with, talked to, and even ate lunch with. But there was no one I spoke with outside of school, or invited over to my house. First, because I wasn't allowed to have friends over, and second, I was scared people would find out what was going on inside the locked doors of my home, scared they would take me away from my mother, who I had to protect.

So I kept myself closed off from others, and for what? To have my mom stand by and say nothing as my stepdad doused my belongings with lighter fluid in the backyard? To wind up living in an apartment not even a hazmat team would enter?

Fuck that.

I lift my beer can. "To friendship."

Emily taps her can against mine. "To friendship."

I tip the beer back and chug the contents until the memory of the bonfire flames—always lurking in the recesses of my mind—are all but extinguished. Until I no longer feel the need to check every knob around me to see if it's been locked, and the ever-tightening band of fear looped around my chest loosens.

It's only then, when the world spins in a blur around me, I find I can finally breathe.

Chapter Five

Lane

It takes me nearly fifteen minutes and two circles around the block before I find a place to park within walking distance of the house party. As soon as I open the door to my truck, I'm assaulted by the pounding of a bass beat. I cringe. "Fucking idiots," I murmur. They might as well call the cops and invite them over, for all the noise they're making. I just hope I can find my sister before the police do show. What would Dad's old work buddies think if they found me hanging out with a bunch of underage drunks?

Annoyance winds around my shoulders. I shouldn't be here—*Em* shouldn't be here. She's lucky Harper's out with her friends and I'm able to check on her and drive her (most likely) drunk-ass home.

As I round the corner and spot the mass of people spilling out the front door of the house and onto the lawn, my hopes of getting in and out quickly are dashed. I exhale through clenched teeth. With a rare night alone, I should be in my garage, underneath my '69 Chevelle with a beer in one hand and a wrench in the other—*not* playing babysitter for a bunch of shitfaced kids doing keg stands on the lawn and fucking in closets.

The thought pushes a memory to the surface of my mind. A blanket of coats lies under my back. The air is thick, hard to swallow. I can't see anything except for the strip of light leaking beneath the closed door. Probably a good thing because with all I drank, the room would surely be spinning. Her lips, sticky with gloss, glide down my neck.

"Yo! Lane!" A voice calls out, dragging me from the past. I swallow the knot in my throat and look up to find a redheaded guy clutching a red Solo cup and pushing through the partygoers who are milling about on the lawn. "So cool you could make it tonight." His eyes are glassy and he wobbles on his feet. "Can I get you something? Beer?" He grins widely. "Oh, I know. A shot of Jäger!"

I make a face. "God, no. I'm not here to party, Pete. I came to find my sister and take her home."

"Aw!" Despite being in his early twenties, Pete still resembles the freckle-faced kid who used to follow his brother and me around on his bike when they lived next door. His brother Michael was always daring him to do stupid stuff like jump across the ravine in the woods and poke the neighbors' sleeping dog with a stick. Pete never turned down a dare, either. As a kid I thought he was brave. Now I'm pretty sure he was just a dumbass. I glance at the girls clustered together by the porch steps. They look like sorority girls. God, *please* let them be old enough to be sorority girls. If not, it's apparent Pete hasn't outgrown his knack for doing stupid shit.

I nod my head over my shoulder. "They legal?"

His grin widens and he shrugs. "Who cares? They're hot."

"Doesn't matter if they're hot. If they're underage and the cops show up, you'll still go to jail."

"You're worried about cops?" He blinks at me, lines of confusion pinching his brow. "What happened to you? You used to be cool."

If he means I was once an idiot, too, he's right. Apparently I'm still cool enough to resist the urge to smack him. Instead, I grunt and head for the house. Some lessons can only be learned on your own. I only hope Pete doesn't learn his the hard way—like me.

A girl with curly bleach-blond hair steps in front of me and holds out a shot glass. "Hey sexy, want to do a body shot?" She tucks the glass between her breasts. I pause because, even if I'm not cool anymore, I'm still male. The added pressure of the shot glass squeezes her boobs against the neckline of her shirt—already tight from the strain on it. If this girl so much as sneezes, there'll be no stopping the boobsplosion.

As the guys around me creep in for a better look, the initial excitement of a potential flashing wears off, leaving me feeling slightly exhausted. Maybe it's because I have Harper, or maybe it's because I've been working my ass off lately, but in all my twenty-six years, I've never felt as old as I do now. "Not interested," I say. Even if I *didn't* have Harper, the girl might as well have "Jail Bait" tattooed across her tits. Unlike Pete, I like to think I've wised up in the last ten years. I'm not about to go to jail for a nice rack.

Apparently the girl doesn't get the hint because she grabs my arm. "Wait. You have to lick me first." She tips her head back and douses her cleavage with salt. Several guys behind me groan appreciatively.

Fucking idiots. All they see are D-cups and a nice ass. Once upon a time, I would have, too. But I've been down that road. Now I see her, and every girl like her, for what they really are—drama. And I don't want any part of that anymore.

"You're wasting your time, angel," I say, as I brush past her on my way to the door.

She huffs. "Queer."

Several people snicker.

Just like I thought. *Drama.* I enter the house without looking back. Inside, people are clustered together so that I have to turn sideways to push my way through. In the living room, a stereo blares and people grind together, a pulsing mass of flesh and limbs.

All of this feels eerily familiar. I brace for impact as a memory I've fought to keep buried slams into me. Ten years ago, at a party similar to this one, I'd been standing in a corner, clutching a lukewarm beer in my bony sixteen-year-old hands, when my eyes drifted across the crowd of dancers and landed on *her.*

She'd been barely sixteen herself, with caramel-colored hair and bubble-gum-pink lips. Even now I can still remember the taste of them, sweet like strawberries.

I shake my head as if to dislodge the ghost of her from my memory. I'm not about to let her haunt me again. Still, my breathing quickens and I glance quickly around to make sure she hasn't materialized. I rub my hands down my face, annoyed that I allow her to get to me after all this time. Absently, I bring my hand to my collarbone and touch the name inked into my skin. Some scars run so much deeper than a needle can drive ink into flesh.

"Hey man!" A fist bumps my bicep. "What the hell are you doing here?"

I'm glad to focus on the dark-skinned guy in front of me. I can't remember his name, but I recognize him as one of Pete's friends from high school—a former football player, only now he's sporting the very distinctive buzz of a military haircut. "Hey." I force a smile. "You enlist or you just sporting the haircut to get girls?"

He laughs. "No. I'm in the Army now. I'm back home for a couple of weeks before they send me to Afghanistan."

"Man." My smile dissolves. "I'm sorry."

"Don't be." He shakes his head. "I love what I do, and I get to see the world."

I nod. That much I can understand. Before Harper, I was filled with wanderlust myself. After high school, I had plans to drive across the country and backpack around Europe before starting college. Of course, none of that happened—not the traveling and not college. Life has a funny way of putting you on a different road before you've even realized you've gone off course.

"Buy, hey!" The guy hits my arm again. "I hear you're making quite a name for yourself."

"I do all right."

"More than all right from what I hear. I'm real happy for you, man. I remember how messed up you were after—" He bites off the words and I stiffen. I've worked hard to prove I'm not the fuckup everyone thought I was all those years ago, but this guy's proven once again, there's no running from your past.

"Anyway," he continues, "I'm not surprised you're doing so well. I remember your drawings when we were kids—they were amazing then. I'll have to stop by your shop before I leave. I've been wanting a tattoo for awhile and it seems only right you should give me my first one."

"Yeah. You should do that." I search over his shoulder for any sign of my sister. "Have you seen Em?"

He laughs. "Man, some things never change. You do realize she's an adult, right? You don't have to watch over her anymore."

I snap my gaze back to him. The heat from my glare makes him stagger back a step with his hands up. Obviously this guy doesn't have a younger sister or he'd know there will never come a day when I don't watch over mine.

"I meant no offense, Lane," he says, all the humor gone from his face. "She's in the kitchen."

"Thanks." I don't wait for him to say anything else before I turn for the door. I'm not trying to be an asshole, but I only have three hot buttons and this guy pushed two of them: my past mistakes and my sister. Lucky for him, he didn't mention Harper, or I wouldn't be walking away.

By the time I reach the kitchen, my muscles are wound tight with anxiety. The sooner I find Em and convince her to leave, the better. The room is small, and it doesn't help that people are clustered together so tightly they're practically climbing on top of one another to get to the keg.

There are shouts from the opposite corner, and I turn to find a small group of people crowded around the kitchen table playing cards. It's there where I spot my sister, eyes glassy, cheeks flushed, and her laugh a pitch too high.

Beside her is the girl Em brought into my shop for the cover up. Ashley, Ashlyn, or something. There's no point asking her now. Given the way she's slumped back in her seat, her eyes vacantly staring at the ceiling, I'd be surprised if *she* knows her name.

The other four chairs are occupied by guys holding cards, though the boulder of a man closest to Ashley-slash-Ashlyn appears far more interested in her than the cards in his softball-sized hands.

My fingers curl into fists and I inhale deeply through my nose. Just great. Instead of one drunk girl to take care of, I now have two. Ignoring the cries of protest, I push through the crowd until I reach the table's edge. "Em? What's going on?"

"Lane! We're playing asshole." She grins up at me and places her thumb on her forehead and everyone around her does the same. "Ah-ah!" She removes her thumb and waves a finger at me. "I'm the president, so now you have to drink!" She picks up her cup and holds it out to me.

I ignore it. "I'm not playing, Em."

"Bah!" She sets the cup down, but not before sloshing beer over the sides so it trails down her hand. She licks the amber liquid from her fingers and turns to the guy beside her. "Lane's a party pooper."

"Not yet." I reach over the stack of cards and grab her cup. "Now I am." Before she can protest, I march to the sink and dump the contents into the drain.

When I get back to the table, Em is giving me the look she'd mastered at three years old. Her arms are crossed and her eyes narrowed, and her bottom lip juts out. "God, Lane!

Just because you hate having fun, does that mean you can't let anyone else have it?"

Here we go—the guilt trip. I roll my eyes even though part of me admires her persistence. You'd think she'd give up after twenty-one years. "Em, you've had your fun. That much is very apparent. I'm just here to tell you that you've had enough."

"I'm not a baby," she fires back. "I'm twenty-one. You can't just show up at a party and tell me when I have to leave."

"Yeah." The long-haired Abercrombie-model-wannabe beside her slides an arm around the back of her chair. "You can't make her go, man, if she doesn't want to go."

I glare at him. "This is a family matter. If you know what's good for you, you'll leave it at that."

He pushes to his feet, nostrils flaring.

"*Lane*." Emily's voice is a warning. She stands. "Just chill, all right? I know how to take care of myself. This isn't high school. I don't need you coming to my rescue."

"She doesn't want to go, man," the guy echoes. "So why don't you get the hell out of here?"

The rhinoceros beside Em's friend slides his massive arm around her chair and pulls her closer to him. She doesn't appear to notice. Instead, her eyes droop sluggishly. "The girls are fine," the rhino growls. "We're watching out for them."

"Hey!" Emily whirls on him. "Who asked you to watch out for us? We're adult women. We're fine on our own."

"Really?" I point a finger at her semiconscious friend. "That doesn't look fine to me."

"Actually, Ashlyn *is* fine. You should have seen her when she got here—she was a mess. *I* calmed her down. Though..." She turns to her friend, scrutinizing her. "I may have overdone it."

I cross my arms. "You think?" It's in this moment I actually feel sorry for Ashlyn. If Em was trying to *take care of her*, the poor girl didn't stand a chance.

"Yeah..." She rubs her eyes. "On second thought, maybe I overdid it, too. Bed is sounding better by the second. Lane, can you help me carry Ash out of here?"

Abercrombie makes a cry of protest. "Are you kidding me? I thought we were having a good time."

"We were." She leans over and pokes his nose with her index finger. "But now I'm done."

That's my girl. I can't help but smile...until I catch a glimpse of the rhino tightening his hold on Ashlyn's chair. "Get your friend on her feet," I tell Em. "I'll help you from there."

Emily nods, but just as she reaches for her, Rhino stands, shoving his way in front of Ashlyn. "Don't you worry about her. I already told her I'd give her a ride home. Didn't I?" He nudges Ashlyn's shoulder. She blinks in response.

Son of a bitch. The guy is roughly the size of baby elephant. While I've been known to hold my own in a fight, I've yet to take on someone the size of a backyard shed. Even so, I'm not about to leave some poor drunk girl alone with him. "Not happening," I say. "She's coming with us."

"No." The dude steps forward, towering over us like a wall of muscle. "She's not." The threat of violence radiates off of him in fiery waves that burn against my skin.

My own muscles coil in response, my knuckles tightening until they ache to drive into his flesh. The fucker glares down at me and I lift my chin and crack my neck from side to side in response. True, I don't know this girl, but I can't help but wonder, what if it were Harper drunk at a party? Wouldn't I want somebody to watch over her? Besides, even if this guy gets a few hits on me, it isn't like I'm going to lose the fight. I *never* lose.

I throw my arms wide, beckoning him to come at me. "I'm taking the girl with me. You don't like it? Try and stop me."

Tension winds between us like a serpent ready to strike. The room falls silent as heads turn in our direction. The Rhino snorts and I half expect to see steam waft out his nose. "Dude, I am going to fuck you up so hard." He presses a fist against his open palm.

I grin. "I'd love to see you try." And I would. It's been so long since I've been in a good fight. My muscles ache to pound out the frustration that's built up inside me.

"Oh my God!" My sister rolls her eyes. "Really? Enough of the macho shit." Before I figure out what's she about to do, she whirls around and drives her knee into Rhino's crotch. "We're taking Ashlyn with us, fuckhead!"

The room draws a collective breath and every guy in the place winces as Rhino's face turns several shades of red before he doubles over with a barely audible squeak.

"Emily!" My shoulders slump. "Damn it. I was taking care of it."

"When?" She crosses in front of Rhino who drops to his knees muttering a continuous line of curses. "Were you going to take care of it sometime this year? Because I want to go home *now*." She drapes Ashlyn's arm over her shoulder and pulls the girl to her feet. "C'mon, honey. Let's get you out of here."

She drags Ashlyn away from the table in front of the

panting Rhino. I want to help her, but at the same time, I refuse to take my eyes off the bent-over man—and I'm glad I don't. As soon as Em passes him, he reaches for her.

I don't hesitate. My fist meets his face with a satisfying crack that sends shockwaves of pain up my arm—not that I let it show. The guy groans and falls backward, crashing into his abandoned chair and splintering it under his weight. He lifts his head and blinks at me with unfocused eyes.

I point at him and notice two of my knuckles are split and bleeding. "If you know what's good for you," I turn and face the crowd of gawkers, "if *any* of you know what's good for you, you'll never screw with my sister, or her friend."

I catch movement out of the corner of my eye and turn just in time to see Abercrombie's fist flying toward my face. I duck, his hand tickling the hair along my scalp as it passes. As I stand, I grab his shoulder, yank it down, and drive my knee into his gut.

Doubled over, the guy lets out a gasp, his eyes bulging. I don't wait for him to recover before I take him by the shoulders and throw him on top of his fallen friend.

"Lane!" Emily screeches. I look to find her frowning at me, with her free hand on her hip.

"What?" I ask. "You started it."

She huffs and struggles to reposition her friend on her shoulder. I can already tell if I wait for her to help the girl out, we'll be here all night. With a sigh, I walk over to them, grab Ashlyn by the waist and hoist her over my shoulder so her legs drape across my chest. The girl grunts softly. "Let's go," I say.

Em searches the crowd of frozen faces. "Hey Pete!" She waves. "This was a really awesome party. I'll be sure to make your next one."

"Yeah…" Pete nods dumbly as we walk by.

Emily bounces ahead of me out the door and onto the lawn. The girl that offered me the shot watches, wide-eyed, as I carry Ashlyn to my truck. I pause long enough to wink at her and watch her mouth drop before I turn away. "So where am I taking this one?" I ask Em.

She stops bouncing. "To her apartment. Duh."

"Which is where?"

"Uh…" She blinks. "Good question."

I pull my keys from my pocket with a sigh. "She can't go home with me. Can you imagine what Harper would think?"

Emily reaches the passenger-side door and pulls it open. "I think Harper is a lot cooler than you give her credit for."

I open my mouth to argue, but she waves a hand, cutting me off. "Calm your tits, Nancy. She can stay at my place."

I press my teeth together so hard my jaw aches as I yank open the quad-cab's back door and deposit Ashlyn onto the bench seat. Her eyes are closed and a thin line of drool trails from the corner of her lips. She's completely wasted. There is no way she would have known if that muscle head had tried– No. I won't go there. The very idea of him touching her without her consent makes me want to go back inside the house and rip his dick off.

"She's cute, right?"

I turn to find Em watching me from the front seat.

I scowl at her. "What the hell are you talking about?"

"Ash." She points at her slumped over friend. "I think she's your type, too. Unfortunately it would never work. She's got a thing about kids, so I told her you were an ass and to steer clear." She spins away from me. "You're welcome."

I haven't a fucking clue what she's talking about, but I don't bother asking. She's so drunk I doubt even she knows. After buckling the seat belt around Ash, I climb in the front seat. Em already has her phone plugged into my stereo. I huff loudly. "This is the thanks I get for coming to this party and getting into a fight, all so I can drag your drunk ass home?"

She snorts. "As far as those two idiots inside, I had things under control. I will thank you for the ride, though." After settling on a song—some techno pop beat that makes me want to grind my teeth together—she leans back and stretches. Her eyelids droop and she yawns. "Wake me when we get home, okay?"

"All right," I say, even though I know I won't. Looking at her, all small and curled up against the seat, she reminds me of the five-year-old girl curled against the hard vinyl of the hospital sofa as we waited for news on our father. When the doctor arrived to tell us they couldn't stop the bleeding from the bullet, I begged my mother not to wake her, to spare her from the pain just a little longer.

Later, at my father's funeral, when his partner handed me his badge, he told me I needed to take care of my sister and mother, a job I take seriously to this day. I adjust my review mirror so I can check on the sleeping girl in the back. *They're safe now.* I might not be a cop like my dad, but that doesn't mean a small part of him doesn't live on through me.

I grip the steering wheel and glance at my knuckles. Dried blood streaks across my skin like torn ribbons. Like Dad, I will stop at nothing to protect the people I love—no matter how much it hurts.

Chapter Six

Ashlyn

The smell of coffee finds me in the darkness of dreamless sleep and pulls me into reluctant consciousness. My eyelashes feel as if they've been glued together. I rub the heels of my hands against them until I can finally pry them open—an act I regret immediately. The light burns my retinas like a laser. I flinch, but I'm too late. A throbbing builds inside my temples, pulsing and grinding the plates of my skull tighter until I'm sure bits of my brain will leak out through my ears.

"Morning, sunshine," a gruff voice greets me. A large hand thrusts a steaming mug of coffee in front of my face. The mug is red with the words *Coffee makes me awesome!* painted in black. Before I can reach for it, a second hand appears with two tiny capsules balanced on the outstretched palm. "Advil. Figured you could use it."

I glance up into Lane's brown eyes and, for a heartbeat,

I feel as if I might fall into them and drown in their dark pools. God, what's wrong with me? I grimace and place a hand against my temple. "I think I might still be drunk. Or having a nightmare. Why else would the asshole tattoo guy be in my apartment?"

"You're not in your apartment." Lane smirks and deposits the pills and mug on the coffee table in front of me—a coffee table I don't recognize.

I jerk back and the blurred lines of the room sharpen around me. The walls of the small living room are painted a warm yellow, and worn, rust-colored drapes hang from floor to ceiling. The small windowsills are stuffed with potted aloes and other leafy green plants. The brown microfiber couch I'm sprawled across is accented with multi-colored pillows. Instead of the stale smell of cigarettes and beer of my own apartment, this one smells of cinnamon and coffee. "Where am I? Is this—is this *your* apartment?"

He laughs out loud. If he wasn't such an ass, I might find the rich sound pleasant. "God no."

"I'm so late!" someone shrieks behind me.

I twist around to find Emily hopping on one foot as she slips a shoe on the other. "Fuck!" She slides to halt in front of a small table and roots through a laundry basket on top. "If I'm late today, that makes three days this week, and that means a warning." She tosses several shirts onto the floor before pulling out her barista apron. She loops it over her head and spins a circle. "Have you seen my keys?"

Lane picks up a cluster of keys off the table and holds them out to her.

"Thanks." She snatches them from his hand and turns for the door.

"Um, Emily," I say. "I know you're late and all, but I kinda need to get back to my car."

She freezes before turning pleading eyes on her brother. "*Please,* Lane. You know you owe me."

He sighs. "Fine. But after this, I want you to know we're even. I don't owe you anything else."

"Thanks, big brother." She leans in and gives him a kiss on the cheek before racing for the door, where she pauses with her hand on the knob. "I hope you had fun last night, Ash. I know I did. We should hang out more."

"Sure," I answer, even though I can't remember if I had fun or not. The night's memories are too deeply embedded in the haze of my hangover for me to sort them out. "How about the next time we hang out, we watch a movie instead of letting trucks drive over our skulls?" I press my palms against my throbbing temples. "At least that's what I think happened."

Laughing, Emily opens the door. "Oh my God, you are so adorable. Isn't she adorable, Lane?"

He grunts.

"Anyway," she continues, "make yourself at home. *Mi casa es su casa* and all that. I hope when you get back to your place, all the naked people have cleared out." She shudders. "Ugh. Anyway, gotta go. We'll talk later."

Before I can respond, she shuts the door behind her, sealing me in with her brother. The quaintness of the small apartment suddenly feels more claustrophobic. Icy panic floods me. If my anxiety shows, it's apparently amusing as hell to Lane, who grins. God, can he be more of an ass? One thing's for sure, I'm not about to spend more time with him than I have to.

"You don't have to give me a ride back to my car," I say. "I can find a lift." The last part is a lie. The only person I know beside Em is my roommate Selena, and she won't wake up before noon for anyone or anything. I glance at the clock to find it's nearly seven in the morning. Yep. I'm totally on my own here.

Lane arches an eyebrow. "So what's this about naked people?"

"Ugh." Typical guy with his selective hearing. I rake my fingers through my hair, only to have them snag on tangles in my bed-head. "If it's all the same to you, I'd rather not talk about it." I fumble on the floor for my missing Toms.

"Looking for these?" Lane reaches behind him and withdraws two red canvas shoes. "You kicked them at me while you were sleeping. I kept them because I thought I'd be safer if you were without ammunition."

With cheeks burning, I snatch them from his hands and slip them on. "Sorry," I mumble. I don't remember kicking my shoes at him, but it's not like he doesn't deserve it.

He stares at me for so long I have to fight to keep from squirming under his gaze.

"What?" I blurt when I can stand it no longer.

He shrugs and sits on the loveseat across from me. "I've just never seen anyone thrash in their sleep the way you do—it was like you were wrestling an alligator or something."

"Some people move in their sleep. What's the big deal?" I quickly glance away before he can read the truth in my eyes. If he knew my real nightmare—the one where I wake up locked in my old bedroom—wrestling alligators would seem tame by comparison.

"Move?" He laughs out loud. "Sweetheart, you were

racing Michael Phelps for the gold."

I scowl at him. "How about we talk about the more disturbing issue. You were watching me sleep? What kind of sick freak are you?"

"You think I was watching you?" He lurches back like I've struck him, and I can't help but feel the slightest twinge of satisfaction. "In your dreams, cupcake. I was trying to sleep in that recliner right there." He points to the chair in the corner of the room. "And I emphasize the word *trying.* It's impossible to fall asleep when someone is moaning and kicking shoes at you all night."

Angry heat burns from my chest and up my neck, until the tops of my ears feel scorched. "What the hell were you doing sleeping here, anyway? Don't you have some girlfriend to get back to?" I thrust a finger in the direction of his tattoo. "Harper, isn't it?"

His laugh is a loud bark and he jabs a finger right back at me. "Please don't flatter yourself. The only reason I stayed was because you and my sister were so wasted, I wanted to make sure neither of you choked on your own vomit while you slept."

It's then, with his hand raised, I notice the bandage wrapped around his knuckles. Spots of blood decorate the gauze in rust-colored splotches. A memory struggles to surface through the sludge of last night's drunken haze. I remember sitting at the kitchen table with Emily and a group of guys. She'd been trying to teach me a card game called Asshole, but I lost every hand. And losing meant more drinking. The big guy to my left kept talking to me, his words floating farther and farther away until all I could do was nod. Then Lane was there, and the big guy suddenly wasn't…

I snap my head up. "You hit that big guy, didn't you?"

Frowning, he drops his hand to his side. "You're welcome."

"You want me to thank you for acting like a Neanderthal?"

He stands suddenly, the muscles in his jaw rigid. "This *Neanderthal* kept that guy from taking you home and having his way with you."

Horror twists around my body like strands of barbed wire. "What?"

"The meathead said you agreed to let him take you home."

"But I never— "

"I figured that. So when I said you were coming with me, he argued." Lane glances at his bandaged hand. "Luckily we came to an agreement."

"Oh my God." Thoughts of what might have happened churn nauseous waves inside my stomach. "Do you think— " The words muffle against my fingers. "That he might of— "

"I don't know." Lane sighs and sits back down, raking his fingers through his hair. "But I wasn't going to take the chance."

My hands tremble and I drop them into my lap. "Why? You don't even like me."

Lane stares at me a long moment, his expression unreadable. "Look… Ashlyn, is it?"

I nod.

"I don't like a lot of people—it's nothing personal. I've been screwed over a time or two, so I've learned to be a little more selective of the people I hang out with. Just because I don't want to get coffee with you doesn't mean I want to see you get hurt. Nobody deserves that."

I hug my chest. I couldn't fault him for that. I'd had my own fair share of assholes come and go in my life.

"Besides"—Lane rests his arms on the back of the loveseat—"it isn't like I did all that much. Em was the one who busted his balls."

My eyes go wide. "No way. Really?"

He nods.

Before I can stop it, a laugh sputters through my clamped lips. The moment I set it free, it becomes its own entity, curling around me and filling the space between us.

At first, Lane only stares at me, blinking. Soon, his lips twitch. The next thing I know, he's doubled over and chuckling along with me until we're both red-cheeked and panting for breath.

After several minutes, our laughter dies down and I'm left wiping tears off my cheeks with the back of my hand. "Your sister is amazing."

"Yeah. I know." He leans back, his grin slowly fading like the sun setting on the horizon. His eyes focus on the plastic wrap still taped to my arm. "How's the tat?"

Reflexively, I touch the corner of the tape, which has curled away from my skin. "Fine."

"Good. You're going to want to wash it with antibacterial soap soon and put more ointment on it. Still up for doing the shading today?"

"Yeah. I mean, if it's still cool with you."

"I wouldn't have offered if it wasn't." He studies me for a moment without saying anything. It takes everything in me to keep from fidgeting. "Listen," he says, after what feels like an eternity, "I have to drive past Pete's house on my way home—that's where your car is, isn't it? You should let me give you a ride. It's not a big deal."

"Um… " I reach for the coffee mug and take a sip to

stall while I come up with an excuse. I immediately regret the action when the acrid liquid hits my tongue. I should have known Lane would like his coffee strong enough to remove nail polish.

"It's not even ten minutes away," Lane says.

I can't drink the coffee, so I grip the mug tightly, hoping to find comfort in the warmth of the ceramic. Sure, Lane won't be nominated for Mr. Congeniality anytime soon, but at least this morning he's been bearable. What would be the harm in spending another ten minutes with him?

"How about this?" Lane extends his bandaged hand. Tattoos decorate the length of his arm, stopping in a sharp line at his wrist. "A truce. I promise to play nice until I'm done shading your tattoo, and then we'll both go our separate ways, never to cross paths again. Sound good?"

I can't help but grin. "The part about not seeing each other again sounds great, actually. So, yeah, I'm in."

He grins back and I slide my hand into his. His palms are rougher than I expect, with calluses that scratch my skin. I'm surprised—I should be disgusted, but instead, I find his hand comforting. Calluses like that signify working hands, strong hands. Before I can stop it, a question floats through my mind; *I wonder what they'd feel like running down my—*

I yank my fingers free from Lane's and shrink back against the couch. He's staring at me curiously, and I only hope my flaming cheeks don't betray my thoughts. "Sorry, I…uh…forgot your hand was hurt." I fight the urge to grab one of the pillows and smother my own face with it.

Lane's still staring at me with that damn unreadable expression. "You're worried about hurting *me*? I'm not exactly made of porcelain, cupcake."

Just when I think my cheeks couldn't burn any hotter, I blush even more. I am certain my skin is on the verge of melting right off my face. "Can part of the truce be that you call me by my name from now on?"

His face softens. "Fair enough." He motions to the coffee mug. "Do you want me to get you a travel mug? We should probably get going."

"No!" I answer a little too quickly.

He quirks an eyebrow. "What? You don't like my coffee?"

"*That's* what it's supposed to be?"

His lips twitch like he's fighting a smile. "I thought we declared a truce."

"We did." I push the mug away. "Sometimes the nicest thing you can do is to be honest."

"Careful. That's a dangerous road to go down."

"Being nice?"

"No." He gives a soft laugh. "Being honest."

Chapter Seven

Ashlyn

After Lane drops me off at my car, I don't bother turning on the radio as I drive back to my apartment. The thoughts swirling through my head are loud enough to drown out all other sound. I keep thinking about last night and the guy who kept inching closer to my chair until my vision blurred and the lines on his shirt melded together in a kaleidoscope of color. What would have happened if he'd been the one to take me home? Granted, he was pretty drunk himself, so the answer might be nothing. Still, there's the possibility that—No! I won't even think it!

I slam my palm against the steering wheel, relishing the sting. While fear is uncertain, pain almost always brings focus. I'd told myself I wouldn't have to be afraid once I escaped my stepdad's grasp. But the more I'm out in the world, the more dangers I realize are out here, and the more

I wonder if I'll ever truly be unafraid again.

That's really all I want—all I've ever wanted. Unfortunately, the demons of my past, as well as the dangers of my present, not only haunt my every waking minute, but they follow me into my dreams, tormenting me through the night. And for someone who gets as little sleep as I do, a good cup of coffee is vital to existence, which is why whatever the hell it was that Lane brewed wasn't going to cut it.

Lane. I think about the bloodstained bandage wrapped around his knuckles and I can't help it—I smile. My entire childhood I'd wished for someone to stand up for me, and now that it's happened, it feels every bit as good as I'd imagined. It doesn't even matter that Lane's an ass—except the more I think about it, the more I realize he's not. An asshole wouldn't try and defend a girl he barely knows, especially when there's no potential for sex as a reward. So I wonder what his deal is? If life's taught me one thing, it's that no one does something for nothing. Everyone has an angle. What's Lane's?

I pull into a parking spot outside my building and turn off my car. Still, I'm in no hurry to get out. It doesn't matter that I've lived here a couple months. This place feels nothing like home. But at least it's not the bedroom prison cell that I grew up in.

I slowly pull the keys from the ignition and stare at the building that houses the few belongings I have left in the world—some clothes, my notebooks with my poetry, and the jar full of cash, where I've been tucking my tip money so I can save up for a better place—a place I can preferably live in alone. So in a way, the glass jar is home.

I walk up the sidewalk, but hesitate outside my apartment

door. I know whatever I find inside won't be good. The skin along my arms begins to itch and I shake my hands to relieve them of the tingling. It doesn't work, so I suck in a deep breath and open the door.

What I see plows into me like a ram, driving the air from my lungs so I'm left gasping in the doorway like a fish dangling from a hook.

The mess from the night before has quadrupled in my absence. The beer bottles that covered the counters now line the floors, some spilling beer into the cracks of the linoleum as well as the carpet. An ashtray has been flipped over on the sofa, leaving behind a ring of cigarette butts and soot in the microfiber.

While the living room is devoid of people, a girl's pink thong sits crumpled in the middle of the floor, right next to a Taco Bell wrapper. A shiny square of cellophane catches the sunlight filtering in through the dusty blinds and winks at me. There's only one thing I can think of that would be wrapped in such a small square. I start to step forward but stop, not sure I want to know whether the package has been opened.

Look at this mess! My stepdad's voice screams inside my head. *What kind of disgusting, worthless person could live in such conditions? And look at you, just standing there, doing nothing. How lazy can you be?*

My heart hammers and I lick my lips. Logically, I know he's not here. Still, I can suddenly feel him behind me, breathing heavily on my neck. I'm scared to turn around. I don't want to see the veins pulse over his temples—don't want to watch as his fingers, one by one, curl into tight fists. My stomach lurches and I close my eyes, hoping to vanquish his presence like a bad dream.

The words continue to echo through my head.

Lazy.

Worthless.

Tears squeeze through the crevices of my eyelids. There's only one thing to do. Opening my eyes, I hurry to the sink and turn the water on.

I need to clean—and fast.

Again, I know it's completely irrational, but I feel as if the mess surrounding me has the power to summon my stepfather, like a demon to blood. The sooner I get rid of it, the sooner I can relax. With shaking hands, I fall to the floor and open the cabinets, rooting through them until I find a garbage bag. I fluff it open and start throwing the bottles, underwear, and wrappers inside. I use the edge of the bag like a glove when it comes to picking up the condom wrapper. The condom itself is nowhere to be found—I can't decide if this is a good thing or not.

Once I've taken care of the trash, I fill the sink with scalding water, plunge my hands in, and start scrubbing. The burn of the water drives fresh tears to my eyes, but I can't stop. Fear drives me, pulse pounding, through the pain. By the time I'm rinsing the last dish, my hands are scarlet and throbbing.

My tears have run dry, leaving tight tracks across my cheeks. Still, I can't rest, not until everything is clean. I plug in the vacuum and go over not only the living room, but the kitchen and hallway, too. Afterward I grab a rag and bottle of cleaner, drop to my knees, and hand-scrub every stain until my knuckles are raw and seeping blood.

Only when I'm finished does my pulse slow from a

gallop to a trot. The pump of adrenaline diminishes, leaving me dizzy. Still clutching the filthy rag, I lean against the wall to keep from falling over.

I glance down the hall at Selena's room. Her door is cracked open—of course—and soft snoring can be heard coming from inside. I don't know if Selena is alone—odds are *no*—so I walk toward her door with the intention of closing it before I get front row seats to another live-action porno.

I make it only halfway when I see my own door and stop. Selena's previous roommate was no more a fan of Selena's party friends than I am, so she had a doorknob with a lock installed. Selena gave me the key when I moved in, and I always lock the door before I leave the apartment. But now it stands slightly ajar.

Dread fills my stomach like a ball of ice. Maybe I forgot to lock it? I immediately dismiss the thought, knowing I would never do such a thing. My room is where I keep my two most prized possessions: the notebooks filled with my writing, and the jar of tip money.

I tentatively grab the handle as a jagged lump wedges inside my throat. Maybe I would be lucky—maybe one of Selena's drunk friends broke in thinking it was the bathroom.

Someone whimpers from inside and I jerk back. "What the—?"

A small pink nose appears near the bottom of the door.

I push the door open and a small, tan puppy with white feet and a white blaze down its nose charges out at me. It jumps and spins circles around my feet, making me dizzy, until I'm forced to bend over and pick it up. I hold the wiggling mass inches away from my face, studying it in the hope that I've fallen into another one of my nightmares.

One sloppy wet swipe of the puppy's tongue across the tip of my nose proves no, I'm very much awake. So where did he come from?

I tuck the puppy under my arm and push my door open all the way. An odor so foul it burns my nose permeates my room. I flick on the lights and discover the puppy has left me several presents on the carpet. Because my bed consists of two stacked mattresses on the floor, there even appears to be a pile on top of my blankets.

Anxiety tightens my muscles, and I breathe deeply through my mouth to keep the panic attack at bay. Whoever decided to leave him in my room hadn't cared enough to even give him a dish of food or water. This puppy has nothing—not even a collar.

Still holding the puppy, I carefully step over the piles until I get to my dresser—the only other piece of furniture in the room. I slide open the first drawer and use my free hand to count the notebooks inside—seven, they're all there. The tight band around my chest loosens a fraction.

I slide the drawer shut and open the one below it. The few shirts and jeans I own are still neatly stacked beside a mound of balled socks. I reach through the socks and my finger touches the lip of a small glass jar. I almost breathe out a sigh of relief—*almost.* But if life has taught me anything, it's to never assume things are what they appear on the surface. Digging deeper, I grab the jar and pull it out.

It's empty.

Shock slams into me like a fist. I stagger back, unable to breathe. My grip loosens on the puppy and I quickly place him on the ground before I drop him. He must sense something's up because he's stopped dancing. His tail droops to the floor and he stares up at me with his large, dark eyes.

Five hundred dollars gone. Every single penny of tip money I've earned as a waitress and barista over the last six months has disappeared, leaving me with nothing. Every hope I've had of moving to another city and starting over is dashed in a few seconds.

I set the jar on my dresser and whirl around, pressing my trembling hands to my face. "What am I going to do?" I whisper.

The puppy cocks its head.

My insides feel as if they've turned to jelly. I grip the edge of my dresser for support. I know I'm seconds from collapsing onto the floor among the piles of shit. I can't continue living in this disgusting apartment among the dog crap, beer stains, and cigarette butts, but without my money, there's nowhere else I can go.

I rake my fingers through my hair, over and over again, as if I can somehow rip the nightmare out of my head. This can't be happening.

Before I realize what I'm doing, I march out my door to the end of the hall, with the puppy dancing at my feet. When I get to Selena's door, I slam it open so it hits the wall with a sharp crack.

Selena is lying alone on top of her covers, and the noise makes her jolt upright. She's wearing a pair of lacy, hot pink underwear and nothing else. Normally, I'd be too embarrassed to talk to her while she's topless, but my anger keeps me rooted in place. She rolls onto her side, blinking puffy eyes. "What the fuck, Ash?"

"Someone broke into my room!" Hysteria squeezes my

voice a pitch too high.

Selena rolls her eyes. "Relax. Nobody broke into your room. I asked Michael to open your door so we could put Diesel inside."

She's not making sense. "Who's Diesel?"

Selena smiles. "My new pit bull puppy. I bought him yesterday. He has shots, papers, everything." She motions to the puppy. "Come here, baby. Come to mama."

Diesel doesn't move.

"What about food?" I ask. "Bowls? A leash? Toys? Did you get any of that?"

She yawns. "I was going to ask if you could do all that for me. Pretty please? Michael promised to take me shopping before work."

I knew it. This puppy was just another one of her impulse buys and now that it's been over twenty-four hours, she's already bored. "Selena! We're not allowed to have dogs at this apartment!"

She makes a face. "The landlord doesn't care. Everyone else in this building has a dog."

I've never seen anyone in our building with a dog. But lying comes as naturally to Selena as breathing. "Look, the dog isn't the point. I keep my room locked for a reason. You can't have someone break into it whenever you want. Especially not to put a puppy inside—who shit all over my carpet, by the way. Because of you, someone went through my drawers and stole five hundred dollars!" My voice catches, and I struggle to swallow the sob that's risen inside my throat.

Selena groans and flings an arm over her face. "Look, I'm sorry about your room. I promise I won't have anyone open your precious locked door again, okay? As far as your money, are you sure you didn't lose it? I know my friends, Ash. And none of them are thieves."

A wave of fury burns through me. "No. I didn't *lose* five hundred dollars. I had it safe in my room before I went to work. And now it's gone. Somebody must have taken it."

Selena pulls her arm off her face. "Jesus, Ash. It's just money. You know, if you'd come work at the club with me, you could make that in a night."

"I don't want to work at your club!" I scream, causing the puppy to duck down and back out of the room. "I just want to come home to a not-trashed apartment, no shit on the carpet, and my money not stolen!"

Selena sighs. "Listen, if someone *did* take your money, they were probably just borrowing it. I'll find out who did and make them pay you back. Happy?"

"No!" I shake my head. "I want my money back now, and I want the parties to end."

Selena's eyes narrow into slits, and she slowly pushes herself up in bed. "You know the rent you pay is only a quarter of what is due, right? You're only renting the room, Ash. You have no say what goes on outside it. If you don't like that, you can find another place to live."

Whatever words I planned to say next dissolve on my tongue. It had been hard enough finding rent I could afford. There was no way I could do it now that my savings are gone.

As if she knows this, Selena gives me a smug smile. "I tell you what. You take that wad of cash over there." She motions to the clutter on her dresser. "Buy Diesel everything he needs, and you can keep the rest until I find out who took your money. Sound fair?"

I know Selena well enough to know she won't be asking

anyone anything, so as much as I hate it, this is the best deal I'm going to get. "Fine."

"Good." She falls back against her pillow. "Would you also mind taking Diesel out for me? You know how late I work. I just want to catch a few more minutes of sleep before my alarm goes off."

I'm pretty sure she doesn't own an alarm. Still, I say nothing as I step over piles of lingerie, shoes, and clothes to get to the dresser. Amidst the clutter of makeup, lotions, and perfumes are crumpled bills I'm sure were shoved in her sweaty G-string only hours ago. I gather every one I can find and leave Selena's room, closing the door behind me.

I can't deal with the mess in my own room at the moment, so I head to the small kitchen to count the money—a little over three hundred bucks.

The puppy looks up at me and whimpers. I pocket the cash and scoop him up. I have no idea the last time he's been let out or fed—given the state of my room, I'm willing to bet it's been awhile. "Let's get you some food. Come on—" I almost say Diesel, but the name doesn't feel right. "Listen," I tell him. "It's not that I don't think you can pull off the name, but you look more like a...Hank. Is it cool if I call you that?"

The puppy wags its entire butt. Apparently it is cool.

I reach for my keys and phone, only to notice I've missed a text. My heart quivers the moment I read the sender's name.

Mom.

She's written only six words, but they're enough to rake knives across my chest.

Please come home. Things are different.

I can feel myself coming undone all over again, muscles loosening from bone, and bone falling from tendon until I'm sure I'll dissolve into a pile on the floor.

God, I'm so tempted. Between the parties, the constant mess, and the sketchy guys, I would endure almost anything to escape this hellhole of an apartment. *Almost.*

This isn't the first time my mom's promised things will be different. *I've talked to him! He's promised to change. He's only hard on you because he loves you and wants you to succeed. He's had a tough life; he can't help the way he is. He's agreed to go to counseling.* These are the pretty words wrapping the box of promises she's offered me time after time. But I know, like every time before, once the words are peeled away and the box is opened, there will be only jagged pieces.

A pretty box full of broken promises.

The memory of the bonfire blazes in my mind with so much intensity I flinch. On top, a stuffed horse, one of my favorites from when I was a girl, crumples and burns into nothing. So much of my childhood—of my life—became nothing that day. I became nothing.

So, no. I won't go back.

As much as I want to believe things might finally be different, I know better. I've been burned too many times before.

Chapter Eight

Lane

I'm outlining a cover-up design in my sketchpad while trying to ignore the ramblings of the scratcher—a novice who stupidly attempted to tattoo himself. He came to me with what he claims to be a picture of his mother on his calf—but it actually looks more like a portrait of Ronald McDonald.

Sadly, I've seen worse.

"I mean," the guy continues, "it's not too bad for a first-timer, right?"

I spin around in my chair and glance at the snarling creature on his leg. "Yeah. It is. Look at that shit. It's supposed to be your mom? It looks like something out of a Stephen King novel."

The guy frowns at me. "I just need more practice is all. I'll start smaller. My girlfriend says I can ink a heart on her ankle—"

"No!" I jab a finger at his face. "You are forbidden from marring any more skin. You want to practice?" I reach across the counter and grab an orange I'd planned to eat for lunch. I'm more than happy to sacrifice it if it means the end of his skin mutilations. "Here." I toss the fruit at him. "Start with fruit and work your way up to pig skin. I swear to God if anyone comes in this shop wanting a tattoo fixed, and I find out you were the one to fuck it up, I'm kicking your ass."

The guy shrinks back against the seat, like I knew he would. Even the biggest assholes are afraid to challenge the guy about to drill into their skin with a needle. I just hope he takes me seriously. Tattoos are art and self-expression, not fucking cattle brands.

I turn back to my sketchpad, but I'm no longer looking at the design I've laid out. Instead, I find my thoughts drifting to Ashlyn and the douchebag she'd let talk her into tattooing his name on her skin. I've seen it many times before. The guys pressure the girls into getting the ink, claiming it will prove their love, but what the guys really want is to claim ownership of their bodies.

I think about Ash sitting in some other artist's chair, getting a tattoo she doesn't want, and my stomach clenches painfully tight. I'd be lying to myself if I said this was the first time I'd thought about her today. I haven't been able to stop thinking about her since I dropped her off at her car. She'd been so quiet on the ride over. She'd glanced at me as she shut the door, and her eyes were so full of worry—like she was afraid of something.

It took everything I had not to follow her home to make sure she was all right. Even now, I can't shake the uneasiness I felt watching her drive away. What if she's hurt? In trouble?

"Um, dude?"

I look over at the scratcher to find him staring at my drawing pad. I glance down and found I've rested my sharpie against the page too long, giving the drawing of his mother what looks like a really big wart on her chin.

"Shit." *Get a fucking grip on yourself, Lane.* I rip the page from the pad. "Don't worry about the drawing. I'll have it squared away when you come back tomorrow." I swallow hard and try to push all thoughts of Ashlyn from my mind. I honestly don't know why I'm giving her a second thought. I've got too much on my plate at the moment to worry about some girl. "Come back at two, and we'll get started."

The guy nods and slides off my chair. I don't bother to watch him leave, so when I hear the front door chime, I assume I'm alone. I roll over to the counter and drop my forehead against it with a thunk. I'm better than this. Lane Garrett doesn't get distracted by the opposite sex—so why is it happening to me now?

"Dad? Are you feeling okay?"

I push away from the counter to find my ten-year-old daughter staring at me with her lips pouted. Lines of concern etch her little brow. Like everything else about her, it's adorable. "Harper! Hey, sweetheart!" I plaster on my biggest smile and squeeze her against me. Her chocolate curls tickle my chin. "No. Your dad isn't sick, he just had a long night babysitting Aunt Emily."

Harper giggles and slides from my grasp. "*Dad.* Aunt Emily is too old to be babysat!"

"You'd think, wouldn't you?"

My mom pushes aside the curtain and steps into the room. She smiles warmly when she sees me. "Hey, Lane.

Sorry for the surprise visit, but she wanted to see you."

"Never be sorry for bringing in my favorite person for a visit!" I grab Harper and try to squeeze her into another bear hug, but she squeals and wriggles free. Avoiding my hugs is something she's started doing more and more since she turned ten, and I can't help it—my heart breaks a little more each time. I look at my mom. "Thanks for watching her for me today." I motion to my schedule book and sigh. "I've got a full lineup."

Harper stops smiling. "Aw! So you'll be home late?"

"Afraid so." I tousle her hair. "Way past your bedtime."

"I'm ten and it's Saturday! What if Grandma lets me stay up?"

"She won't." I jab a stern finger at my mom. "You won't."

She smirks and waves my warning away. "Please. Grandmas are known for their stern enforcement of bedtimes."

I make a face. "*Yeah.*" I turn back to Harper, who's still giving me puppy eyes. Damned if it doesn't make me want to cancel all my appointments and lock the shop up right now.

"Can you at least give me a tattoo?" she asks, bottom lip stuck out.

Warmth swells inside me. At least she's not too old for some things. "Sure." I open a drawer, searching for the washable markers I've used to give Harper "tattoos" since she was a toddler. As for the real thing, she's not allowed to get one until she's eighteen, just like everyone else. "I've only got fifteen minutes until my next appointment so it will have to be fast. What do you want?"

She points to the edge of her name peeking out from my shirt collar. "I want your name, Daddy, like you have mine."

I freeze with my hand clutching the black marker so

tightly my knuckles turn white. Very slowly, I swivel around to face her. "Sweetheart, what does Daddy say about getting someone's name inked on your body?"

She flops onto the chair with a huff. "That getting someone's name is a bad idea because you can't be sure they'll be with you forever. But we're going to be together forever, right?"

Damn it. She has me there. I look to my mom for help but she's too busy trying to cover her smile with her hand. I give her a look that clearly states, *Thanks a lot,* before I turn back to Harper. I take her hands in mine and pull her close so our foreheads touch. "Yes, sweetheart, we're going to be together forever. I promise."

She traces her name along the edge of my collarbone. "Is that why you never got my mom's name? Did you always know she was going to leave?"

My mom stops laughing, and I feel as if an invisible fist has ripped through my chest and taken hold of my heart. This isn't the first time we've had this discussion, but that doesn't make it any easier. "Sweetheart," I struggle to say, "when your mom found out she was pregnant, she was very, very young and scared. In her own way, she wanted to do what was best for you, and she thought that was to let me take care of you."

Harper nods slowly, her eyes roaming my face as if searching for the truth. Someday, when she's older, I'll tell her about the two sixteen-year-olds who made a reckless mistake and paid for it. Crystal and I barely knew each other when we hooked up at that party all those years ago. When she found out she was pregnant, she insisted on giving the baby up for adoption. After all, what the hell did two sixteen-year-olds know about raising a baby?

Initially, I agreed, but only until the moment I first saw Harper and knew I could more easily saw off my limbs and give them away than I could give up the baby who was just as much, if not more, a part of me. I tried to make it work with Crystal so Harper could have a mother, but in the end there was no fixing what had never worked in the first place. Crystal eventually left, leaving me with sole custody. After Dad died, with Mom unable to work while receiving chemo treatments, I dropped out of school so I could work full time to provide for my family. I went through hell to make sure Harper, Em, and Mom never wanted for anything. And I'd do it all over again.

In ten years, Crystal has never visited, called, or even written to check on her daughter. Even though Harper doesn't remember her, her mom's absence has left a hole in her heart. I can see it in the way her brows draw together when she's studying other mothers at the playground or in restaurants. I can read on her lips the questions that she refuses to ask. The biggest one is why. And no matter how much I want to, I just can't answer.

Because I don't *have* an answer. Apparently, there are people who can cut out a piece of their heart, throw it in the trash, and forget it ever existed. I am not one of them.

But they're out there.

Which is why I've worked so hard to create a good life for us, to make sure Harper has all the security and love she needs. I can't afford to let someone else in to our family and risk them undoing everything I've struggled to build. I know relationships come with risks, which is why I've vowed to avoid them.

Harper is my number one priority. She needs stability, and I owe it to her to make sure she has it. The fact that her mother gave her up hurts her, so I've dedicated my life to loving her enough for two parents. Maybe I'll be enough, maybe I won't. Either way, I'll be damned if I let anyone else into our lives and risk them walking away with another piece of my daughter's heart.

Chapter Nine

Lane

I'm sprawled across the tattoo chair, dicking around on my phone in an attempt to keep my fury at bay. I told Ashlyn to be here at ten o'clock for her shading appointment. But here I am, alone, at nearly ten forty-five. I shove the phone in my pocket. *Fuck this, I'm going home.*

But no sooner do I stand when I hear the front door chime. My muscles tingle as I try to get a grip on my agitation. I stride to the curtain and rip it aside. Ashlyn stands at the front door, twisting the handle open and closed. "What the hell are you doing?" I ask.

Inhaling sharply, she releases the knob. A flush creeps into her cheeks. "Sorry, I was just checking— " But she bites off the words before she finishes. "Never mind. It's silly."

"Do you have any idea what time it is?"

"I do. I'm so sorry." She leans against the door and

combs her fingers through her hair. "Work ran late and I had to rush home after. My roommate got this puppy that she's not going to take care of. I knew she probably hadn't let it outside the entire time I was gone, so I drove home really quickly so I could—"

"Save it." The words come out harsher than I intend and she flinches. "I don't want to hear your excuses when you obviously don't care about my time. Did it ever occur to you I have better things to do than sit around all night and wait for you to show up?"

"No, I—" She snaps her mouth shut. "I'm sorry." She twists her fingers together and shrinks against the door. "Maybe I should go?"

There's something about her that looks so fragile, vulnerable. My anger dissolves and I'm left feeling like an asshole. I sigh and shake my head. "No. Look, I'm sorry I snapped at you. I've had a long day and I thought you were blowing me off.

"I would never!" She shakes her head and that's when I notice the exhaustion pulling at her shoulders, and the dark circles beneath her eyes. Maybe she's still suffering from last night's hangover—or maybe it's something else entirely.

My dad the cop would never turn away from someone in distress. While I hate to get involved in other people's business, there's that part of him that lives on in me. I take a step toward her and her eyes widen, startled. "Are you okay?"

She gives a nervous laugh. "Of course I'm okay. I'm fine—better than fine. So do you still have time to do some shading or do you want me to come back another night?"

It's obvious this girl doesn't have a lot of experience

lying. The truth is written across her face like on the page of a book. "Don't bullshit me. You don't look fine."

Two tiny lines crease above her nose as she frowns. "Not that it's any of your business, but my roommate and I keep very different hours. It's taking a little getting used to."

I don't buy for a second that's the extent of her problems. But she does have a point. Whatever is going on with her is none of my business. I shrug—my attempt to drop the subject. I can't force her to open up to me, and I paid my duty to the old man by asking. Still, I can't shake the gnawing feeling she's in some kind of trouble. Even worse, I can't figure out why I care.

"Come on." I wave a hand for her to follow, and head into the back room. When she enters, I point to the chair. "Make yourself at home. Some people get sick to their stomach when they're getting inked. Nerves or whatever. Sometimes a soda helps—you want one?"

She nods as she walks to the chair. "Please," she says and perches on the end. She picks up one of the markers I used for Harper's "tattoo" and raises an eyebrow. "Doing some coloring?"

I cross the room to the mini fridge. "They're for the kids that come into my shop."

An unreadable expression crosses her face, and I'm reminded of Em's drunken warning from last night.

She's got a thing about kids.

I hesitate with my hand on the fridge. What kind of thing? Does she not like them? Did she have an abortion? Did she abandon her baby with the father and take off across the country, never to be heard from again?

I want to ask about this, but I know that would violate

the conditions of our truce. Besides, after tonight I'll never see Ash again, so it's not like it will matter.

I open the fridge. "What kind of soda do you want?"

She shakes her head and sets the marker down. "Doesn't really matter. I was in such a hurry after work I didn't have time to eat, so I'll be happy with anything."

I turn away from her so she can't see my frown. I know she's feeding me more lies. As skinny as the girl is, she either forgets to eat a lot, or there's something else going on.

Not my problem, I remind myself as I grab two Dr Peppers from the fridge. I also snag the Snickers bar I'd been saving for later and toss it on Ashlyn's lap.

She flinches—something I realize she does a lot—before grabbing the candy. "That's really nice of you, but I'm fine, really." She says this, but I can see the hunger in her eyes and the way she can't look away from the chocolate bar. "I'll just eat something when I get home."

"Keep it." I set the sodas down on the counter and pop both tabs at once.

"Are you sure?"

"It's a fucking candy bar, not an engagement ring. I'm sure." I turn to hand her the soda and find her staring at her lap, lips tight, and cheeks flushed red. *Jesus H. Christ.* I don't know what I find more annoying, that this girl is so sensitive, or that I actually feel shitty for making her feel bad.

My stool cushion makes a little hiss of protest as I drop onto it. "Look, I'm sorry. We've both had long days, and we're both tired. The sooner we get done here, the sooner we can both go to bed."

She nods, her gaze still glued to her lap. "Okay."

Thank God. "Here." I thrust the soda at her.

She looks up and, maybe she wasn't expecting to find me so close, but she lets out a startled squeak and her hand flies up. Her fingers hit the edge of the soda can and knock it from my grasp. Dr Pepper spirals through the air, raining across the chair and my lap until the can hits the floor, where the rest of the soda pools in a brown lake.

I don't move. Maybe because I'm the father of a young child, spills are nothing new to me. In fact, the look of horror on Ash's face makes me crack a grin. "Well, fuck," I say, laughing softly. I expect Ash to join in—I mean, my crotch is soaked in ice-cold Dr Pepper, making me look like I pissed my jeans. That shit's comedy gold. If Harper were here, she'd be giggling her ass off.

But not Ash. She doesn't move for several seconds, doesn't appear to breathe. The blood drains from her face until her skin matches the white paint on the walls. I stop laughing. "Hey. You all right?"

She jumps to her feet. "I…I'm so s-sorry." Her eyes are impossibly wide as her head whips back and forth, searching for— I have no idea what.

What the fuck? I slowly rise to my feet. "It's not that big of a—"

"I'll clean it up! I promise!" Her voice has risen to a shriek and she's visibly shaking. She runs to the counter and rips handfuls of paper towels from a holder on the wall. In the process, she bumps a glass jar of alcohol swabs onto the floor where it shatters. She freezes, her eyes clenched shut.

"Oh my God," she whispers. The paper towels slip from her fingers and she falls to her knees, I'm pretty sure landing on top of broken glass.

"Holy shit." I'm momentarily frozen because I have no

idea what to do. It's like she's coming completely undone before my eyes. I take a tentative step toward her and confirm that yes, she's kneeling in glass. What I can't figure out is how she hasn't noticed.

She reaches for the paper towel roll only to bump it further away with her shaking hands. "I'm so sorry. I can be so clumsy, so s-stupid." She chokes and pulls her hands away. A flush burns up her neck and bleeds into her cheeks. Tears shimmer in her eyes and cling to her lashes. "I'll clean it up. I promise. I'm just so sorry." She covers her face.

"Hey." I walk toward her slowly, as if approaching a frightened animal, until I'm directly in front of her. "Hey!" I try again. "Ash, look at me."

But she only shakes her head and mumbles more apologies behind her hands.

Okay, fuck this. I tried the gentle approach, but I'll be damned if I let this girl continue to fillet herself. Before she can stop me, I bend down and scoop her up in my arms. She weighs practically nothing, confirming my suspicion she's not eating enough.

She lets out a small yelp and drops her hands. "What are you doing?"

I don't say anything as I carry her across the room and deposit her back in the chair. Honestly, I don't know how to answer her question because I'm not sure myself. I point a finger at her. "I'm going to clean this mess up." She opens her mouth as if to argue, but I quickly cut her off. "Do *not* move. I mean it."

Her eyes widen and she wipes at her tear-streaked cheeks. "I'm so—"

"Sorry," I finish for her. "I know. But it was an accident,

Ash." I grab the paper towels from the floor and look into her frightened eyes. "Don't you get that? You don't have to be sorry for accidents."

"I should be cleaning," she says, and starts to rise.

My anger burns like acid—anger not directed at Ash, but whoever made her this way. "*Sit.*" I growl through clenched teeth.

She shrinks against the chair, her eyes unfocused. Whoever she's seeing, it's not me.

I try again, this time gentler. "I got this."

Instead of answering, she wraps her arms around her chest.

Moving as quickly as I can, I mop up the soda on the floor with the paper towels and use a brush and dustpan to gather the glass. Ash doesn't move or make a sound the entire time. When I finish, I grab my first aid kit from the cabinet and scoot my stool next to her before sitting.

"I'm going to look at your knees now, okay?" I say in the same voice I use to soothe Harper when she wakes up from a nightmare. It must work, because Ashlyn's eyes meet mine and for the first time since spilling the soda, they're clear and focused.

"Why?"

How the hell is it possible she doesn't know? "Just look at them."

She glances at the torn fabric of her jeans and the blood seeping into the denim. "Oh my God," she whispers. "I didn't…I just…I'm so sorry. I'll clean up the blood. I swear." Her face crumples.

Fuck. This was not my intention. "Ash, please don't cry. It's just a little blood. We'll get it cleaned up."

She shakes her head and chokes on a sob. "I'm so sorry."

Seeing her fall apart like this does something to me I can't explain. Maybe it's my desire to live up to my dad's honor, maybe it's because I'm a father, or maybe it's something else entirely. Before I realize what I'm doing, I set the first aid kit aside and pull her into my arms, cradling her head into the curve of my neck. I have a split second to think, *what the fuck are you doing, Lane?* before I decide to shut down my brain entirely. God, for once I don't want to analyze every fucking thing. I just want to do what feels right, regardless of the repercussions. And this feels right. I don't know why, I don't want to know why, I just know it does.

"No one is going to hurt you," I whisper against the top of her head. "Not while I got you." And I mean every fucking word. In this moment, while cradling this broken girl, I would rip the arms off anyone who tried to lay a finger on her.

Her shuddering stills, and Ashlyn loops her arms around my neck and claws her fingers into the fabric of my T-shirt. Her tears trail down my neck and bleed into my shirt collar. Her grip on my neck is almost choking, but I don't say a word. In this moment I will be whatever she needs me to be—even if that's just something to hold onto.

I wrap my arms around her and pull her tight against me. She feels too skinny and too frail in my grasp. A small voice in my head screams at me to stop, to let her go and walk her straight out of the shop, locking the door behind her. But the strength required to release her is more than I can gather.

I'm not sure how much time passes. Minutes? A half hour? Gradually, her sobs die down and her grasp loosens from my neck. I can feel her head shift beneath my chin so that she's looking up at me, but the moment I lean back to look down, she averts her gaze.

"I feel like such an idiot," she says, her voice barely a whisper. "Y-you don't even like me."

"That's not true," I say. I reach for her face and use my thumbs to wipe the tears from her eyes.

Irritation pinches lines above her nose. Damned if it isn't adorable. "*Please.*" She pushes against my chest, forcing my arms open, and slides off my lap. I suddenly feel hollowed out, and I grip my knees to keep from reaching for her.

"Look," she continues. "I don't need your pity. This situation is awkward enough without that."

"You think I pity you?"

"Of course," she says matter-of-factly. "Why else are you being so nice to me?"

I sigh and rake a hand through my hair. I'm not sure how to answer. A moment of weakness? Hormones? Who the hell knows? "Not out of pity," I mumble.

"*Right.*" She rubs the heels of her hands against her swollen eyes. "If there's one thing I can't stand, it's a liar, Lane."

I know exactly what she's doing because I've done it myself, too many times. She opened herself too wide and I got too close, so now she wants to push me away before anything else happens. I should be happy she's pulling away, something I should have done all along. But instead, my fingers curl into the denim of my jeans as anger swells inside my chest. "You're calling me a liar?"

She stops rubbing her eyes and makes a face. "I may be many things Lane, but I'm not stupid."

"Good." I slide my hand behind her head, entwining my

fingers in her hair so there's no escape. Her eyes fly wide. "Then you'll have no trouble at all deciphering this."

"What are you—?"

Before she can finish, I pull her to me until I feel the heat of her startled gasp against my lips. I tell myself it's because I can't stand to be called a liar. I tell myself it's because I want to prove her wrong. But in the end, it doesn't matter what I tell myself. The second our lips touch, a fire ignites inside of me and I know *exactly* why I kissed her—because I fucking wanted to.

Her hands go rigid on my chest, like she might pull away, and I might have to let her, then they soften, sliding up the fabric of my shirt, leaving a trail of shivers in their wake. Her mouth is hot, a delicious burn of sweet candy on my tongue. I know I should let her go, that no good can come of this, but then her slender fingers crawl along the back of my neck and curl into my hair. She's not going anywhere.

I wind my fingers through the belt loops in her jeans and tug. Ash responds by swinging a leg over my lap, straddling me. The heat of her skin melts into mine, tightening things low inside me with need. A growl spills from my throat and Ash swallows it with her kisses. They become frantic, devouring. And for a moment, I consider letting her consume me.

Her hands slide from the back of my head and trace my jaw. She rises up a fraction, rubbing against my jeans and the throbbing ache locked behind the zipper. A hiss spills from between my teeth as I run my fingers under the edge of her shirt to the silky skin beyond. I slide them slowly upward until I find the lacy edge of her bra. Gliding my thumb along the curve of her breast, I hear her gasp, a sound which drives me wild and makes me dizzy. I want to make her cry out again and again.

I free one hand from her shirt, wind it into her hair, and gently pull her head back, exposing her throat. My dick pulses in time with her heavy breaths. I'm not sure I'll be able to stop myself from exploding.

I run my lips along the arc of her throat, and her fingers fall to my shoulders. Her nails dig into my skin just to the point of pain. I'm seconds from crying out when she thrusts her hips forwards, grinding along my lap and sending a wave of heat surging through my body. Without meaning to, I bite down on her neck.

Ash moans and bucks against me, building the ache inside me to an unbearable level. This time I can't fight the groan building in my throat. I know we should stop, before we reach the point of no return. But for once in my life, I've lost complete control. I grab the edge of her shirt and rip it over her head.

Her breasts, like the rest of her, are absolutely perfect. I run my hands along the swell of them, feeling the way she quivers beneath my touch. She takes the hem of my own shirt in her hands and, with my help, tugs it from my body.

She pulls on her bottom lip with the edge of her teeth as her gaze roams appraisingly across my chest. The hunger in her eyes rips through me, pulling every muscle in my body taut with need. "Ash—" I need to warn her, need to make sure she wants this as much as I do, because we're dangerously close to the edge.

She traces a finger across my collarbone. A feeling like satin ribbons trails after her touch. She slowly leans closer; her swollen lips part. I tighten my hold on her in anticipation.

But our lips never meet.

I shift back to find her staring at something specifically. At a point on my chest. "Ash?"

"Oh my God." She shakes her head. "I'm such an idiot." Before I can ask her what she's talking about, she slides from my lap and skitters across the floor for her T-shirt.

I'm still tight with desire, so I can't move as fast as her. It takes me several seconds before I'm able to stand. By then, she's already got her shirt on and is moving for the door. She's not making sense. One second we were all over each other, stripping off our clothes and the next second, not. "Ash, wait. What's going on?"

She shakes her head. "I was just confused and upset—you made me forget that. But I just can't be *that* girl for you, Lane. I have more respect for myself than that." The darkness that had disappeared from her eyes a moment ago is back.

She's not making any fucking sense. "What do you mean, *that* girl?"

She points a finger at my chest and I follow her gaze to where Harper's name is etched on my skin.

"The *other* girl," Ash says and brushes past the curtain. A moment later I hear the front door chime and I know she's well and truly gone.

Alone, I sit on the edge of the tattoo chair and run my fingers though my hair. "Fuck." I can't say I didn't see this coming. In fact, I should be glad Ash had the strength to end it because I clearly didn't.

So fucking weak. I sigh and shake my head. Not to mention stupid. This never could have worked out. *Ash has a thing about kids.* And so do I. I place my hand over Harper's name. I can't believe I allowed someone to get to me, to break down the walls I've carefully constructed. I'd told Ash what Harper and I have is special, that it's forever, and it is.

I will love that little girl with my last dying breath. I will do anything to protect her from being hurt, and I will never get involved with a woman who might leave us wounded all over again.

And if Ash proved anything to me tonight, it's that she's a runner.

Chapter Ten

Ashlyn

Fuck. Fuck. Fuck.

The words run on a loop through my head as I exit my car and walk to my apartment. What the hell was I thinking? Well, I know exactly what I was thinking. Every time I close my eyes, or even blink, Lane fills the darkness. I bring a hand to my lips to find them still swollen from his kisses. It's as if I can still feel the heat of Lane's fingers trailing along my ribs, and the hardness of him swelling between my straddled legs. A shudder ripples through me and I sway slightly.

Fuck!

I shake my head as if to rid myself of the memories. Yes, he's unbelievably sexy, and yes, with just a look he can tighten things inside of me to the point of snapping, but that doesn't make him any less unavailable. I've been used before—too many times before—and I'm done. I made a promise to myself after Chris, that I was going to get my life in order before I even considered a relationship.

I open the door to the building and am greeted by the thump of a bass beat. Dread twists inside my gut as I walk down the hall. I know which apartment is hosting the party before I even reach the door.

I grip the knob but can't bring myself to turn it. Beneath the pulse of music I hear voices rising in laughter. Wisps of smoke waft from under the door. If I had any tears left in me, I might cry. All I want is a quiet night alone in my bed to get my head straight. The last thing I want to deal with is Selena's drunken, doped-out friends. I consider turning around, but where would I go? Besides, there's Hank, and the odds Selena even remembers she has a puppy are slim to none.

I suck in a gulp of air and brace myself as I push the door open. As expected, a wall of smoke barrels out at me, an acrid fog of cigarette and pot that I'm forced to inhale when I can hold my breath no longer.

"Ash!" Selena shouts over the music. She waves a cup at me, the contents sloshing over the plastic rim. The sickly-sweet smell of alcohol permeates the air, making my stomach roll in nauseous waves, reminding me of my drunken escapade the night before.

"Hey." I keep my eyes trained on her face so I don't have to look at the mess.

Selena's on the couch, sitting on a guy's lap—he's new, and so are half the other people in the apartment.

"Hey, sexy." A skinny, long-nosed guy leans against the wall next to me. "Where'd you come from?"

I brush past him. *So* not in the mood for that.

"Where you going?" he calls behind me.

"To find my dog," I answer. It takes me a minute to realize what I've said—*my* dog. But as soon as I speak the words, I realize it's true. It doesn't matter that I never wanted a pet and I can barely take care of myself. Both of us were dragged into shitty situations and forgotten by the very person who was supposed to look out for us. I know what it's like to be left to fend for yourself, to be tossed aside the second you become inconvenient, and I won't turn my back on Hank.

"The pit bull?" the guy asks. "Little shit pissed on the floor so somebody threw it in the bathtub. You should leave it there so it learns its lesson."

It takes everything in me not to grab the guy by the throat and lock *him* in the bathroom. Instead, I push past him and open the door. The smell of shit smacks me in the face as I enter the small room and find Hank cowering in the back of the tub, his eyes wide in terror.

Several piles of his runny stool streak the bottom of the tub, run through with paw prints.

The guy laughs behind me. "Told you he was a little shit."

Without responding, I slam the door in his face and lock it behind me. Even through the pulse of music I hear him call me a bitch. As if I care.

I turn to the shivering puppy. "Oh Hank, I'm so sorry I had to leave you alone here." Guilt rips through my heart. I know exactly what it's like to be locked inside a room, alone and scared. I kneel beside the tub and the puppy hops along the side, desperate to get to me.

I turn the water on warm. "I'm going to get you cleaned up and then we're going to go… " I really have no idea where. After giving Hank a thorough scrubbing and towel drying,

I gather his bowls, food, and leash, as well as a change of clothes for myself, and head for the door.

"Hey!" Selena calls out to me. Her eyes are glassy and red-rimmed. "Where are you taking Diesel?"

"For a walk." I don't tell her where to or for how long. She's too fucked up to notice.

"Okay." She grins and reaches for the joint the girl beside her holds out. Maybe by tomorrow she'll forget she ever had a dog.

When we get outside, Hank prances and spins around my legs. Apparently he's just as happy to get the hell out of there as I am. I pause in the grass long enough for him to do his business before loading him in my car.

He grins happily, his tail thumping against my seat.

I sigh. "While I appreciate your enthusiasm, I'm afraid we're not going anywhere exciting." Hotels are expensive, and with no family other than my mom and stepdad in the area, it looks like we are destined for a night in the car, something I'm no stranger to. When I was first kicked out of my house, I learned pretty fast there are certain places you can sleep in your car without getting harassed by cops or anyone else.

After a fifteen-minute trek down the interstate, I turn off onto a ramp for a rest stop. Having frequented many in the area, I know this particular one is the nicest, with the cleanest bathroom stalls, the most vending machines, and best-lit parking lot.

I park at the end of the row and carefully drape T-shirts over the side windows, keeping them in place by rolling the window up on the fabric. Next, I unfold a sun visor across the windshield.

Hank watches me, cocking his head in interest.

"This isn't my first rodeo," I tell him. "I don't like people watching me sleep—some of them are pretty sick fucks." One of the first times I'd slept overnight at a rest stop I'd awoken to find a truck parked next to my car and a guy staring at me through the window, his hand clearly groping his own lap.

A shudder of revulsion ripples through me and I hit the door lock. "Sorry there are no mints for the pillows," I tell Hank. "This is the best I can do."

The puppy climbs across the center console and curls into my lap. I can't help but smile as I stroke his soft fur. This is the first time I haven't been alone while forced to sleep in my car. I have to admit, with Hank here, it's not nearly as bad.

I recline my seat and settle against the hard cushion as best I can. In fact, compared to the loud party going on at my apartment, the quiet comfort of my car is almost peaceful.

Too bad it doesn't last.

The second my eyelids close, I find Lane waiting for me in the darkness behind them. Lane, whose eyes blaze with hunger and whose touch ignites fire beneath my skin. I can almost feel the ripple of his chest muscles under my fingers and smell the earthy spice of his cologne.

"Bah!" I open my eyes as cold droplets of sweat prick along my skin.

Hank yawns and gives me an annoyed look.

"Sorry," I mutter. But I'm even more sorry I let Lane get to me. Emily warned me to stay away from her brother, and Lane himself told me he was involved with someone. My only excuse is I'd been vulnerable. After spilling the soda, I could feel my stepdad's angry presence in the tattoo studio, feel the fury radiating off of him like a thousand pin pricks digging into my skin. But the second Lane put his arms around me, my stepdad was gone. For the first time in my life, I felt safe.

And then I felt other things...*lots* of other things. But who could blame me for losing myself in the moment and in Lane's arms?

I scratch my fingers along my skull as if I can pluck the memories out and fling them from my head. God, I'm such an idiot. Lane is probably laughing his ass off at me right now—the stupid girl he thought he could play.

"Stupid! So stupid!" I slam my hand against the steering wheel.

Startled, Hank jumps up and licks my nose.

I blink at him, surprised, before I bust out in a laugh. "You're absolutely right, Hank." I scratch behind his floppy ears until he settles back onto my lap. "From now on, I'll be saving my kisses for puppies, *not* dogs."

Chapter Eleven

Ashlyn

The sunbeams filtering through the T-shirt covered window warm my skin and pull me into consciousness. My back aches, and I bring my hand to my neck to massage the knot that's formed. God, sleeping in a car sucks.

The lump of fur on my lap stirs and lets out a whimper.

"Right." My voice is thick with sleep. I fumble my hand along the center console and grab my phone and the leash. After snapping the leash to Hank's collar, I push the door open. Hank bounds outside while I stumble after. We walk to the grassy area designated for dogs. While Hank searches for the perfect spot, I glance at my phone to discover I have a text message. With my phone on vibrate, I guess I slept through the buzz.

At first a flicker of excitement jolts through me when I think the sender might be Lane, before I realize A, he doesn't know my number, and B, he's already involved with someone. *Ashlyn, you idiot!*

I read the name of the sender. The single word sends anxiety plummeting into my stomach.

Chris.

We dated on and off throughout my senior year of high school, and even rented an apartment together for three months after graduation, before I got tired of trying to force myself into the mold Chris set out for me. His subtle suggestions for how I should live my life became more and more persistent until I figured out it wasn't me he loved, but some ideal he thought he could shape me into. Turns out I wasn't clay. The more he sculpted, the more I broke.

I thought we were done. While I know I should leave well enough alone, my curiosity about what he could want with me *now* is overwhelming, so I click on the message.

Hey Ash, I was cleaning out my closet when I found some clothes of yours I thought you might want back. I won't make you come here. How about we meet for lunch? Panera at noon? My treat. No strings attached.

I chew on my lip and reread the text several times. I moved out of his apartment in such a hurry I left behind my favorite green sweater. I really would love to get it back—but not at the expense of having to put up with any of Chris's bullshit. Still, he *did* say no strings attached. And can I really turn down a free lunch?

My stomach twists painfully at the thought; it's been nearly twenty-four hours since I last ate anything. Really, the second he mentioned food, he had me. "And you'll go with me, right?" I ask Hank. "Chris wouldn't dare mess with me while I have such a vicious guard beast, would he?"

As if in response, Hank flops over and rolls his back along the grass.

Yeah. Chris is sure to be intimidated by that.

Chris is already sitting on the restaurant patio when I show up. Two plates of sandwiches and chips sit on the table. Despite being starving, a flicker of annoyance twinges through me. I always hated how he ordered food for me without asking—looks like some things never change.

He smiles and stands when he sees me. His blond hair is gelled perfectly in place and the creases ironed into his shirt are so sharp they look like they could cut bread. Nothing new there—Chris always did like everything just so. But I can tell by the way his smile withers when he spots the leash in my hand and the puppy trailing behind me, our meeting isn't going according to his plan—and he always has a plan.

"You have a dog now?"

"Yes." I slip the loop of Hank's leash under the chair leg before I sit down.

"I hate dogs," Chris says, his eyes accusing. "You know that."

Actually I didn't. Happy coincidence. I pick a piece of turkey from the sandwich and give it to Hank, who happily gobbles it up.

Chris groans. "Don't do that. You shouldn't feed it table scraps. You're going to make it a beggar."

Wow. I've only been with him for thirty seconds and he's

already telling me what to do. That has to be a new record. I pull another piece of turkey from the sandwich and feed it to Hank.

Chris scowls. "You always do that, Ash. You always ignore me when I'm just trying to help."

I take a big bite of the sandwich—the entire reason I agreed to this meeting. It's been months since I've eaten in an actual restaurant. The flavors of the lettuce, tomato, and turkey should be exploding on my tongue, but with Chris sitting so close, the food tastes like dirt. "I don't need your help," I say between mouthfuls.

Chris leans back in the chair and folds his arms across his chest. "First of all, you shouldn't talk with your mouth full."

I roll my eyes and take another bite.

"Second," he continues, "I know that's not true because your mom called me. She says you won't return her calls—she's worried about you."

The bite of turkey sinks into my stomach like a stone and I set the sandwich down. "What?" I never imagined my mother would call my ex-boyfriend to check up on me. Then again, because I haven't spoken to her since my stepdad threw me out, she probably didn't know Chris was my ex.

He leans across the table. "Where are you living, Ash?"

I jerk back. "That's none of your business."

"It is my business. Just because we broke up doesn't mean I don't still care about you. I miss you, Ash. I know we got off to a rocky start, that I was too hard on you, and I'm here to tell you I'm sorry." He reaches for my hands, which I quickly recoil into my lap. "I'll change, I'll do whatever you need me to do so you'll move back in. I'll take care of you,

I promise."

His words wrap around my ribs and pull tight, suffocating me. I've heard enough promises in my life to know putting faith in them is like walking a tightrope made of licorice. Sure they're sweet, but they never hold weight.

"It won't be easy," Chris admits, "but I know we can work this out. Relationships are about give and take, so of course you'd have to give a little, too. This dog, for example." He nods at Hank. "He'd have to go. But I'm willing to help find him a good home. My uncle lives on a farm, I'm sure he'd be willing to take him. Also, you're not still serious about this writing thing, are you? You can still go back to college."

For a moment, the lure of Chris's always clean and quiet apartment is enough to make me wonder if all the struggle I've put myself through in the attempt to live my own life is worth it. I slept in my car last night because it was a better option than my current apartment. I'm a long way from having the money I need to live on my own, and I haven't written a word of poetry in weeks. What the hell am I fighting for?

Hank whines, pulling me from my thoughts. My gaze travels to the leash looped beneath my chair leg, and I realize *this* is why I'm fighting. No Hank. No writing. Go to college. Even though I know Chris would never hurt me physically, the leash I would wear under his roof would only be a prettier version of the one I wore under my stepdad's.

And I'll sleep in a million truck stops before I let someone tie me up and try to control me ever again.

"Chris." I lean forward.

"Yeah?" He grins, that cocky grin, as if he can already see my bags packed.

"I just really want my green sweater back."

Chapter Twelve

Lane

Harper scans through my truck's radio stations and settles on some sappy ballad sung by a boy band. I press my lips into a thin line and grip the steering wheel to keep from turning the music off. I'm hardly in the mood to listen to a bunch of fourteen-year-olds sing about everlasting love.

Harper sits next to me smiling and singing along with the words—something about a Friday night party and *Girl, you're so beautiful.* If only things were so simple. My mind pulls up the memory of Ash on my lap, her hands roaming my body, and I cringe inwardly. I still don't know how I could have been so stupid, could have let my hormones overpower me, and for what? A fuck?

It isn't like I have any real feelings for Ash—I barely know the girl. From what I do know she's impulsive, damaged, and very obviously running from something or someone—not exactly the pillar of stability I'd want around my kid. At the same time, there's no denying Ash is a few other things—smart, beautiful, and if she'd gain a bit of weight she might be one of the sexiest women I've ever met.

"I'm hungry," Harper announces.

"Okay." I drum my thumbs along the steering wheel, hoping the flush of my skin and rapid beat of my heart won't give away my thoughts. *Relax, Lane, she's ten for Christ's sake!* I exhale slowly. "What do you feel like?"

"I don't know." She shrugs. "Maybe a hamburger or—Ooh!" She points at the window. "What about Panera?"

"Panera it is." I hit the blinker. "It's a nice day. Maybe we can sit outside."

"Yeah." Harper grins. "And look! Someone has a puppy. Isn't he cute, Dad? Why can't we have a puppy?"

I follow the line of her finger and spot a little fawn pit bull puppy curled beneath a girl's chair. I like dogs, but I barely have enough time to devote to Harper. "I don't know. A puppy is a lot of work." I park the truck and pull the key out of the ignition.

"I'll take care of the puppy myself. You wouldn't have to do a thing!"

I sigh. "Puppy's need a lot of attention. You're so busy, Harper, with gymnastics and piano—"

"When you love someone, you make the time," she answers. "Like you do with me."

I grab my wallet from the cup holder and look at her—*really* look at her. She's got her mother's pointed nose, but I'll be damned if the rest of her isn't all me.

Harper turns to the window. "When we do get a puppy, I want one just like that."

I follow her gaze, only it's not the dog my eyes land on, but the girl sitting in the chair—the girl clearly having lunch with another guy.

Ash.

Fuck. A surge of jealousy that I don't understand burns through me like acid. After all, what do I have to be jealous over? It's not like she's *my* girl or anything. All we did was fool around—something we both realized was a huge mistake. So why the fuck should I care that she's sitting across from some blond, white-collared douche?

Except I do. I feel it in the way every muscle in my body tightens, like I'm on the verge of ripping through my skin. And that only pisses me off more. I never asked for this. I've got too much shit going on in my life to waste time on feelings—especially worthless emotions like lust and jealousy.

It doesn't help Ash is pushed back against her chair, her posture rigid. Everything about her body language screams she doesn't want to be there. So why is she? Does she need help? Can I really walk away if she does? I sweep a hand through my hair. "Harper, honey, there's been a change of plans."

"What?"

"We can't eat here."

Her face crumples in disappointment. "Why not?"

I reach for the door handle. "I'll explain it to you when you're older. In the meantime, I need you to promise me you'll sit in the car and under no circumstances get out. Do you understand?"

She frowns. "Why are you acting so weird?"

"Thank your grandpa," I grumble too low for her to hear. I slide my phone out of my pocket and hand it to her.

Most of the apps on there are hers, anyway. "Keep yourself occupied and I'll be back in a minute. If you stay in here like I asked, I'll take you to that cupcake shop you like."

Her eyes widen. "For real? Promise?"

"Promise. I'll be right back."

I get out of the truck and lock the door behind me. Harper's already got my phone in her hands, playing some game. I turn in Ash's direction and breathe deep, trying to loosen some of the tension pulling across my chest. I'm halfway across the parking lot when my steps falter—I didn't exactly think this through. What the hell am I supposed to say that's not going to make me look like a gigantic stalker?

Before I can come up with a good answer, her eyes meet mine.

"Lane?"

Fuck. Trying to play it cool, I nod as I stride over to her table. "Hey."

The guy sitting across from her narrows his eyes and gives me the once over. He leans forward, flexing the tendons along his jaw, and everything about him screams *Mine!* As if I care about some douchey frat boy's display of dominance.

Ignoring him, I crouch beside Ash's chair and scratch the puppy's head. "Who's this?" The puppy licks my hand, his tail thumping happily against the sidewalk.

"He's yours," the guy answers. "Our apartment doesn't allow dogs."

"No, he's not." Ashlyn scoops the puppy into her arms and cradles him against her chest. "He's my puppy and his name is Hank. *Your* apartment doesn't allow puppies, Chris, but I don't live with you, remember?"

Chris? The prick whose name she tattooed on her arm?

If so, what's she doing having lunch with him? I fold my arms across my chest and slowly stand. "Am I interrupting something?"

"No," Ash answers the same time Chris says, "Yes."

He swivels toward her. "Ashlyn, I thought we were discussing our future."

"Chris, there's no *our* anything, anymore."

He sinks lower in his chair and glares at me.

I smirk. Definitely no love lost here.

Ash sighs and presses two fingers against her temples. My hands curl into fists. I don't like this dude and it's obvious Ash doesn't either. The fact he's stressing her out makes me want to pound his face a little. "I'm sorry, Lane, *what* are you doing here?"

"Uh—" I wasn't expecting the question and I rack my brain for an answer. But the truth is, I don't quite know the answer myself. For ten years I've focused on building my business and taking care of my family. I've built a nice life for myself and Harper, so what is it about Ash that makes me so reckless? I did my good deed and made sure she was okay. Now that I know she is, if I know what is good for me—what is good for Harper—I'll leave well enough alone.

So how do I end it? I've never been the type of guy to screw around with a girl and blow her off after. Ash came to me for a tattoo, and I owe it to her to finish what I started. When it's done, I can forget all about her.

"I was out running some errands," I say. "When I saw you I remembered we never finished your shading."

Her eyes drop to her arm and the tattoo hidden beneath her sleeve. "Right. The tattoo." I might be wrong, but I think I hear a touch of disappointment in her voice.

"Tattoo?" Chris asks. "What tattoo?"

I ignore him. "Anyway, I can finish it tonight if you can make it in." The sooner I get it done, the sooner I can get her out of my head.

"Yeah, okay." Ash nods and a strand of her hair tumbles forward, hiding her face.

It takes nearly all of my willpower not to reach forward and tuck it behind her ear.

Chris stands so suddenly, the feet of his chair scrape against the concrete. "What fucking tattoo?" he shouts.

Ash shrinks against the chair.

My body tenses and I lift my chin. "Easy, buddy."

"Don't call me *buddy,* you piece of white trash." His nostrils flare and he whirls on Ash. "What the hell are you thinking getting another tattoo? Do you want to end up looking like this trailer park loser? What will people think?"

I slowly ease myself in front of Ash, pressing my fist against my palm, cracking my knuckles. My arms actually ache with the desire to hit him, but with Harper in the car, I can't risk it. "They'd *think* she's her own person, not an object for some asshole to sign his name on."

"What the fuck does that mean?" Chris asks.

Ash stands and moves to my side. "It means we're over, Chris."

His face softens. "You don't mean that. You're upset. You're not thinking clearly."

"No." She shakes her head. "For the first time ever, I think I'm starting to figure things out." She thrusts the puppy into my arms. Startled, I hold his wagging body close to my chest. "Watch Hank for me," she tells me. "I'm going inside to get a to-go box. I am eating my fucking lunch—just not here." She turns to Chris. "When I get back, a green fucking sweater better be right there." She points to his vacated chair. "And you better not be."

Before either of us can reply, she turns on her heel and marches toward the restaurant.

"That's not the Ashlyn I know," Chris mutters between clenched teeth. "Whoever the fuck that is, you can keep her."

I can't fight off the grin pulling at my lips. "Something tells me I'm getting the better deal."

Chapter Thirteen

Ashlyn

With my green sweater slung over my shoulder and Hank cradled in my arms, I get out of my car, but I'm in no hurry to go inside my apartment and deal with the mess sure to be waiting for me.

Instead, I sit down in a shady grassy area just outside the main apartment doors and unhook Hank's leash. He bounds around me, hopping and rolling in the grass. The sight of the tumbling puppy brings a smile to my face—no one deserves to be leashed all the time.

Despite his new freedom, Hank never strays more than a few feet from where I sit. He finds a stick and lays beside me to chew on it. While he's occupied, I open my to-go box and finish my sandwich. The bread's a little soggy, but it sure beats the instant mac and cheese I'd planned on eating.

As I open the bag of chips, my mind drifts to my earlier

encounter with Lane and the way my breath caught in my throat at the sight of his muscles rippling beneath his T-shirt as he approached my table—muscles I'd traced with my fingertips only the night before.

A shiver courses down my body, and I quickly grab the pickle spear out of the box and tear into it. I hate that even the memory of Lane can raise my body temperature. It's so stupid. Of all the guys to get under my skin, why is it the one I know is the least good for me? Like Emily said, I should leave him alone—which I plan on doing the second my tattoo is finished.

I gather my trash, stand, and brush the grass from my jeans. If I hurry and get the apartment cleaned, I might have time to go to the coffee shop to get some writing done before I have to meet Lane. Because that's what I *need* to do—focus on the things I want, like getting my poetry published, and not the things that are so obviously bad for me, like Lane.

I call Hank over with a pat on my leg. Once I've gathered him in my arms, I open the main door to the apartment. If I want to write today, there's no delaying the inevitable.

Hank squirms when I enter the long hallway, as if he doesn't want to be here anymore than I do.

"Don't worry," I tell him. "We're not staying long." Our apartment is one of the last ones down the hall. As we draw closer to the door, I notice an overweight bald man crouched outside doing something to the knob with a power tool.

"Hey!" I quicken my pace to a jog. I've already been robbed once. I don't need it happening again. "Stop! What are you doing?"

The guy turns to face me and it's then I notice the

nametag sewn on the front of his blue shirt. He has a grease-stained tool belt strapped to his hips. "I'm replacing the locks." His eyes narrow on the puppy in my arms. "You know there're no dogs allowed in the building."

I ignore him, as dread swells inside my stomach. "Why are you changing the locks? Did someone break in?"

"Naw." He lines the drill up with the screws. "It's policy to change the locks after an eviction."

I nearly laugh in relief as I place my hand on the doorknob, blocking him. "We haven't been evicted. You must have the wrong apartment."

The guy huffs and pulls a square of paper from his pocket. He unfolds it and his eyes scan the page before he holds it out for me to see. "Nope. Apartment 32A. Says so right here." He thrusts it close to my face. It smells like cigarettes. "Says you were given your notice thirty days ago."

No. That can't be right. I feel as if the floor has disappeared from under me, and I'm suddenly plummeting through the earth. Hank whimpers and I tighten my hold to keep him from slipping through my arms. "I never saw an eviction notice," I say.

The guy flips the sheet over. "Says here it was delivered to a Selena Garcia. She hasn't paid rent in three months."

My knees wobble and I lean against the wall before they can give out. "B-but that can't be right. I've given her rent money for the last two months!"

"That may be," the guy says, folding the paper and cramming it back inside his pocket, "but she hasn't been paying it."

This can't be happening to me. Not again. My eyes burn hot with fresh tears. I set Hank down and press my palms against my eyes to keep the tears from falling. A sob wells inside my throat and I struggle to swallow it down. "What am I supposed to do now?" I mumble.

The maintenance guy must hear me, because his face softens. "Look, I'm not really supposed to do this, but I can give you thirty minutes to grab whatever stuff you can, okay?"

It's not a solution, but at least it's something. I bring my arms to my side and manage a weak smile. "Thanks."

The man brings the screw gun to the doorknob. After several metallic screeches, the knob falls off the door. It lands next to the fallen screws. He fiddles with the inner workings of the lock and, a second later, the door opens.

He gestures me forward. "I'll wait out here."

I nod, grateful for the privacy should I suffer another breakdown. I step inside the small kitchen and, as expected, it's a mess. Hank follows at my heels, rising up on his hind feet to sniff at the empty beer bottles and fast food wrappers lining the counters. Only this time, the dirty dishes are absent from the sink. I open several cabinets to find all the dishes missing, as well as the food—even the instant mac, Cheerios, and ramen noodles belonging to me.

I step around the corner into the living room. The couches and television are missing, liquor bottles and ashtrays are scattered across the floor in their place. It's apparent Selena knew this was coming, but having spent my rent money on God knows what, she didn't have the decency to let me know.

I turn away from the living room and walk to my room. I press my hand against the door and it swings inward. There's a gash in the doorframe where the lock was kicked through.

The dresser and mattress, the only furniture in the room, are gone. This doesn't bother me, as they weren't mine to begin with. What does is the fact my clothes look like they've been dumped from the drawer into a pile on the floor.

The edge of my notebook sticks out from beneath a pair of my jeans. This time I'm not worried about my tip money being stolen, as I've learned to keep it hidden in my car. I realize, though, this means I won't ever get back the full amount taken from me—which leaves me a long way from having enough money to get my own place.

Once again, I'm homeless.

The realization falls heavy on my shoulders, and I sink to my knees on the thin carpet. Still, I will myself to hold back the tears. I can't break down, not here, not when I have so little time to get the rest of my things out. The breakdown will have to wait. I don't have a bag, so I gather as many of my clothes as I can hold and carry them out to my car.

The maintenance man is outside smoking a cigarette as I throw my clothes into the trunk. He frowns, watching me. "Do you, uh, need any help?" he asks.

"That's okay," I say as I walk back to the apartment for another load. I want to hold onto what little pride I have left, and there's no dignified way to let a strange man grab fistfuls of your underwear.

Hank's belongings are already in my car, so it only takes me a couple trips to carry out the rest of my clothes, my notebooks, the few toiletries I have in the bathroom, and my pillow and blanket. When I'm finished, I shut the back passenger door to my Jetta and stare at my car. This is it. My entire life is reduced to the contents of a trunk and backseat. I'm completely packed, but literally have nowhere to go.

The tears that I've been fighting for the last half hour finally break free. I want to punch something, to let loose the scream swelling inside my chest. This isn't how my life is supposed to go. Once I escaped the hold of my stepdad, things were supposed to get better, but here I am, with a puppy, a pile of clothes, no food, and nowhere to live.

I pull my phone out of my pocket and stare at the screen. Both Chris and my mom offered me a place to stay, but I know in reality they're offering me a choice between two cages. For a brief second, I consider calling Emily, but her apartment is too small for more than one person, and it's not like our friendship is on the level where I can ask to crash on her couch for—God, I have no idea how long it's going to take me to find a new place.

I pick up Hank and climb inside the car. After placing him on the passenger seat, I stick the key in the ignition, but don't turn it. I know I can't stay here—but where can I go? I have my tattoo appointment this evening, so I can't drive around town all day and waste gas. I wrack my brain for a solution, but nothing comes to mind.

I pull a wad of napkins from my glove box and wipe the tear streaks from my eyes. God, I can't even remember the last time I went a whole day without crying and I hate it. I hate that tears have become as much a part of my daily routine as brushing my teeth. The only thing that's changed is the reason *why* I cry. First it was because I was a treated like a prisoner inside my own home and, when I finally broke free, I cried because I no longer had a home.

Pathetic, my stepdad's voice whispers inside my head. With a gasp, I pull the napkins from my face. I meet my own eyes in the review mirror. I am not pathetic, nor am I defeated. I dig my nails into the tear-soaked napkin and rip it into strips. I've survived worse, and I'll survive this.

Hank whines at me from the passenger seat.

I toss the ribbons of napkin into the side door compartment, reach over, and pet Hank's head. "I'm scared, too," I tell him. "Just give me a little time, okay? I'm sure we can figure this out."

I turn the key in the ignition and pull out of the parking spot. When I reach the edge of the lot, I flick on my blinker and make a left toward Lane's tattoo studio. My appointment isn't for several hours, but I'm pretty sure there's a park nearby where I can let Hank run around while I figure out my next move.

My fingers are tight on the wheel and my gaze locked on the road as I drive. I refuse to look in the review mirror. I promise myself I won't look back.

I won't *ever* look back.

Chapter Fourteen

Lane

Harper sits in my tattoo chair, humming another one of her damned boy band songs while I finish up another Sharpie-drawn tattoo on her forearm. Only this time, because I'm working, the song doesn't make me want to grind my teeth. That's why I love drawing so much, be it with a needle or pen—I can lose myself in the slope of lines and wash of color. Nothing can touch me there, not boy band music, fourth-grade science projects, or thoughts of making out with mentally unstable girls.

The memory of Ash's lips, hot on my skin, flashes through my mind and the pen slips. "Goddamn it," I murmur.

"Uh-oh, Dad." Harper grins. "That's five dollars for the swear jar."

In an attempt to watch my language around Harper, I instituted a swear jar policy several months ago. If things keep going the way they are, we're going to have enough money for our Disney vacation by the end of the year.

The front door jingles, and every muscle in my body goes rigid. I say a silent prayer Ashlyn isn't early. I refuse to let my hormones betray me like they did last night. Which is why I need to get my shit together before I face her again. Thank God, after tonight she'll be out of my life, and out of my head, forever.

"Where's my favorite niece?" my sister calls before pushing the curtain aside.

"Aunt Em!" Harper jumps out of the chair and wraps her arms around Emily's waist as I cap the Sharpie in my hand.

"Who's ready for a sleepover?" Emily asks. "I have popcorn, candy, and tons of movies. We can stay up all night."

I grunt. "If all night is ten o'clock."

Emily makes a face. "Just because your dad doesn't know how to have fun, he thinks no one else should, either."

I swallow my response—that it's kind of hard to have fun when you're a parent at sixteen—because I don't want Harper to think I blame her. Instead, I silently glare at my sister until she eventually looks away.

"Where are your things?" she asks Harper.

My daughter is bouncing on her toes. "I'll go get them." She brushes past the curtain to where I tucked her overnight bag beneath the counter.

Once she's out of sight, Em turns to me with an impish grin. "According to Mom, you've been working late quite a bit this week. If I didn't know better, I'd think you have a hot date."

I roll my eyes as I turn to shove the Sharpies back inside

their container. "But you do know better, don't you? I don't date."

The smile melts off her face. "Geez, Lane. How long are you going to make yourself suffer for a mistake you made as a kid?"

Anger flashes through me, and I whirl on her. "First of all, that was the best *mistake* I ever made. I am the father of a fucking amazing kid. Second, I'm not punishing myself. I'm protecting her. Harper's mother was a psycho bitch in a world full of psycho bitches. Why on earth would I risk subjecting my daughter to another woman like that? Why would I invite someone into our lives only to have her walk out on us? How could I do that to Harper again?"

Emily sighs and flops into the chair abandoned by Harper. "Yes, there may be plenty of psychos in the sea, but there are also good, decent women, too. You're doing Harper no favors by putting off your own happiness."

"Don't you get it?" The markers rattle as I slam the box against the counter. Nothing pisses me off like when my sister becomes a know-it-all. "When you become a parent the only thing that matters is your kid's safety and happiness. Relationships bring risk, and I won't do anything to hurt my daughter if I can avoid it. If protecting Harper means I'm going to be a hermit for the rest of my life, I'll do it—I'll do anything for her."

Again I think about the night with Ashlyn when I almost lost control, and a hot wave of shame washes over me. I won't allow myself to be weak again.

Harper pushes the curtain aside, her backpack slung over her shoulder. There's a strange expression on her face, which makes me wonder if she heard what I was talking about.

I turn away. I don't want to discuss my dating life with my daughter any more than I do with my sister.

The vinyl chair creaks behind me as Emily slides off. "Ready to go, girlfriend?"

"Yeah," Harper answers. Behind me, the sounds of her footsteps approach. Seconds later, her small arms slide around my neck. "I love you, Daddy," she whispers in my ear.

As if by magic, the knots wound into my muscles slowly unwind. "Love you, too, babe."

Her arms slip from my neck. "I don't want you to be lonely anymore. One of these days I'll have to go to college and then I won't be able to take care of you. Then you'll be all by yourself."

The shock of her words freezes me in place. Seconds later, when the air returns to my lungs and I can finally move, I turn to see that she's already left, leaving me exactly as she said she would: completely by myself.

A half hour later, the door chimes. I push the curtain aside and walk to the front of the shop. Ashlyn stands in the foyer, her long hair in a loose braid that tumbles over her shoulder. The haunted look is back in her eyes and it tugs at me. Immediately my body tenses with an ache to go to her, to touch her, and pull her against me.

I ball my hands into fists and shove them into my pockets. Fucking pheromones, or hormones, or whatever the hell it is that draws me to her. I'm stronger than that—I have to be.

She's holding the leash of the puppy she had at the restaurant. His nose is to the floor and he's circling her ankles as he sniffs. She bites her lip and motions to the dog. "I'm sorry. Is this okay? I didn't know what else to do with him."

A sort of nervous tension hangs in the air between us. But it's not strong enough to keep either of us, or both of us, from crossing over. Just looking at her, smelling her damn apple perfume, makes my fingers itch to reach for her.

There's a softness to her that draws me in. She's an uncut diamond, raw in her beauty. She stands before me with wispy hair, little makeup, and an oversize sweatshirt that hangs off a shoulder, and yet I'm literally stunned by her.

I want to say something snarky, something like, *You could have left your fucking dog at home for starters.* Not because I mind her dog being here—because I don't—but I need her to hate me. I want to see the disgust she held in her eyes the first night she met me. Because, God help me, right now, watching her nervously tug the hem of her shirt, I want her.

I want *her.* There's this primal part of me that wants to lay claim to her, to fucking tear into any other guy who would mess with her, because she's *mine.* But that's not right. I shouldn't want anyone else—Harper is the only girl I want in my life, the only girl I need.

"Should we get started?" I take a cautious step back. I need to get her out of my shop, and out of my life, as fast as possible. If only I could dig a spoon into the parts of my brain she's infected and scoop her out of my head.

"Um, sure." She crouches and unhooks the puppy from his leash. He immediately sets about exploring the shop. When she stands, she keeps her gaze locked on the floor. "I was just thinking, we could, um, talk about last night first?"

My body goes rigid. Last night is the last thing I want to talk about.

She must see something on my face that amuses her because she smiles. "Don't worry, it's not like I'm going to try and rope you into a relationship because we kissed. Actually, I was hoping we could just forget it even happened."

My muscles relax. "Forget *what* happened?" I brush the curtain aside and motion her into the back room.

She grins and moves forward, stopping in front of me. Her sudden closeness winds ropes through me, all of them connected to her, tugging me closer. Despite the pull, I clench my jaw and stand my ground. "Thanks," she says, and then pauses. "Just so you know, I don't think you're an asshole."

"Thank God. Now I can sleep at night."

Her grin widens. "So we're back where we started. Perfect." She walks to the chair and climbs into it.

I want to agree, but the second she stretches out against the black vinyl my thoughts drift back to the night before, when she straddled my body on that very spot, her fingers burning trails along my skin.

A pulsing ache along my jaw pulls me from the memory. It takes me a second to realize the pain is from clenching my teeth. And that's when I realize something else: she's wrong.

We'll never be back where we started. When you ignite a fire, you can never rebuild out of the ashes left behind.

Chapter Fifteen

Ashlyn

I stare at the typewriter on my arm. Blood mixes with the ointment, blurring the image beneath the plastic wrap taped to my skin. Still, I can tell the drawing is absolutely perfect. No trace of Chris's name remains. Like Lane said the night we first met, I feel like this tattoo really has been a rite of passage. While I'd lost my home, as well as most of my belongings, at least I'd reclaimed my body.

"You're all set." Lane slides away from me on his rolling stool and pulls his black latex gloves off with a snap. "You remember what I said about the antibacterial soap and lotion, right?"

I nod, realizing I'll have to pick them up at Walgreens. This sucks because I'll be depleting my already nonexistent funds. Still, without insurance, a trip to the emergency room for a preventable infection would be far worse.

He stands. “Looks like we’re all done here.”

His words catch me off guard, and I sit up. We *are* done. In more ways than one. “I guess so.” I slide off the chair as a wave of disappointment rolls through me. Stupid, I know. Lane already has someone and I need to figure my life out before I get involved in a relationship. Still, the memory of his lips grazing down my neck is seared into my mind like a brand.

My breath quickens, and I look away before my thoughts betray me. *God, Ashlyn, for once in your life can you not be such a pathetic embarrassment?* I jerk back with a gasp, not certain if the words whispering through my head are mine, or the resonating scars left by my stepdad.

Lane narrows his eyes. “Something wrong?”

Only everything. But I don’t tell him this, and instead shake my head. My problems are my own. “Thanks for everything, Lane.” I like the way his name feels sliding off my tongue, and I silently mourn the fact I won’t get to say it to him again.

He’s focused on dismantling the needle from the tattoo machine, so he doesn’t look up as he nods.

So I guess that’s it. We really are done. It’s what I want—but if that’s really true, why is there an ache growing in my chest as I walk away? Hank bounds after me. I scoop him up before I brush through the curtain into the lobby.

Lane doesn’t follow. When I open the front door and the chime sounds, he doesn’t call out to me to stop, either.

Good, I think as I step out into the cool fall evening. A nice clean break—that’s exactly what I want. Logically, I know he’s no good for me. Emily stated as much. Still, when I’m with him, I feel safer than I’ve ever felt. After all, hadn’t he risked a fight to get me home safely the night of the party? Hadn't he given me a ride to my car, covered up my tattoo, and held me during a massive freak out all the while not asking for anything in return? How bad can he really be?

And then I think about his hands roaming my body and wonder how bad do I *want* him to be?

Jesus, Ash! Pull yourself together.

I shake my head to clear all thoughts of Lane as I fasten Hank's leash. I set the puppy on the ground to do his business before we get in the car. As he sniffs the grass, I can't help but look over my shoulder, hoping to see Lane watching me from the door.

Of course he's not, and I scold myself for hoping he would be, or for hoping last night meant anything to him at all. Why should it? He has a girlfriend, I remind myself for the millionth time. He was just trying to make me feel better after my freak out, and things got a little…out of control. Besides, what did it matter if he cared or not?

It's not like I need the headache of another guy in my life, anyway. They only want to change you, control you, and keep you tied down. And now, for the first time in my life, I'm free.

But as I climb inside my car with Hank and put the key in the ignition, it occurs to me, wings are pretty useless when you have nowhere to fly.

"Shit." I lean back in my seat and close my eyes. I can always spend another night in my car at the rest stop. But where would I go tomorrow? And the day after that? I have several more months of work before I'll have enough stored away for an apartment deposit. Can I live out of my car for that long? And what about Hank? What am I supposed to do with him while I'm at work?

I open my eyes and glance at the sleeping bundle of fur curled in the passenger seat. A pang rips through my chest as I realize I have no choice but to give him up. He deserves better than this. I wonder if he'll think I abandoned him, that I lost interest like Selena.

I reach out to stroke his fuzzy head. "I love you, Hank," I say. The words feel foreign on my tongue. I can't remember the last time I uttered them about anyone—or anything, for that matter. Chris said them to me once, but we'd been having sex so I don't think it counts.

There were kids in high school who would slink down in embarrassment when their mom or dad would tell them as they got out of the car that they loved them. I remember thinking I would never shrink away from such affection if I had some of my own. Instead, I imagined the words as a blanket, something I could wrap myself in, to shield myself from the world.

The words in my home were never so soft. They pierced my skin like porcupine quills, jagged and sharp. No matter how hard I tried to pull them free, they stayed a part of me. *Stupid. Lazy. Worthless.* Even now, months later, I can still feel their sting.

My face grows hot and I rub my palms against my eyes to keep the tears from spilling. *No more tears.* I promised myself. I can feel myself cracking, on the verge of breaking into a million tiny pieces. But I can't let myself fall apart. If that happens, I'm almost certain I won't be able to put myself back together.

Someone raps on the window next to me and I jolt upright with a startled gasp. I grab the pepper spray I keep tucked beside my seat. I'm no stranger to being harassed while in my car. "Go away!" I raise the pepper spray and turn to the window.

Outside my car, Lane frowns and folds his arms. "Go away or what? You'll mace yourself? Your window is up."

"I know *that.*" Embarrassment burns up my neck into my cheeks. I scowl at him as I roll my window down. "I was going to use it if you broke into my car and tried to pull me out."

Hank opens his eyes and, upon seeing Lane at the window, wags his tail.

Lane's frown deepens. "Is that something you really have to worry about? What kind of neighborhoods are you driving through?"

If he only knew. "You can never be too prepared," I mutter.

He leans forward, bracing his hands on my car door. The tattoos on his arms are nothing but dark shadows in the night. "I'll say. Look at all the stuff you got back there." He motions to mountain of clothes piled across the backseat.

"It's laundry day." I turn away so he can't read the lie on my face.

"Uh-huh." I can tell by his voice he has anyway. "So you're going to the laundromat with your toothbrush"—he leans closer to me and peers over my shoulder—"and dog food bowls?"

I shrug. "You see how much laundry is back there. It's going to be an all-nighter."

Actually, laundromats in good neighborhoods aren't half-bad places to spend the night. Some of them have bathrooms, vending machines, and televisions—and all it costs to stay is a handful of quarters.

"Cut the shit, Ash." Lane slaps a hand against my car, forcing me to look at him. "What the hell is really going on?"

Shame rolls through my gut. *I'm a big fucking failure, that's what. I tried to make it on my own and, for the second time in three months, I'm homeless.* Still, the words won't leave my tongue. This is my problem, not his.

"Ash." Lane's voice is noticeably softer, and I can't help but shiver at the way my name sounds on his lips—like the word means something beautiful, rather than charred remains. "Are you in some kind of trouble?"

I can feel the damn tears welling in my eyes at the same time I will myself not to blink. Why is he asking me this, picking a scab that's sure to bleed? We agreed we weren't going to have anything to do with each other.

Lane sighs. "Well, that answers that. Where are you running to?"

I laugh, even as the burn of my eyes becomes too great. I blink and fresh tears course down my cheek. If only it were that easy—that a place exists where I can run and my problems won't follow.

He scowls. "I don't understand. What's so funny?"

"That you think I'm running away." I wipe my wet cheeks with the back of my hand. "I already tried that—turns out, I got nowhere to go."

He stands and murmurs something under his breath that I can't make out. He turns away from me and jams his fingers through his hair.

This is exactly what I don't want—anyone, least of all Lane, inconvenienced by my sucky life. I reach for the keys in the ignition and turn them. The engine roars to life.

Lane swivels on his feet. "Where the hell do you think

you're going?"

I shrug. "Don't worry about me, okay? I'll figure it out. I usually do." I give him a weak smile and place my hands on the wheel.

"No." He closes the distance between us and bends down to stare at me. "You're not going anywhere."

It's my turn to frown. "Are you unfamiliar with how a car works?"

"Goddamn it, Ash." Before I can stop him, he ducks through the window, leans across my lap, and snatches my car keys from the ignition."

"Lane! What the fuck!"

He backs away from my window and jingles my keys in his hand. "Out of the car, cupcake."

Anger rolls over me in hot waves as I fling open my door and step onto the asphalt. I'm thankful for the heat of it, a welcome distraction from my earlier tears. I hold my hand out. "Give them back."

"In a minute." He tucks them in his jeans pocket. "First, you're coming with me."

"No, I'm not." I'm so tired of everyone telling me what to do. I don't know what Lane has planned, but I do know the best thing for both of us is to go our separate ways, *not* to prolong our time together.

He shrugs. "Fine. Stay out here then." He turns around and walks back to the tattoo studio—*with* my keys.

"Lane!" I take a step forward. My blood feels on the verge of boiling. "Don't you dare! You come back right now and give me my keys!"

He keeps walking. When he reaches the front of the tattoo studio, he veers to the right and climbs a wooden staircase alongside the brick building. I wait, sure he's going to come back. Instead, he unlocks the door at the top of the stairs and disappears inside.

Son of a bitch! I stand there, blinking, unable to believe he left me without my car keys. I consider my options, only to realize I don't have many. I can stand in the middle of the street all night, or I can go after him.

Not wanting to leave Hank alone, I pull him from the car and walk across the street to the side of the building. Up close, the stairs Lane ascended do little to instill confidence. The brittle steps creak beneath my feet. I touch the handrail only to recoil as splinters stab my skin.

I hug the squirming puppy closer to my body. Just why does Lane want me to follow him up here anyway? My mind races as my steps slow. How dumb am I to follow a guy I barely know into an unknown room? I am considering going back for my pepper spray, when Lane ducks his head out of the door.

"Can you be any slower?"

"Yes." I slow my climb to a crawl.

He sighs and disappears back inside.

With a smile, I finish climbing the stairs at my normal pace. I enter the open door and find myself in what looks to be a tiny, dim, studio apartment. A threadbare loveseat stands across from an old tube television backed against a peeling wall. A single light illuminates the room, as well as several dark stains on the wall. Lane's examining the faucet in the small kitchenette. A dead plant sits in the window above his head. At the opposite end of the room, an unmade bed stands in the corner, with a folded, faded quilt and sheets stacked on top.

My pulse quickens upon seeing the bed, and my throat tightens. I've been offered money before in exchange for *favors.* Of course I didn't accept then, and I won't accept now. I back slowly toward the door as disappointment washes through me. I can't believe Lane is the kind of guy to even make this kind of offer.

"I'll fix this leak tomorrow." Lane looks up from the faucet and, after catching sight of me moving toward the door, his eyes narrow. "Where are you going?"

I shake my head and pull Hank to my chest. "I'm sorry. I know things got heated between us yesterday, but that doesn't mean I'm like that."

Lines of confusion pinch his brow. "Like *what*?"

"I'm not going to sleep with you for money or whatever."

He makes a choking noise. "Sleep with me? Fuck, Ash! That's not why I brought you here." He strides across the room, and my muscles tighten with each step. He stops inches away from me, dipping his head to meet my eyes. "Is that really the type of guy you think I am?"

I frown because I don't really know *what* kind of guy he is. The only thing I know for sure is my body temperature spikes several degrees whenever he is near. My heart flutters when he says my name, and my chest tightens when we touch. In short, he makes me absolutely miserable. At the same time, I realize I was so drunk the night of the party, if he wanted to take advantage of me, he could have easily done it then.

"Why have you brought me here?" I ask.

"To show you this!" He holds his arms out wide. "I know it's not much, and it needs a little bit of work, but the apartment is yours if you want it."

An apartment? Of my own? It's as if the room transforms before my eyes, morphing from a dark, paint-peeled room to a brilliant place of endless possibilities. The frayed couch only needs a throw to brighten it up. The floors just need a good cleaning and I can easily give the walls a fresh coat of paint.

I blink, trying to catch hold of my racing thoughts. That's when a niggling doubt creeps in and all but squashes my blooming excitement. I turn away. "Look, Lane, I really appreciate your offer, but there's no way I can afford to rent a place on my own right now."

"I haven't even told you what rent is."

I look at him. "My roommate had a party and someone broke into my room and stole all of my savings. Even if the rent is super cheap, I can't afford a deposit. It's been my experience that when people offer to help me, they usually want something in return. I don't know what you want, Lane, but it's probably more than I'm able to give."

I don't give him a chance to argue before I turn and walk out the door. It's not like there's anything he can say that will change my mind. I have nothing. I can pay nothing. Even if I could, people have been taking pieces of me ever since I was a kid. If I give anymore away, there might not be anything left.

Chapter Sixteen

Lane

I stand there, unmoving, for several seconds after she leaves. Goddamned if this girl didn't walk away from me again. That in itself should be enough warning for me to leave well enough alone. Once a runner, always a runner. But instead of listening to common sense, rocket scientist that I am, I follow her out the door.

She's halfway down the stairs when I call out. "Where are you going now?"

She turns to me, puppy clutched to her chest. "I'll figure it out."

"Sure." I pull her car keys from my pocket. "I guess you're going to have to figure out how to hotwire a car while you're at it."

She pauses, looking uncertain.

I sigh and walk down the stairs. I hold the keys out for

her, but when she raises a hand, I pull them back to my chest. "Before you take off, can you do me a favor and shut up for one fucking second?"

Frowning, she strokes the puppy's head. "Fine."

"I don't want anything from you, Ash. As I've told you before, I've got enough shit on my plate. However, my dad was a cop, and the best goddamned man I ever knew—there wasn't a beggar on the street he wouldn't find a shelter and hot meal for. I'll be damned if I dishonor him by turning my back on someone who clearly needs help."

She opens her mouth but I cut her off before she can talk. "Look, if you can't afford to pay, I can really use some help around the shop. My schedule is a wreck and I haven't touched my books in weeks. If you can help me with that, we'll call it even. I don't want anything else from you. No strings."

She's quiet a moment. It's a fucking miracle.

The puppy whimpers in her arms.

"What about Hank?" she asks.

"Who?"

She motions to the dog.

"Hank is welcome to stay, too." I drop her keys in her hands. "The decision is yours."

Her fingers slowly curl around the keys. She bites her lips and looks from me, to her car, and back to me again. "I think—I'd like to stay."

I only realize how badly I wanted her to say that when relief washes over me. "Good. Like I said, the place isn't the greatest. Renting it out got to be too much of a hassle so I haven't spent a lot of time cleaning it up. I'll fix the leaky faucet tomorrow, and if you notice anything else, you tell me, okay?"

She places Hank on the top step and grins. "Okay. And I can help clean it up."

I nod and smile back. "Great. So would you like help carrying your stuff up?"

Her eyes widen. "I can move in tonight? Just like that?"

"Just like that."

She squeals and throws her arms around me. Before I can stop myself, I wrap my arm around her shoulder, pulling her to my chest. The realization of what I've done, our sudden closeness, makes my arms go rigid. Ash stiffens in my grasp. The awkward tension between us grows thick, pushing us apart.

I slide past her and descend the stairs. "I'll just go get your stuff."

"Yeah. Okay." I hear her footsteps disappear into the apartment above me.

I walk to her car, open the backseat, and pull out a backpack and forty-pound bag of dog food. I carry both upstairs, drop them just inside the door, and head out for the rest. After several trips I've emptied her car, and yet the apartment barely looks any different.

"You sure this is all you have?" I stare at the mound of clothes I piled on the mattress. "I thought girls had no less than thirty pairs of shoes."

Ash shrugs while folding the clothes and stacking them in the dresser. I notice the knob to the drawer wiggles in her hand, and I make a mental note to fix that tomorrow, too. "I travel light," she answers.

I know there's more to it than that. I can see it in the tightness of her expression, but I don't press.

Someone knocks at the door and Ash gasps, dropping the shirt she was folding onto the floor.

I frown and fight the urge to go to her. Instead, I walk to the door as a new surge of anger rolls through me. I'd sure love to meet whoever made her so afraid. I crack my knuckles just thinking about it.

Outside the door a delivery guy waits with the pizza I ordered when I first entered the apartment. It'd been wishful thinking Ash would still be here when he arrived. But even if she decided to leave, I'd still have pizza.

I pay the guy and shut the door behind me. Ash watches me with a curious expression. I shrug. "There's no food in the apartment."

"I can feed myself."

"Can you?" I arch an eyebrow. "When's the last time you've eaten?"

She turns away, a flush burning her cheeks. So now I know why she's so damn skinny. I make another mental note to pick her up some groceries tomorrow before work. I open the box and, after offering her a slice, I go downstairs to the studio to retrieve two sodas, but after remembering the incident from last night, change my mind and grab two water bottles instead.

When I return upstairs she's curled in the old brown recliner that used to belong to my dad. I'd rescued it from the curb where my mom had placed it. Mom argued it was time for a change, that the chair was old, ripped, and she was better off with a new one.

Maybe. But seeing Ash tucked into it, with her knees drawn to her chest, I'm glad I brought it up here. Some things are worth holding onto.

I notice she hasn't touched the pizza box sitting on the chipped coffee table, despite the fact her eyes are practically boring into the cover. I flop on the couch and push the box toward her. "Don't you like pepperoni? Eat."

She shakes her head, still not looking at me. "I'm not allowed to eat first, especially when the food isn't mine."

What the fuck? "What are you talking about? I bought it for both of us."

She blinks and shakes her head. "Sorry. Just forget it." She reaches for the box, flips the lid open, and takes a slice. She holds it in her hands, staring at me, waiting.

I grab a slice of my own and lift it to my lips. Ash smiles when I chew, and bites into her own piece. She devours the slice in a matter of seconds and eagerly reaches for the box. She pauses with her fingers hovering over the pizza, and looks up at me. "This okay?"

I nod without saying anything and she digs in. I'm afraid if I open my mouth, I'll let loose with the flurry of insults I have for whoever did this to her. She acts as if eating is a privilege—something that has to be earned. Who the fuck made her believe that? Chris? Her parents?

Watching her devour another slice, I tear into a piece of my own. I chew with more force than necessary, using my teeth to expel the anger building inside me.

We finish the entire pizza in silence. I clear off the coffee table, slipping the pizza box and the empty water bottles inside a plastic bag. "I'll take these with me when I leave. Just so you know, there's a recycling bin as well as a dumpster behind the shop."

I glance at the clock blinking on the stove. It's creeping toward midnight. Slowly, I stand. "I should get going."

Ashlyn squeezes her knees to her chest and nods. "Yeah." Even though she's looking at me, her eyes are unfocused and I know she's somewhere else entirely. I wonder what she sees when she falls into herself like that. Given the tight way she's holding herself, it can't be good. I wish to hell I could go inside her mind and chase the demons away.

I start for the door only to stop. Something keeps me rooted to the room, a force I don't understand—and I'm pretty sure I don't want to. I turn and she's still curled into the chair staring at nothing I can see. She looks so vulnerable, and it's all I can do to stand my ground and not go to her and scoop her in my arms. "Ash—"

She blinks, her gaze flicking to my face.

"Are you going to be okay?" I ask. "Do you want me to stay?" I regret the words the second they leave my mouth. What the hell am I thinking? I'm supposed to be putting distance between us, not spending the night with her.

The corner of her mouth twitches, and she quirks an eyebrow.

"Not like that," I add quickly. "It's just, I know staying in a new place can be tough the first night, even a little scary."

"No scarier than sleeping at a rest stop," she says.

"And you know this how?"

She purses her lips, a flush warming her cheeks as if this isn't a secret she'd planned on letting slip.

"What happened to you?" I ask. "A girl your age shouldn't be without a place to live, or sleeping out of her car."

She turns away, but not before I see the shame, heavy in her eyes. "We don't get to choose what happens to us, Lane. We only decide what we're going to do with the shit handed to us. I'm not going to let my past own me." She glances at me over her shoulder. "It doesn't matter where I've lived before, I live here now." She holds her arms out, gesturing to the shabby apartment, and smiles. "Thanks to you."

I'm not quite sure how to respond, so I don't. Besides, I've dealt with my own fair share of shit and know where she's coming from. Do I want to be judged for being the screw-up teenager who had a one-night stand, or for working hard to give my daughter the best life possible? If she doesn't want to discuss pasts, I'm only too happy to comply.

Minutes pass. It's well past Harper's bedtime, and I silently scold myself for not calling her to say good night before Emily put her to bed. I hope Harper isn't mad. I'll have to get donuts in the morning to make it up to her. I don't know what it is about Ash, how she can distract me in ways no other woman's done before. It's not a good thing, for me or Harper.

"I'll check on you tomorrow," I say, and Ash nods. "My number is taped to the fridge if something goes wrong with the apartment or you need—" I bite off the end of the sentence, as I'm not sure exactly what I have to offer her—what I *can* offer.

"Thanks," she says, seeming not to notice my fumble.

I walk to the coffee table and set the apartment key down beside a dried stain of purple nail polish. "Lock the door after I leave, okay?"

She hugs her arms around her chest and nods.

I hesitate at the door. The pull to stay feels like a rope tied around my chest. Still, I have Harper to think about. It's bad enough I let the one girl I can't seem to stop thinking about move in above my studio. I'll have to be careful. She's already in my head. She can't invade my heart, too.

"The answer is yes." Ash speaks the words so softly, I'm not sure my mind isn't playing tricks on me until I look up and find her large eyes locked on mine.

"The answer to what?"

"Your earlier question." She hugs herself tighter. "You asked if I wanted you to stay, and the answer is yes."

I open my mouth to respond, not that I even know *how* to, but she shakes her head and cuts me off. "But you can't. I know. You already have someone in your life." It's then I realize it's not my face she's looking at, but Harper's name on my chest. "If you—if we—" She shakes her head. "No good can come from it."

"No good," I echo. We stare at each other, seconds turning to minutes, as if we're both trying to figure out how much of ourselves we really have to give.

Slowly, she turns away from me and I have my answer.

Nothing.

Chapter Seventeen

Ashlyn

I'm in the middle of brewing a café Americano when my phone buzzes in my pocket. I place the lid on the steaming cup and slide it over to a man in a business suit, who barely gives me a nod of acknowledgement before he leaves.

I smile at his retreating form and yell at him to come back soon. His mood can't bring me down—nothing can. Funny how having a place to live can do that.

I slip the phone from my pocket and give the screen a glance—my mother. My smile dissolves. Well, almost nothing can bring me down. I hit the decline button and slip the phone back inside my apron. This is the third time she's called me in a week. Doesn't matter. She can call every minute of every day and I'll still never move back into that hellhole with her—not as long as she remains with *him.* And thanks to Lane, I don't have to.

Emily's at the register ringing up the last person from the morning's nonstop stream of customers. When she's finished, I make the woman's chai tea and hand it to her. She smiles and hands me a dollar, which I tuck into my apron pocket. It's been a week since I moved into Lane's apartment, and he still hasn't given me a definitive answer as far as the cost of rent, telling me my bookkeeping and light cleaning of his shop makes up the difference. Since he won't take my money, I've decided to make small improvements to the place when I can. I refuse to be a freeloader, after all. So first up is a fresh coat of paint.

The second the woman walks out the door, Emily groans and jumps on the counter. "Jesus. I thought we were never going to get a break."

I nod, even though I'm more focused on the puddle of spilled cream on the counter. After I wipe it clean with a rag, my chest loosens and I can breathe more easily.

Emily watches me, nibbling at piece of pound cake she pulled from the pastry case. "What's with the cleaning thing? Is it OCD?"

"Probably," I say, because it's easier than admitting the real reason I clean—to keep the voice of my stepdad from surfacing.

"Huh." She swings her legs, crumbs dribbling from her chin. "I read about a guy with OCD who woke up in the middle of the night to comb the tassels of his oriental rug."

I roll my eyes and reach past her for a cake pop. "I'm not combing rugs in the middle of the night, if that's what you're implying."

She shrugs. "I don't judge. Besides, I know my brother's shitty-ass apartment doesn't have tasseled rugs."

I stare at the cake pop a moment, realizing the ever-present gnaw of hunger is no longer chewing at my stomach. It must have something to do with the fact that Lane stocked the fridge and cabinets with food—and not just peanut butter and Ramen noodles. The fridge is packed with cheese, lunchmeat, fruits, and veggies. The cabinets are filled with pasta, sauces, and boxes of Hamburger Helper, plus popcorn, chips and cookies. I couldn't help but notice the amount of high fat items he purchased, almost like he's trying to tell me something.

I shrug and pop the ball of icing-covered cake in my mouth. "It's not a shitty-ass apartment."

She rolls her eyes. "Says the girl who was going to live out of her car. Jesus, Ash! You should have said something to me before it got to that point!"

I drop my gaze to the floor. It's not that I didn't want to ask for help, it's just I don't know how. When you've been beaten down your entire life, you learn it's easier to accept things the way they are than to suffer the consequences of speaking out. The image of my stepdad appears in my mind. He towers over me with his neck stretched taught and his nostrils flared. His eyes are impossibly wide and streaked through with red webs of blood vessels. His lips are pursed, and I know I have seconds before they open and spew cutting words that will leave scars deep below my skin.

My pulse quickens and the cake turns to dirt in my mouth. The cord around my chest pulls tight, and I try to think of something positive to chase the memory away. "I'm going to paint," I blurt around the stick in my mouth.

"Cool." Emily jumps down from the counter. "Want some help? I've got nothing going on tonight."

My first instinct is to refuse. After all, why would she want to help me paint a dingy apartment on a Saturday night? What's in it for her? The familiar refrain of *when people offer help, they usually want something in return,* plays in my mind.

I shake my head to silence it. *No.* I can't think like that, always suspicious of everyone's intentions. That's the old Ash, and I don't want to be her anymore. The refusal is halfway up my throat when I swallow it back down. "That would be really great."

"Awesome." She smiles. "I'll meet you at your place tonight. You bring the paint and I'll bring the beer. Sound good?"

Her grin is infectious, and I smile back, despite the niggling insecurity weaving through my head. I still can't understand why she would want to give up a Saturday night to help me paint.

Maybe, a small voice inside my head whispers, *she just likes you.*

I want to dismiss the thought, ridiculous as it is. Why would anyone like me? I'm stupid, lazy, ungrateful—a pang of realization stops me before I can add to the list. Those aren't my words, those are my stepdad's words. And as a writer, I should know the difference between making words and becoming them.

I won't become them.

"I can't wait," I say.

Later that night, I exit my car, lugging two gallons of sage green paint with me. The thin wire handles dig into my palms as I trudge across the street. I place them at the foot of the stairs leading up to my apartment.

A lump forms in my throat as I walk the short distance to Lane's shop door. Knowing I'm going to see him has that effect on me, which I hate. Why should I waste the skip of my heart or the hitch of my breath on a guy I can never have? Not only that, but he's my landlord now, and I know better than to mix business with pleasure. This apartment is the best thing to ever happen to me, and I'm not about to do anything to risk losing it.

I swallow hard and open the glass door. The curtain dividing the lobby from Lane's studio is closed, and I can hear the buzz of his needle pulsing behind it. I don't dare cross the threshold. I made the mistake of pushing through several days ago to find him in the middle of driving a barbell through some guy's dick. Lane was too busy concentrating on his work, and the guy's eyes were clenched shut, with tears rolling down his cheeks. Neither one noticed my intrusion, but an impaled penis isn't an image the mind easily forgets. Needless to say, I vowed never again to open Lane's curtain without announcing myself first.

"Lane!" I call out.

The buzzing stops. "Yeah?"

All it takes is the sound of his voice and my throat goes dry. "Uh, I got some paint…for upstairs."

"Cool. Leave the receipt on the counter and I'll reimburse you." The buzzing starts again before I can argue.

I frown. I came here to make sure he doesn't mind the painting, *not* to ask him for money. That's the point—if he won't take my rent money, I at least owe it to him to improve the apartment.

I turn away from the counter. I'm almost to the door when I hear a long sigh behind me. Glancing over my shoulder, I spot a young girl sitting in one of the chairs along the far wall. Her head is thrown back and she's staring at the ceiling. A notebook is balanced on her skinny knees and a pink backpack sits on the floor between her feet. What the hell is a kid doing in a tattoo parlor?

"Um." I take a step toward her. "Is something wrong?"

She slowly pulls her head up and looks at me with large blue eyes. Springs of curls have escaped her ponytail and frame her freckled face. I don't have a lot of experience with kids, but I guess her to be around nine or ten. "Every year we have to draw a picture of our family." She taps the blank page on her lap. "It's stupid and I hate it."

"Where is your family?" I ask, slowly lowering myself into the chair beside her. Despite what I told Em, I really like kids. And this one, with her little lips jutted into a pout, looks too miserable for me to just ignore.

She shrugs and points to the curtain. "Dad's in there. I'm just waiting for Grandma to pick me up."

I fight to keep from frowning. I may not know anything about good male role models, but I'm pretty sure taking your daughter with you when you get a tattoo isn't exactly quality time.

Still, it's not my place to judge. "Why is the assignment stupid?"

She shrugs and gazes down at her notebook. "Everyone in my class has a real family with a mom and a dad—though Olivia's got two dads. And all of them have brothers or sisters and stuff. All I have is my dad."

I'm not sure what to say to that. Comforting others has

never been a skill of mine. Where I come from, words are used to hurt, never heal. This, above all else, is why I'm sure I'd make a horrible mother. How could someone who's spent her entire life broken know the first thing about mending? Still, I want to help, even if that means just sitting beside her. I motion to her notebook. "Can I draw with you?" She shrugs and I rip a sheet of paper from her pad, place it on a stack of tattoo magazines, and pull a green colored pencil from the box in her backpack.

I settle back against the vinyl chair and begin drawing a field while the girl beside me watches. Something about the smell of the paper and the feel of the pencil between my fingers transports me back to my early childhood days. The days when I was happy—the days before *him*.

After sketching several stems, I grab a pink pencil and add daisies to my drawing. Daisies have always been my favorite flower. They're not delicate like tulips and roses, which need constant care and perfect conditions to flourish. Some even consider them weeds. I'll admit they may not be the prettiest flower out there, but there's no denying beauty in their strength.

"You know," I say as I shade the petals, "I don't think it's the size of the family that matters, but the amount of love the family members have for each other."

She plucks a blue pencil from the box and begins outlining a figure on her own paper. "What do you mean?"

"Well," I trade my pink pencil for yellow and draw a sun. "I had a mom and a stepdad. He wasn't very nice to me at all."

The girl gasps. "That's so sad."

The tip of the yellow pencil snaps off in the center of my

sun, startling me. Immediately, I suck in a deep breath and relax my grip. "Yes, it was. The point is, I don't think more family always equals more love. I would have been so much happier with just my mom, who did love me, as I'm sure your dad loves you."

She nods and finishes drawing an oval face. "He does love me. He works a lot, but when he's home he plays games with me and reads to me. We have a lot of fun."

I smile, happy there are actually decent fathers out there. I've never known one, but it fills me with hope to know they exist. "And you mentioned a grandma, too."

The girl grins. "Yeah. She's really nice. She takes care of me when my dad can't. She helps me with my homework and takes me shopping for clothes. She also cooks, which is good because Dad never does."

I laugh, and she does, too. "Your dad sounds like a pretty cool guy."

"He is. You would like him." There's a mischievousness to her grin. "He doesn't have a girlfriend, and you're really pretty. I bet he would take you to a movie if you asked."

A strangled choke escapes my throat and I set the yellow pencil aside. The conniving little cupid! "I'm sure your dad is really great, sweetie, but I'm not dating at the moment."

"Why not?" She sits grinning at me, blinking her long lashes innocently.

"I…uh…" How the hell do you explain emotional baggage to a ten-year-old? "I just got a lot of stuff going on right now."

"What kind of stuff?"

"Well, I just moved, and I'm trying to get a handle on my finances. Then I'd like to focus on my writing and maybe college—" The girl scrunches her eyes, as if trying to make sense of my words. "Besides, you'd need someone in your life who can take care of you. I can barely take care of myself."

She tilts her head. "Take care of me? I'm not a baby."

I fidget in my seat. This conversation is going to become incredibly awkward if I don't find an out and fast. I point to a fourth figure on her paper. "Who's that?"

She glances her drawing of a girl with short, blond hair, and her face lights up. "Oh! That's my aunt. She's really silly and fun," she says, laughing. "When she watches me she always lets me stay up late."

I cheer inwardly that the distraction worked. "Sounds to me like your family is pretty awesome."

"Yeah." She grins down at the drawing of herself with her family and smiles. "They really are."

I can't help but smile. I'm almost tempted to peek behind the curtain to see who the mystery guy is that Lane's working on. After all, I can think of a worse dating prospect than someone who's so obviously a good father.

But then I immediately realize the fault in that logic. I could never date a man with a kid. What if things got serious? What the hell do I know about raising and caring for child? And what if my toxic upbringing infected me somehow? What if I'm destined to hurt my kids the way I was hurt?

The knife-edge of panic twists inside my chest, and I climb to my feet. I can't do it. Getting involved with someone with a kid would be the absolutely worst thing I can do. I know this now. Maybe on a subconscious level, I've known the truth all along—that I'm broken beyond repair. That the real reason I've never had a serious relationship is because

I'm like my stepdad, and I'm not capable of love.

The thought crashes into me, and I waver on my feet. *That can't be true. I love Hank, don't I?*

The girl is watching me curiously. I force a smile and hand her my drawing. "This is for you."

Her grin widens as she takes my completed picture of a sunny field of daisies. "You're pretty good. Not as good as my dad—but good."

I'm still shaken from my epiphany, but I laugh. The girl is adorable—all the more reason to get as far away from her and her dad as fast as possible. "I appreciate your honesty."

"But I really do like it," she adds quickly, folding it and tucking it inside her notebook. "I'm going to put it up in my room."

I shrug. "You do whatever you want with it. It's your drawing. I just wanted to thank you for letting me draw with you. I had fun."

"Me, too." She grabs a red pencil and returns to her sketch, a smile on her face.

I stare at her a moment longer. I was about her age when my mom married my stepdad and everything changed. Between the endless rules, locked doors, forbidden rooms, and massive amounts of chores, drawing became a thing of the past for me.

But at least I had my notebooks. I'd been fed so much poison during my time in that house. If I hadn't been able to bleed it out onto the pages of my battered journal, there was no way I would have survived.

But this girl, with her colored pencils, funny aunt, loving grandma, and dad who can't cook, well, she's going to do more than survive. She's going to live.

I push the door open and step outside, making a mental note to buy myself some colored pencils. Because from now on, I am going to do more than survive, too. It's my turn to live.

Chapter Eighteen

Lane

The guy in my chair opens his clenched eyes. "Something the matter?"

It's only after he asks me that I realize I'd turned my needle off and haven't moved in the last couple of minutes, haven't even breathed. All that stopped the moment I heard Ash talk to Harper. "Hang tight." I set my tattoo machine aside and strip off my gloves, leaving his old tribal tattoo nearly covered by a dragon in flight.

The door chimes, and I know Ash is gone. The only question is how much information she took with her. The thick curtain dividing the rooms blurred their conversation into muffled words. Does Ashlyn know Harper's my daughter? Does it even matter, since I vowed to not get involved with her?

Not that the vow's been working.

Each night I visit Ash's apartment before I go home. The apartment's been empty for so long it was in desperate need of repair. As Ash's landlord, I have a moral obligation to make sure everything is in working order. The only problem is, now I'm running dangerously low on things to fix. So I might have purposely pulled the towel rod anchor from the wall and stripped the screw out of the kitchen cabinet hinge just so I have a reason to come back tonight.

I'm not proud of the fact. But it's obvious that somebody hurt Ash. She seems so vulnerable, and she's all alone up there. I wouldn't be living up to my dad's name if I didn't check on her.

At least that's what I tell myself. Because it's easier than admitting there's an invisible cord that pulls me up her stairs at the end of each night, that the tug in my chest eases just a fraction when she opens the door and smiles up at me.

I stand and make my way to the lobby.

"Where you going?" the guy asks.

"I'll be right back." I push through the curtain. It's not like he can't use the break. He's had more tears rolling down his cheeks than a toddler with a skinned knee.

Harper looks up at me as I enter the lobby, a pencil poised over a drawing on her lap. "Hey, Dad."

"Hey, Angel." I force a smile, hoping my face doesn't betray the unease rolling through me. "Just thought I'd check on you."

She frowns at me. "Why?"

"Can't a dad miss spending some time with his girl?" My muscles are coiled, tense. I sit beside her, stretching my legs in front of me. "Besides, Grandma's running late and you've been sitting out here by yourself for a while."

She shrugs. "Just doing my homework."

I look at her drawing and mentally cringe. The yearly family portrait. I know from past experience it's one of Harper's most dreaded assignments. She's never made her longing for a more complete family a secret. In the beginning I tried. But good women my age who are accepting of a guy with a kid are few and far between. The breakups that followed left Harper devastated, and that's when I decided dating wasn't worth putting my daughter through hell. Which is exactly what I need to remind myself now—and why the conversation about Ash can wait.

"Family portrait, huh?"

She nods, shading in what looks to be a pink daisy—one of several drawn in patches around our feet.

"Want to talk about it?"

"What about?" She places the pink pencil back in the box and grabs a yellow.

"Well, I know you sometimes feel bad that you don't have a mother or brothers and sisters like the other kids in your class."

She shakes her head, drawing a sun above our heads. "Not any more. That girl talked to me."

I lean back, surprised. This assignment has bothered Harper for years, and I've never seen her handle it so well. "What did she say?"

She shrugs. "She told me it doesn't matter if you have a mom and dad, it just matters if you have love. Some families—even with moms and dads—don't take care of each other. That's really sad." She looks at me. "You, me, Grandma, Aunt Em, we all love each other. So we have the best kind of family."

Ash did the one thing I've been trying to do since the moment Harper was born—she convinced her my love is enough. I won't forget that. My throat tightens to the point I almost can't squeeze the words out. "The very best." I smile and smooth her curls back with my hand.

She returns to her drawing. "I like that girl. She's nice."

"She certainly seems that way." I think again about Emily's warning. Whatever Ash's issue with kids is, it can't be that she doesn't like them. Otherwise why spend time with Harper trying to make her feel better?

"Too bad you can't ask her out." Harper shakes her head sadly as she finishes shading the sun. "She has too much going on right now."

"How do you know that?"

"I asked."

I nearly choke. "You asked her out for me?"

She sets the pencil down and makes a face. "No. I'm ten. I don't know how to ask people out."

Apparently that's not the case. "Harper, did she ask your name? Did you tell her you're my daughter?"

"No. Why?"

I sigh, relieved. If Ash told Harper she doesn't want a relationship, and I feel the same, there's no need to complicate things further. Especially given Ash's unknown issue with kids. Besides, what guy wants to be known as the dude who has his ten-year-old daughter ask girls out for him? Pathetic. "I can't date, either. I've got my own stuff going on, honey."

"What stuff?" She folds her arms across her chest and levels her gaze with mine.

She's ten and I'll be damned if I don't flinch. Sometimes I think she has more of me in her than I'd like to admit.

"Stuff! Like a business to run and a family to take care of."

She sighs and goes back to scribbling. "If everybody who worked and had families to take care of didn't date, there would be no more married people."

Ropes of irritation wind around me. There's nothing quite like being psychoanalyzed by a ten-year-old. Since I know better than to argue, I stand and kiss the top of her head. "I got to get back to work."

She nods without looking up.

"Tell Grandma to give you—"

"My vitamins and allergy medicine," Harper cuts in, rolling her eyes. "Got it, Dad."

Clearly I'm not the only one irritated. Throwing my hands up in defeat, I retreat into my studio. I'm not sure what I did to piss off God in a past life, but it must have been something bad for Him to surround me in this one with women who, no matter what I do, I can't ever seem to make happy.

I sit back down on my stool, put on a fresh pair of gloves, and pick up my machine. Inhaling deeply to loosen my strained muscles, I start the needle and place it against the guy's arm. For a big guy, he sure squeaks like a girl. I ignore his moans as I continue with the dragon, thankful I have my work to get lost in.

Still, as hard as I try, I can't stop thinking about Ashlyn—and the way she sat with Harper and made her feel better about her assignment. She didn't have to do that—she could have walked past her, like so many other women coming through my shop. Somehow, whatever shit she's had to endure in life, it didn't harden her, or bury her kindness behind a wall of scars—like it did me.

As I shade the scales down the dragon's spine, I try to push all thoughts of Ash from my mind. But I can't. I can hear her muffled laughter upstairs, feel the pull of her through the drywall and wood separating us.

I accidentally dig the needle in a little too deep and the guy yelps. I grab some gauze to wipe away the blood, biting on my cheek to keep from smiling. At least I have my job. With all this pent up frustration, I don't know how I'd make it through the day if I didn't get to make people bleed.

Chapter Nineteen

Ashlyn

"Two walls down. Two to go." Emily tips her beer back and takes a long swallow. "I have to admit, I think the place is actually starting to look livable."

I grin from my perch on the couch and take a swig of my own beer. Hank is sprawled across my lap, staring miserably at the fries I refuse to share. Feeling slightly guilty, and with a mental promise to give him extra treats, I scratch under his chin and lean back to admire our work. It's taken a couple hours, but half of the apartment's walls are now a light-green sage color.

I read online green is supposed to create a feeling of comfort and calm, and I feel as if the new paint is doing just that. Well, the paint coupled with the cool breeze wafting through the open windows. I sink deeper into the worn couch, feeling more at peace than I can ever remember feeling before.

"Should we keep going?" Emily asks.

I nod, gently pushing Hank off my lap before grabbing another fistful of fries and cramming them in my mouth. My neck is stiff and my muscles ache from the painting and furniture moving. Still, I'm eager to get the painting done. My stepdad refused to let me hang posters or pictures, saying they'd damage the walls, and changing the eggshell color was out of the question. I guess that's why I've been in such a hurry to paint. The more personal touches I add to this apartment, the more it begins to feel like mine. "Let's do it."

Before I can stand, there's a knock at the door. I glance at the clock on the oven. My heart skips a beat when I realize it's a little after ten. He's right on time. Every day this week Lane's come up to the apartment after he closes the shop. The first night he fixed the leaky faucet, the next he changed the air filter, and the third night he rewired a faulty switch. The fourth and fifth nights he installed a garbage disposal, and last night, despite my protests that it was unnecessary, he replaced the lime-crusted showerhead with a brand new one.

Each time he's come over, he's set about his work with few words to me. The same goes for when I'm working in his shop balancing books and organizing his schedule. We'll say hello and maybe mention the weather, but that's the extent of our interaction. Logically, I'm relieved an invisible boundary has formed between us. He's involved, and I'm renting his apartment. The complication of anything more would be a disaster. Still, my body mourns the memory of his touch, which plays through my mind whenever he's near.

Even now, just knowing he's on the other side of the

door sends my heart into palpitations.

"Hey, everything okay in there?" Lane calls out. His voice is muffled through the door. "Sounds like there's been a herd of elephants stomping around over my head all night."

I cringe as I walk to the door. We did make a lot noise moving the bed away from the wall.

"Lane?" Emily turns to look at me. "What's he doing here?"

I shrug, hoping to appear more nonchalant than I feel. "He's been coming over after work to fix a few things."

"How often does he come over?"

I pause. Hank has beat me to the door. His nose is jammed in the crack as his tail spins like a propeller. "Um, every night."

For the first time since I've met her, Emily says nothing. She turns away, but not before I see the confused lines furrowed across her brow.

I open the door, and my throat squeezes tight. Lane stands inches away, looking very much like the sex god he always does. Every inch of him radiates a heat that tingles against my skin. Reflexively I pull back, not because I'm afraid, but when he's that close, *I'm* dangerously close to forgetting the rules I've set into place for myself. Number one, don't get involved with taken guys and, number two, don't get involved with your landlord. The second rule is relatively new, but it's important nonetheless.

But God, if the sight of his taut chest peeking through his gray V-neck T-shirt doesn't make me want to forget all of my damn rules long enough to explore the muscles beneath with my hands.

"Laney!" Emily calls, reminding me I haven't spoken a word since I opened the door.

With my cheeks burning, I back out of the way so he can enter.

"Em?" He steps past me, his eyes lingering on my face just long enough to make my stomach flutter. "I know you were painting, but what's with all the noise?"

Emily raises a paint roller. "We're throwing a rave. What do think we're doing, genius? We had to move some things around to reach the walls."

He turns to the painted walls and folds his arms as he appraises our work. He's quiet, his face unreadable.

My heart plummets in my chest. "You hate it, don't you?" He looks at me but I don't give him a chance to respond. "I should have asked you before I picked the color. Shit. Don't worry. I can change the walls back to white as soon as the paint dries."

"No." He turns back to the walls. "I love it."

"You do?"

"It's an amazing color—really brightens the place up." He bends down and picks up a roller from the paint tray. "Where can I start?"

"There." Emily points to the unfinished portion of wall in the kitchen. "We were saving that for last because neither one of us could move the fridge."

"Wait." I step forward. My heart pulses an electric rhythm in my veins. "You don't have to stay. Emily and I have this under control. Besides, I know you have someone to get home to."

"Harper?" Emily arches an eyebrow. "But she's with—"

He cuts her off. "I'm happy to help."

Emily gives him a peculiar look I can't interpret.

Lane looks away. Either he doesn't notice, or he's

choosing to ignore her.

"That's it, I'm going home." Emily throws her hands in the air. "I thought I heard my brother say he's happy to help someone. That's how I know I'm exhausted."

"What? No!" I move in front of her, blocking her path to the door. I can handle working in Lane's shop because he's usually too distracted with a customer to notice I'm there. And then later, when he works on the apartment, I make it a point to position myself in the opposite side of the room with a book—far from accidental groping range. When I watched him work, bent under the sink with his muscles flexing, I couldn't think of anything but running my fingers over his muscles. Which is exactly why I can't be alone with him now.

"You can't leave," I say. "We still have two more walls to paint."

She shrugs. "We only have two rollers, Ash. Besides, Lane is a much faster painter than I am. You'll be done in no time." She steps around me. "You need to call me tomorrow." She jabs a finger at Lane. "We have *stuff* to talk about."

"Sure. Whatever." He glances at his boots. He actually looks embarrassed.

"B-but the beer!" I stammer. "You bought that whole case and you only had one."

She makes a face. "Meh. You keep it. I'm just not feeling it tonight." She walks to the door.

I take a step toward her, my mind racing to find any excuse to make her stay. But short of saying, *Please don't go. Your brother is sex on legs and I'm worried I'll do unspeakable things to him once you leave,* I have nothing.

She opens the door and steps through. Looking over her shoulder, she shrugs. "I don't like to get involved in other people's lives," she says, in a whisper only I can hear. "Just be careful. This could go one of two ways; fucking amazing, or fucking messed up as shit. I'll be rooting for you." She shuts the door without giving me a chance to reply.

One of two ways? Rooting for me? What the hell does any of that even mean? Unfortunately, I don't have time to decipher Emily's cryptic warning. I have more pressing matters at hand—mainly the six-foot-something sex on a stick I've suddenly found myself alone with. Son of a bitch.

My palms are sweaty, and I wipe them on my jeans as I slowly turn around. Lane's already at the wall, gliding the roller down plaster with quick, strong strokes. The knots of anxiety inside my chest loosen just a fraction.

It's okay, Ash. Nothing is going to happen. Sure Lane is the hottest guy you've ever met, and just looking at him tightens things low in your body, but hey, you're a big girl now. You can control your urges like a mother-fucking adult.

In an attempt to steady my nerves, I inhale deeply through my mouth then grab the other roller and slide it along the paint pan. When the foam can hold no more paint, I walk to the opposite end of the wall and begin working. Still, in an apartment this small, Lane is closer than I like. I glance over my shoulder, momentarily mesmerized by his flexing biceps as he works the roller along the wall.

Holy hell. I involuntarily lower the roller to my side. Even through the paint fumes I can smell his cologne, warm and spicy. The scent of it travels through my nose, filling my lungs, making me dizzy. I close my eyes and fight to suppress a shudder. When I'm sure I have myself under control, I open my eyes and resume working. Several minutes pass and silence fills the space between us, thick and pulsing.

"So," Lane says finally, his focus never leaving the paint gliding onto the wall. "There's beer?"

"Yes!" I practically shout, dropping my roller into the pan. I already drank a bottle with Emily, but that was nearly an hour ago. One more can't hurt, especially when I so desperately need something to take the edge off.

I rush to the fridge, pull two bottles from inside, and twist off the tabs. After taking a long draw from my own bottle, I walk the second one over to Lane.

He reaches for it without looking and our hands touch, his fingers wrapping around mine. Our eyes meet, tightening my throat and locking the breath inside my lungs. It's not until he shimmies the bottle from my grip I realize that was his intention all along. The corner of his mouth quirks into a grin as he lifts the bottle to his lips and takes a lopsided swig.

A flush creeps along my neck, and I duck my head, hoping to hide my embarrassment behind a curtain of hair. I quickly grab my abandoned roller and retreat to my corner of the room.

Lane starts to whistle as he spreads the paint across the walls. Is he playing with me? Arrogant jackass. Too bad my annoyance does nothing to squash my arousal. With renewed vigor, I work furiously on my own section. Unfortunately, it doesn't distract from the man beside me, the man whose shoulders pull taut each time he rolls out a long, even stroke of paint. Maybe I'm imagining things, but I would swear he's deliberately slowed his pace.

Which is bad. Very bad. In response, I quicken my own. With my resolve draining away, I have to finish this wall and get Lane out of the apartment as fast as possible.

Before I don't have any resistance left.

Chapter Twenty

Ashlyn

Lane steps back and admires his work. He's already moved the fridge and stove away from the wall, and his side of the room is nearly complete.

Thank God, because I don't know if it's the paint fumes, the beer I chugged, or the dizzying effects of watching Lane's arms strain against his shirtsleeves as he moves the fridge, but I'm having trouble concentrating through the swirling inside my head. The sooner Lane leaves, the better.

After Lane pulls the fridge several feet from the wall, he turns to his roller sitting in the empty pan. "You got any more paint?"

I nod, not trusting my voice due to the tightness of my chest. I grab the paint can from the corner and return to his pan. The can is still half full, and the small wire handle digs into my palm. My breathing is unsteady, making my hands shake. I turn the bucket on its side, but the paint moves faster than I expect, falling into the pan only to splatter over the side and onto the floor.

I let out a gasp, and clutch the bucket against my chest. The green droplets glare at me from the floor like a dozen angry eyes. *You're such a clumsy idiot!* a voice screams inside my head. *A child can pour paint into a pan without spilling it. But not you, because you're absolutely worthless.*

The words are ghosts of those spoken to me before, but they remain inside my brain like razor blades, always cutting, and too deep to pull out.

"Ash?" Lane's in front of me—funny because I don't remember him moving. "It's fine. It's just a little paint. We can clean it up with a wet rag."

My arms tremble and I set the paint can on the ground before I make more of a mess. He's missing the point. It doesn't matter that I can clean up the mess. What matters is that I made it in the first place. "I'm so sorry. I'm such an idiot."

He frowns and grabs my arms. "Who told you that?"

I don't answer. I'm too transfixed by the paint to form words.

"Ash." This time he gives me a small shake, forcing me to look up at him. His eyes are narrowed, and anger radiates in warm waves that prickle against my skin. Immediately my heart jumps inside my throat, and I try to shrink out of his arms, but he holds me fast. He says something, but I can't make out the words over the beat of my own pulse. I can't run, can't escape—I'm trapped.

I've been in similar situations with my stepdad, and the outcome was never good. Fear paralyzes me and my legs give out. I crumple in Lane's arms. He secures me against him with an arm around my waist and he reaches for the paint can with the other. I just know he's going to dump the entire thing onto the floor and force me to clean it up—that's what my stepdad would do, after all. And it's what I deserve for being so clumsy.

Instead, he sets the paint can on the kitchen counter. I try and curl into myself, to disappear, but his arms hold fast. My fingers are balled into fists and tucked under my chin. He wrenches one free and pulls it toward the paint can. His face is blurred, but I can see his lips continue to move, spilling words I can't hear over the crash of static inside my head.

He tries to pry my fingers open with his thumb, but I won't budge, so he dunks my entire hand into pail. I don't understand what he's doing. The paint is thick and cool against my fingers. He lifts my wrist from the bucket and paint trails green ribbons down my arm. Before I can stop him, he places my hand against his cheek.

The warmth of him seeps into my skin, spreading throughout my body. Green paint stains his cheek and dots his whiskers. He releases my wrist and yet my fingers stay, exploring the line of his jaw and the tendons flexing beneath my palm. He covers my hand with his, the paint turning sticky and sealing us together like glue.

Slowly, my breathing steadies and the rush of sound inside my head begins to quiet. His face falls into focus, the anger that was in his eyes only moments ago is gone, replaced instead with concern. "Ashlyn."

The sound of my name from his lips loosens something in me, and my hand falls from his face, leaving a wide, green stripe in its wake. "I don't—I don't understand."

"It's paint, Ashlyn. Just paint. It doesn't matter." He takes his hand, dips his finger into the paint bucket, and lightly taps my nose with it.

Reflexively, I jerk back. "Hey!" I swipe at his face with my paint-covered hand, miss, and make a wide streak on his gray shirt.

With a smile, he swings at me and manages to catch my cheek, creating a long, sticky trail all the way to my chin.

"Lane, stop!" I fight the grin pulling at my lips.

His own smile turns wicked. "Make me." He reaches for me, but I duck under his grasp.

I dart to my own paint pan and grab the roller, brandishing it in front of me like a sword. "Don't you dare take a step closer."

Without hesitation, he takes one exaggerated step toward me. Throwing his arms wide, he asks, "Now what?"

I can't help but giggle as I swing the roller in front of me. "I mean it!"

"Oh yeah?" Lane glances around until his gaze lands on an abandoned paintbrush in the sink. He grabs it and dunks it into the paint pail, saturating the bristles. He holds it in front of him, paint dripping to the ground.

My throat tightens. "The floor."

"I'll buy you a new one. Whatever kind of floor you want—laminate, linoleum, ceramic, you pick." Before I can respond, he lunges for me. I squeal and dart out of the way just as his paintbrush streaks by my face. As he stumbles past, I slap him with my roller and paint a stripe down his back.

He turns around, eyes wide, and pulls his T-shirt at the shoulder, eyeing the stripe. "I can't believe you did that."

He looks ridiculous, with a green handprint on his face and wide stripe down his shirt. I can't help but laugh.

There's something about the amusement in his eyes that transforms his face. I thought he was good-looking before, but when he laughs he makes my stomach fall into my knees in an oh-so-nice way. "You think this is funny?" He quirks an eyebrow—a small movement, but it sends jolts of electricity through my chest. "You're really asking for it," he says.

God, if he keeps smiling at me, I'll do more than ask for it—I'll beg, plead, whatever it takes. I lick my suddenly dry lips.

He lifts his chin and stalks toward me. My heartbeat ricochets off my chest with each step. I tighten my hold on the roller. "You better stay back," I warn. "You saw what happened last time."

He laughs, a deep rumble from his chest. "You think I'm scared."

I push my shoulders back, displaying a confidence I definitely don't feel. "You can't handle this."

He chuckles. "We'll see." He lunges for me.

With a shriek, I skitter backward and collide with the wall.

Lane's grin widens. "No use running now—you're trapped." He cups his chin in his hand and tilts his head, like an artist appraising his work. "And you know that wall is still wet, don't you?"

With a gasp, I lurch forward. Lane grabs my arm and swipes a streak of paint across my cheek. In response, I swing wide, and roll a line of paint down his arm. I'm giggling so hard my lungs burn and I'm heaving for breath. We're both laughing as he pulls me closer, threatening my face with his freshly painted arm. I'm struggling against him when my foot slides in a pool of paint.

I start to fall when Lane, still holding my arm, manages to twist his body to keep me from hitting the ground too hard. Unfortunately, the move knocks him off balance, and he topples to the floor beside me. Smiling, he rolls to his side and props his head up on his hand. "You look ridiculous."

I'm sure I do. Even if I can't see the green streaked across my face, I can feel the paint tightening on my skin as it dries. "You're one to talk. You look like you're about to move back to the swamp with your talking donkey."

He barks out a laugh. "Is that so? Well, what's an ogre without his ogre princess?" He grabs for the paint pan and dips his hand into it. "The transformation is almost complete. Looks like we missed a spot." He points a paint-covered finger at my forehead.

"Don't you dare!" I kick my legs in an attempt to scoot away.

"No you don't!" With sticky fingers, Lane grabs my wrists, pinning them to the floor. He swings a leg over my waist, straddling me. He leans down, his chest heaving. "Are you going to say 'Uncle'?"

A charge of electricity passes between us, buzzing beneath my skin and catching my breath in my throat. My smile fades as a flush courses over me. The heat from his hands feels as if it's searing my wrists, and yet I don't want him to let go. Even as the room wavers and the entire world feels like it's falling away, he holds on.

"Uncle." The word is barely a whisper as it leaves my throat.

"Too late," he says, and I know he's right. The wall I've

worked so hard to build between us is crumbling with each breath I take. I actually have to fight the urge to buck my hips toward his, to close the cruel distance between us. I've been falling for so long and he's the first person to hold on.

Without warning, his lips crash against mine like a tidal wave. He swallows my gasp of surprise as his tongue meets mine. His mouth tastes sweet, and there's an urgency to his kiss. His hands grip tighter and his mouth works harder against mine, almost as if he's trying to drink me in. I kiss him back, just as hard, because if he can drink me in, I'll let him. And then I'd remain there for always, a part of the man who wouldn't let go.

He joins my wrists together and readjusts his hold with one hand. With the other, he trails his fingers down my paint-streaked arm. An ocean of shivers follow in his wake as I claw at the air and writhe between his legs.

His hand finds the curve of my breast and I groan under his touch. His head lifts a fraction, his lips dark and swollen. I arch against his fingers and brush my tongue against his neck. A growl rumbles from between his clenched teeth and he lowers his hips against mine. The second the hardness of him falls between my legs, a burning ache ignites low inside me.

A whimper escapes my throat and I know I'm on the verge of losing control like I did the other night. Only this time, I don't want to stop. His hands find the edge of my T-shirt and inch it up over my torso. He slides his hand along my waist, his fingers taking their time, exploring every inch of my skin until they stop at the edge of my bra.

I hold my breath, my body tense in anticipation. My chest is actually quivering, desperate for his touch, aching for it. Until, finally, he slides his hand under the wire rim of my bra and cups my breast in his hand.

I moan, arching into his touch, trying to pour myself into his hands. His thumb grazes the edge of my nipple, and I shudder and buck my hips against his, grinding against the bulge beneath his zipper and tightening the need between my legs.

His grip loosens on my wrists and that's all the invitation I need to slip free, grab the edge of his T-shirt, and tug upward. He helps by sliding his arms out of his sleeves and throwing his shirt across the room. His entire chest is covered in ink. I trace my fingers along the various tattoos. Lane said all tattoos should have meaning, and I can't help but wonder about his. A police badge is centered over his heart, a pair of sparrows take flight from his ribs, and a skeletal woman, face painted like a candy skull, stares at me with parted red lips on the left side of his abs, just below the name Harper.

My fingers freeze beneath the delicate script. *What the fuck are you doing, Ashlyn?*

As if sensing my thoughts, Lane places a hand on my face, guiding my gaze back to his. "I know what you're thinking. With Harper, it's not like that."

I want to ask what he means, but he cuts me off. "Tonight, there's only you." His lips find mine and swallow any argument on my tongue. "Tonight, I belong only to you, and you only to me."

I wish I were strong enough to refuse, to tell him that's not enough—that one night will never be enough. But the temptation is too great. To have Lane as my own, even for a night, is too much to resist. "Tonight." I whisper the word against his neck. "I'm yours."

"Mine." The low growl of that one word renews the ache inside me. His hands rip my shirt over my head and the delicious warmth of his skin burns into mine. I slide my palms along his muscular back, pulling him as tightly to me as I can. If I only have tonight, I want to feel every inch of him, to memorize every ripple of muscle with my fingers.

He thrusts against me, the firmness of him grinding between my legs. A heaviness grows low inside me. I gasp, which he takes as invitation to push again, and again, until I'm worried I'll lose myself right there on the kitchen floor. And I don't want that. Because if I only have tonight, I want all of him—every hard, pulsating inch.

I slide my hands between us, grab the button of his jeans, and pry it apart. He tenses when I slip my fingers beneath the elastic of his briefs. When I encircle his swollen shaft, he inhales sharply before letting out a groan as I slide my fingers along the velvety skin.

"Ash." Lane closes his eyes and dips his head against my neck. His shoulders shudder and he groans. "You're killing me, I want you so bad."

I keep moving my hand, bucking my hips upward. The pressure inside me swells into a balloon of sweet agony. "Then take me."

He shakes his head. "I never expected…I don't have anything."

It takes me a minute to understand what he's talking about. "A condom? I've got one in my purse." I read somewhere that keeping condoms in a wallet broke them down over time. Ever since then I decided to keep some in my purse, just in case.

He sweeps an arm behind my back and lifts me off the ground in an instant. Before I can blink, he's tossed me over his shoulder.

"Lane!" I can't help but laugh. "What the hell?"

He ignores me. "Where the fuck is your purse?"

"Over there." He can't see me point, as I'm draped over his back. "On the nightstand."

He crosses the room in several long strides and slides me off his shoulder, placing me gently on the bed. He grabs my purse off the battered nightstand and hands it to me. "I wouldn't feel right searching through it. But I'm perfectly okay with this." Before I can ask what he's talking about, he unbuttons my jeans and slides them from my body.

After tossing them aside, he stands above me, lines of ink and muscle woven into a man too gorgeous to be real. His eyes are wild, hungry, and every cell in my body aches for him. At the same time, a small sliver of fear coils around me. This isn't like me, to sleep with a guy I barely know, especially when the terms he's set are quite clear. We belong to each other only for the night.

I fumble inside my purse with shaking fingers. Unzipping an inner pouch, I root around until I find the cellophane square holding the condom. I grab it and hold it out to Lane.

He takes it, climbing onto the bed and straddling me. My muscles quiver in anticipation. "Are you absolutely sure you want this?" he asks, a huskiness to his voice.

Oh God, yes. Still, a thread of hesitation weaves through me. It's not like I haven't been with a guy before, but something feels different with Lane—dangerous in a way I can't explain. Every guy I've ever been with I've been able to walk away from without regret, without sorrow, without any feeling whatsoever.

With Lane, I have this fear that if I open myself to him, even a little, he'll take more than I'm able to give. And then what will I be left with? What will I be?

Nothing at all.

Lane must read my uncertainty because he frowns. "God, Ash. I'm sorry. If I'm moving too fast…"

He starts to slide off of me and I quickly wrap my arms around his neck. *No. No. No.* I won't let him go. "You're mine for the night. You promised."

He eases back against me, the firmness of him pressing against the thin cotton of my panties, making my eyelids flutter. "You're right. I did promise. But we don't have to do this if you don't want to."

"I do. Please." I pull him tighter against me. That's the entire problem, I realize. I want him too much. And when I want things, they tend to get taken from me.

He lowers his head and the scruff of his cheek gently scratches the line of my jaw. "What do you want?" His breath tickles my skin, making me shiver. "Say it." His fingers find the edge of my panties and slowly work the elastic band down my hips.

My breath hitches in my throat as a wave of desire washes through me. Every muscle and nerve pulses with a burning ache. "I want you, Lane."

He smiles, a sly quirk of the lips. He shifts to his side, fumbling, and I hear the crinkle of cellophane. A second later he leans on his elbows, his fingers entwining in my hair. I feel the tip of him settle between my legs and it's all I can do not to squirm downward and guide him in. "Say it again."

He throbs against me, igniting pulses of pleasure where

his skin meets mine. I close my eyes and arch my back. I don't know how much more I can take. "Please, Lane. I want you."

And then I have him. All of him.

With a groan, I dip my head back and cling to him, rising up to meet him like a wave crashing into the shore. I raise my leg, hooking him around his waist as a warm pressure builds low inside me. With each thrust it grows, expanding between my hips until there's no room left, and it spills over. I cry out, back bowing, as my nails dig into his skin.

He kept his promise. Tonight, he belongs to me.

I only hope in the morning I'll have the strength to let him go.

Chapter Twenty-One

Ashlyn

The next morning at the coffeehouse, I'm still thinking about my night with Lane even though I know I should be concentrating on the iced vanilla latte I'm pouring. Lane was still asleep, tangled in the covers, when I'd slipped out of bed to get ready for work. He slept on his stomach, his arms wrapped around his pillow, and Hank was nestled in a ball against his legs. The thin sheet covering him had fallen to his hips, exposing his muscular tattooed back all the way to the dimples just above his tailbone.

I shiver at the memory and vanilla latte sloshes over the rim of the cup, soaking my fingers. I jerk back, spilling more liquid on the counter. *Jesus, Ash, pull it together.* I grab several napkins, mop up the mess, and seal the cup with a lid. After calling the customer and handing off her drink, I spin around to find Emily staring at me with a strange expression.

"What's up with you?" she asks, quirking an eyebrow. "You're acting weirder than normal—which is pretty fucking weird."

"I don't know what you're talking about." I grab the spray bottle and spritz down the counter to keep it from becoming sticky. "I'm just tired. I was up late last night—painting," I add quickly.

"Uh-huh." She folds her arms across her chest. "Just how late was that?"

I shrug, and rummage along the shelves for another pack of coffee cup sleeves. We have plenty stacked on the counter, but I need something to do to avoid her narrow-eyed gaze. "I don't really know. I lost track of time."

"Really? Because painting is so interesting?" A ghost of a smile pulls at her lips.

I scowl at her. I know she's fishing for details, but I'm not about to give her any, especially when the guy in question is her brother—a guy she specifically warned me to stay away from. Even though my night with Lane was amazing, I'm not exactly proud of the fact I let my hormones overpower my better judgment. I mean, he has another girl's name tattooed across his heart for Christ's sake! What kind of girl does it make me that I would still fool around with him knowing this?

Emily gives me a questioning look and I turn away from her before she can read the guilt in my eyes. Lane did say his relationship with Harper "wasn't like that," whatever the hell that means. Still, he also only promised me a night, and now that it's over, I know better than to expect anything more. It was by far the hottest night of my life, and I should be happy with the memory and leave it at that.

Emily touches my shoulder. "Hey. You okay? You want to talk about anything?"

I'm about to shake my head when the front door chimes.

Emily curses under her breath. "Later then, okay?"

I nod and turn to face the customer.

Only I realize immediately the woman walking into the shop isn't a customer. My heart plummets to my ankles.

The woman clutches her cardigan together with a bony hand, even though the weather is far too warm for a sweater. It's probably a Ralph Lauren or Calvin Klein. Her wheat-colored hair is cropped above her ears, and dark circles rim her eyes. She glances around the shop, taking everything in, her eyes alert, as if she's never been inside a coffee shop before in her life. I'm willing to bet she hasn't.

Emily approaches the register. "What can we get started for you?"

The woman twitches, her eyes widening at the attention. "Actually, I was looking for someone."

Every muscle in my body coils, desperate to make a run for it. I grip the counter to keep from fleeing.

The woman's head swivels in my direction, her eyes meeting mine. Her shoulders slump slightly. "Ashlyn."

I lick my lips before I answer. "Hey, Mom." The word tastes like bile on my tongue.

She lets go of her sweater, revealing the skeletal frame beneath. "Do you have a minute?"

I'm falling. The second I saw her I felt as if the floor disappeared from beneath my feet. I keep plummeting farther and farther, bracing myself for the painful landing to come. "What are you doing here?"

She bites her lip, looking uncertain, like she's not quite

sure herself. "I hope you don't mind me stopping in like this. One of the women at church, Muriel, saw you working here and told me. I just need to talk to you. It won't take long, I promise."

Anger rises inside of me until I think I might explode from the force of it. How dare she show up at my work, expecting to get a moment of my time, when she only stood by, sobbing, as her husband physically shoved me out the door of our home? She has no idea what I've been through over the last six months—how I've been forced to survive by sleeping in truck stops and rooming with strippers. I owe her nothing.

And yet, I find myself nodding. "Yeah. Sure. But just a minute." Because as much as I want to tell her to go fuck herself, she's still my mom. I glance over my shoulder at Emily to see if she's cool with it.

She nods, her forehead creased with lines of worry. "Go ahead. I can handle things."

I untie my apron, wad it into a ball, and shove it under the counter before I step around the register. "I can talk to you outside." I motion to the outdoor seating. If there's going to be a scene—which is always a possibility with my mother—I don't want to risk losing my job over it.

"Sounds good." Mom follows me out of the coffee shop. I sit at one of the metal tables outside and she sits across from me. Emily and I haven't had a chance to put the table umbrellas up yet, so the midmorning sun forces me to squint. All I have to do to fix the situation is crank the umbrella up, but I don't. I'd rather have my retinas burned with hot, white light than make eye contact with the woman who stood by and did nothing as everything I owned was burned to cinders.

Mom fidgets with the strap of her purse before resting it on the table. "You look too skinny."

I frown. Of course I'm skinny. That's what happens when you're forced to skip meals so you can pay rent. At least now, thanks to my rent agreement with Lane, I actually have money for real food. But I don't tell her any of this. The moment I left the house, I left her, too. "I only have a few minutes," I remind her, in case she's looking for something else to criticize.

"Right." She shifts uncomfortably in her seat. She's looking awfully skinny herself, not from diet but from whatever cocktail of antianxiety and bipolar medication she happens to be on at the moment. "I hate the way things ended between us. I worry about you struggling to survive on your own. If you want to come home—"

"I don't." I'd rather sleep in a thousand truck stops and eat nothing but crushed glass than put myself through that hell again.

Mom's shoulders slump. "I understand things have been rough between your stepdad and you. You know he's had a very rough life, don't you? That his mom was an abusive alcoholic? Maybe if we all went to therapy together—"

I stand so abruptly, the chair tips back before righting itself with a bang. I should have known she'd come here trying to make yet another excuse for his behavior. Each time my stepdad called me stupid and worthless, the words slid into my heart like a knife. When he grew tired of the abuse, Mom would swoop in with her excuses, "He had a very hard life. He's under a lot of pressure from work." Words make good weapons, but, excuses make shitty Band-Aids.

For years, I believed her, praying my stepdad would wake one day transformed into a man who didn't need to belittle or control me. At ten years old I tried to convince myself his negative attention was better than none at all. I craved a father so I took his abuse, greedily even, because it was more attention than I'd ever had from a man. But I was wrong. Neglect would have been kinder. The problem with verbal abuse is it festers inside you like poison, spreading through your blood, infecting your brain until you believe the very words that cut so deeply.

I am stupid.

I am lazy.

I am worthless.

These words have lived inside me for the last ten years. Even now I can feel them squeezing my heart like so many strands of barbed wire. And excuses are the hands that pull them tighter.

No fucking more. I've been beaten down enough in my life. I won't let anyone take what little bit of me I have left. "I've got to go."

"No!" Mom's reaches across the table for me, but I'm too far away for her to touch. "Please. I'm so sorry." Tears well in her eyes. "You're my baby. I can't lose you. Tell me what to do to make it better."

A wisp of anger uncurls inside me. My fingers clench so tight my nails dig into my flesh. I'm so sick of her tears. My mother's cried every day of her life for as long as I can remember. If for once she actually did something, rather than cry about it, I wonder how different our lives would have been. "Leave him."

Her eyes flutter wide as the tears spill down her cheeks.

"What?"

I grip the edge of the table and lean toward her. "You want to know how to make things better? Leave Charles."

She recoils as if I've slapped her. "I…I can't do that. What would I do? Where would I go? Besides, he needs me. I know he has anger issues, but it's not his fault—"

"Enough excuses!" I slam my palm against the table, rattling it. A lifetime of anger has built up inside of me only to erupt in this moment. "He's a monster and he's not going to change. You know it and I know it."

Mom's face crumples and the tears wind down her cheeks. She's quiet—I'm sure she's searching for another excuse—then she nods. "You're right."

Her voice is so soft I'm sure I've misheard. "What?" Slowly, I lower myself back into the chair.

"You're right," she says, louder. She wipes her tear-streaked cheeks with her hand. "He's not changing." A sob chokes up her throat. "We were on welfare when I met him. I knew he had a temper, but I thought I could soften his edges. I thought he'd be able to take care of us, give you the life I never could. I was wrong. God, how I was wrong."

She buries her face in her hands, her chest heaving. She looks so fragile sitting there, like a porcelain puppet with broken strings. Still, I've been submerged under a sea of her tears in my lifetime, and I refuse to drown in them anymore. "So leave him."

To my surprise, she laughs. "Ashlyn, I'm fifty years old and work at a department store. Women in my position don't leave their husbands. It's too late for me…" She swallows hard. "But not for you."

I frown. "What does that even mean?"

She glances over her shoulder before reaching inside her purse and withdrawing a bank envelope. She slides it across the table. "It's not much, but it will buy you a ticket to Atlanta."

I stare at the envelope, afraid to touch it. Charles keeps obsessive watch over the bank accounts. If Mom withdrew any money, he'll find out, and there will be hell to pay—especially if he finds out the money is for me.

"Don't worry." Mom slides the envelope closer. "I've been tucking this cash away for awhile. He doesn't know about it."

"Why Atlanta?"

Mom turns away from me, her eyes focused on something distant in the parking lot. "I've been talking to your Aunt Linda ever since you left."

Got kicked out, I want to scream. Instead, I press my lips together so hard my teeth bite into my skin.

Mom fidgets in her chair before continuing. "Aunt Linda says you can live with her—in Atlanta—for as long as you need. She's happy to have you and, if you agree to take some college courses, she won't even charge you rent. You can start over."

Start over.

The words tumble through my head like jagged stones. All I've wanted my entire life was a way out, a chance to start my life over. And now, my ticket is quite literally in front of me. Still, I'm hesitant to take it. I'm finally at a point where things are falling into place for me. I have a good job, a friend, a dog, time to write, and an apartment all of my own.

And Lane.

I brush the thought aside. Lane made it perfectly clear what we had was only for the night. Even if Lane and I *were* together, I'd have to be pretty stupid to throw away this perfectly good opportunity for a guy I barely know—one who is sure to hurt me like all the guys before.

"Take the money, Ashlyn."

I glance up from the envelope to find my mom watching me. "There's nothing for you here."

Her words bite into my heart with razor-edged teeth. Is she right? Aunt Linda's always been nice to me. I'm sure we'd get along. Maybe I can even talk her into letting me bring Hank. Sure, I'd be leaving Emily behind, but maybe I'd make more friends. And it would be nice to go to school and not worry about bills. I curl my fingers around the envelope and slide it toward me.

But what about Lane?

I shake my head, as if I can somehow push all thoughts of him from my mind. Lane doesn't matter, I remind myself. He's not mine.

Mom clears her throat. "Aunt Linda's having some renovations done to her house for the next couple of weeks, so she won't be ready for you until the end of the month. Will you be okay on your own until then?"

I nod.

"I'm happy to hear that." Mom grabs her purse and hikes the strap over her shoulder. "I really should get going. I told Charles I was making a quick run to the grocery store. I'll have to pick up some things and get back before he gets suspicious."

His keeping track of her every move proves nothing's changed.

She stands to go. I want to stand, too, but a cold numbness seeping through my body keeps me locked into place.

There's nothing for you here. Her words echo in an endless loop inside my head. I really don't know what I expected—for her to tell me she was leaving Charles and I was welcome to move back in with her? No. I know better. But to have her tell me in so many words that our relationship is *nothing* does more than sting. It shreds my heart like a cheese grater. It's bad enough she didn't do a thing as my stepdad threw me out of the house, but she had to contact me again and make a point of choosing him over me all over again.

Just when I think I can finally begin to heal, she finds another way to break me.

"Oh." Mom pauses. "I found a few of your things when I was cleaning out the attic last weekend. Just some old stuffed animals and a few yearbooks. I hid them for now but I think it's safer if I send them to you before..."

They get burned, like the rest of my stuff?

Of course, Mom doesn't say this. She licks her lips. "Anyway, if you give me your address, I'll put them in the mail for you so you can take them with you to Atlanta." She pulls out her phone. "Where can I ship them?"

I don't want to give her my address. I've given her enough of myself today. Still, the temptation of getting a few of my childhood belongings back is too great to resist. I mumble the address quickly before I can change my mind. "Four-seventy-five Sixth Street. Don't use it for anything else but sending me my stuff."

Mom nods, her eyes meeting mine. We're done. We're both silent as the finality passes between us, a feeling so uncomfortable I shiver to get it off my shoulders.

She turns and heads for her car. In a way, that's fitting. Because, really, when a relationship is done, so are the words.

It's the broken pieces that stay behind.

Chapter Twenty-Two

Lane

My last client of the night left hours ago, and yet I can't bring myself to go home. I pretend I need to place orders and file receipts, but I can't lie to myself. I have more than enough ink and needles to get through the end of the month. It's not until I hear the door to the upstairs apartment creak open above me, followed by the sound of footsteps, that my muscles unwind from tense knots I hadn't realized I carried.

She came home.

I sweep my hand through my hair, aggravated for caring at all. It's bad enough I woke in a panic when I discovered Ash missing from my arms this morning. It resurfaced the memory of the day I came home from work to discover Harper, face red and swollen from crying, strapped in her car seat, alone in that very apartment for God knows how long. All of her mother's belongings were gone with nothing but a note left in their place. A note with only two hastily scribbled words:

I can't.

As a high school dropout, barely seventeen and working fulltime, I was fairly certain I couldn't either. Only, from the moment I first saw my daughter, and I fell in love with everything from her long, dark lashes to her tiny, curled fists, I knew I owed it to her to try.

Harper's mother leaving really came as no big surprise. After all, we only moved in together because her parents kicked her out when they found out she was pregnant. We had nothing in common other than a few drunken moments alone in a closet, which would forever link us together. I only hope wherever she is, she's happy. She may not have been the love of my life, but Crystal gave me someone who I'll love for a lifetime.

And that's enough.

Or, at least I thought so until I find myself locking the shop doors and climbing the steps to the apartment above. Because the second she arrived home, I had to see her. I don't even have an excuse ready tonight—no leaky faucet to fix or air filter to change. With my fist raised to knock against her door, I stop myself and ram my hands into the back pockets of my jeans.

Just what the hell am I doing? Ash and I have an understanding: we only had one night, and now it's over. I get that. If only the rest of my body would get the message.

Sure, I can try to pass it off as desire, because, damn, every cell in my body craves that girl. But it's more than that. If all I wanted was a good fuck, I got it. So why am I back for more? Why am I almost crazy with the need to throw her door open, take her in my arms, and kiss her like I did last night? I could lie and say I feel some sort of obligation to take care of her, to watch over her like I do my sister. But the hard truth settles into my stomach like a block of lead. With Ash, I don't want to protect her out of obligation or sense of duty. With Ash, I want to take care of her, protect her, because the thought of anything happening to her wrenches something deep inside my core.

I care about her. More than I should.

Fuck. When the hell did that even happen?

The realization startles me so much, I turn to walk back down the stairs. Behind me I hear the door open.

"Lane?"

Damn it.

Slowly, I turn to find Ash standing outside the door with Hank's leash in hand. Her hair is pulled back and the fabric of her shirt is so worn I can see the outline of her body beneath—a body I became all too familiar with last night. Desire coils around me as the memory resurfaces.

The puppy lets out a yip, pulling me from my thoughts. He strains against the leash, tail wagging, in an attempt to get to me. "Hey. I thought I'd stop by and..." My brain spins, searching for something that won't make me look like a pathetic stalker loser. "Check on Hank. I wasn't sure you were home from work yet." The lie sounds forced, even to me. I lean over to give his ear a scratch, which starts him into a licking frenzy.

"Oh." It could be me, but I swear there's a hint of disappointment in her voice. "I was just about to walk him." She's quiet for a minute while I fend off Hank and his tongue. "Do you want to come with us?"

It's not a good idea. The more time I spend with her, the more embedded in my head she becomes. Still, I nod. No matter how badly I want to, I just can't refuse her. Besides, it's late, and I don't like the idea of her wandering the dark streets alone.

She gives me a hint of a smile, and something inside me constricts. It's then I realize I'm completely ensnared by her, and that really puts me in a bad situation. I've done nothing these past years but devote myself to one girl and one girl alone. Didn't I promise Harper I wouldn't let anyone come between us? That I wouldn't let anyone hurt her and run out on us again?

Ash walks past me and I inhale her dizzying aroma of apples and coffee. My arms strain with desire to reach for her. Now that I know what it's like to have her curled beside me, head on my chest, I ache to have that closeness again. She's only a couple of feet ahead of me but it's too much. I quicken my pace to close the distance, and it's a good thing I do. When Ash reaches the bottom step, Hank surges ahead and yanks her off her feet. I grab her arm, steadying her before she can fall.

She looks up at me, large blue eyes blinking in surprise. "Thanks."

I nod and loosen my grip on her elbow, but find myself unable to let go. Instead, I slide my hand to her wrist and pause. "Is this okay?" Before I explain, I weave my fingers through hers.

Her eyes widen, and her voice is soft when she answers. "What happened to just one night?" Still, she doesn't let go, and I tighten my hold, the heat of our palms melting us together.

We start down the sidewalk hand in hand. I can't remember the last time I held hands with a girl who wasn't in grade school. I have to admit, it's nice—actually, better than nice. It feels right in a way nothing else has until now. Even the fucking hot sex from the night before. With Ash's hand in mine, I feel…complete. And I'm not ready to give that up.

"What if it's not just one night?" I ask.

Hank stops to sniff a light pole and Ash lurches to a halt beside him. "What?"

Shit. That wasn't exactly the reaction I was hoping for. At least she doesn't slide her fingers free from mine. "Would that be so bad? If we saw more of each other?"

She frowns at me. "Are you looking for a nightly booty call or something? Because, despite last night, I'm not that kind of girl."

"What? No!" I give her hand a tug and draw her to me. She braces a palm against my chest and sparks ignite beneath my skin where she touches. "Ash, I wasn't talking about sex. I'm talking about…hell, I don't really know. Going out. Getting to know each other better. Dating."

Her eyes widen, pools of blue so deep I can almost feel myself falling into them and drowning. "But what about…" She swallows hard, and her gaze drifts to the name tattooed below my collarbone.

Harper.

I realize now is the moment to tell Ash about my daughter. But first, there's something I need to know. "Ash, my relationship with Harper isn't what you think."

She frowns at me and I find myself sweeping an arm behind her back, pulling her closer. "I don't know what that means," she says.

"I know. And I want to explain it to you. But first I need to know you're not going anywhere. We've—" I shake my head. "I mean *I* have been run out on before. I guess that's why I've kept women at a distance. But the more time I spend with you, the harder it's becoming for me to let you go—and I don't *want* to let you go. I just need to know you're not going to run away."

Her gaze drifts to the puppy tugging at the end of the leash. "God, Lane, I—" She blinks, and tears well heavy on her eyelashes.

Seeing them, my stomach winds into a painful knot, and I release her hand. I know whatever she says next, I'm not going to like.

Ash turns away from me and allows Hank to lead her down the sidewalk. I follow a half step behind. "My mom visited me today," she says without looking at me. "She says my aunt offered to let me live with her in Atlanta, rent free, so I can go to school."

Her words hit me like a punch in the gut, and I inhale sharply. Anger follows the pain, clawing through my chest. Though it's not Ash I'm mad at, but me, for allowing myself to be put in such a vulnerable position. *God, I'm such a fucking idiot.* At least I found this out before I got Harper involved.

"You're leaving." Miraculously, the words come out flat, without emotion.

She ducks her head. "I don't know. I have every reason to leave, but only one to stay." Her eyes flick to mine before she quickly looks away. "And I didn't even think you were a reason up until a couple of minutes ago. You made it plenty clear what happened between us was only for the night."

She stares at me, as if waiting for me to argue, and I want to—God, how I want to—but how can I put up a fight when I feel as if my heart's just been torn out?

"Right." I rake my fingers through my hair. At least we know where we stand. And if she leaves, maybe that's for the best. If she moves several states away, it'll be a clean break, no accidental run-ins at the grocery store or the gas station. Gradually she'll fade from my mind and it'll be like we never met. I can cover her mark on my heart like I did the tattoo on her arm.

I force a smile to my face. "I guess I just really suck at one-night stands."

She opens her mouth to say something, but apparently changes her mind. An awkwardness hangs between us, heavy and thick. We both turn to Hank to find him sitting, watching us expectantly. Apparently, his business outside is done.

She gives the leash a gentle tug and turns back toward the apartment. I don't want to follow, but I can't help myself. "How long?"

She sighs and gives a half shrug. "A week. Maybe two. I want to thank you for giving me a place to stay. I promise I'll pay you back for whatever rent I owe."

I shake my head. "I don't want your money. I only want… " *You,* I think, but I'm not man enough to voice the word out loud. She cocks her head, waiting for an answer, so I give her one. "More time," I finish.

She rolls her eyes. "Come on. You and I both know this could never go anywhere. We had an amazing night. Why tempt fate by asking for more?" She looks up at me. "Maybe it's better this way—that things end now before they go any further. I mean, I'm a fucking disaster. You don't need me in your life."

She's not telling me anything I haven't already told myself. Still, I can't stay away, no matter how hard I try. There's her beauty. The soft gentleness of her. They way she made Harper feel better when I was unable. Then there's the feel of her bare skin against mine and the softness of her lips and even the taste of her—these are drugs I can't quit. Even now my body aches to close the distance between us. Because I can't stand not touching her, I reach out and brush a strand of hair behind her shoulder. "My past hasn't exactly been a picnic, either."

She grins. "See, we're a nuclear bomb waiting to go off. Continuing… whatever this is would be a huge mistake."

"Huge," I echo. Still, I'm haunted by the way she felt in my arms last night, and the weight of her head against my chest as she slept. For a moment, she was well and truly mine, and nothing has ever felt more right.

Heat stirs inside me and I grab her arms, pulling her slowly toward me. She comes willingly, biting her lip as she cranes her neck to stare up at me. I trace my thumb along her shoulders, up the curve of her neck to her jaw.

She shivers beneath my touch. "Lane. I thought we agreed this is a mistake."

I curl my fingers into her hair. "For the last ten years, I've worked my ass off to provide for my family. I've sacrificed everything to make sure they were happy and had what they needed. Don't get me wrong, I don't regret it and I'd do it all again in a minute. But during that time, I forgot what it was to want something for myself. That is, until I met you, Ashlyn. I want you. Even if only for a short while longer."

She pauses before sliding her hands along my chest and

wrapping her arms around my neck. "If we do this, it's only going to make my leaving that much worse."

She's right. A small voice begs me to listen, but in this moment, nothing short of the end of the world can make me let go of her. I gave up everything to provide for Harper—and I was glad to do it. I had dreams of going to college, of becoming a cop like the old man. But those dreams were flimsy and easy to lose. Not Ash. I wasn't lying when I said I've never wanted anything as much as I want her.

And I'll hold on for as long as I can.

Chapter Twenty-Three

Ashlyn

I walk inside my apartment, unhook Hank from his leash, and grab the plastic bin where I keep his food. Everything about Lane feels like a dream, and I'm scared if I turn around he won't really be there. But when I walk across the kitchen to Hank's bowl, Lane's leaning against the door, watching me with a hunger that has nothing to do with appetite.

Relief unwinds the tight band around my chest. Stupid, because I know it would be better if I just ended things with Lane. Still, I'm not ready to let him go.

I scoop a cup of kibble into Hank's bowl and he eagerly shoves his face into the food.

I set the container aside, and Lane moves toward me, his jaw tight and shoulders rigid. Electricity pulses between us, prickling my skin and tightening things deep inside me. The look in his eyes is all heat and desire.

He stops in front of me, close enough to touch me, but he doesn't. "Last night I was yours," he says, voice husky. "Tonight I want you to be mine. But I want your permission first."

My throat constricts, and I lick my suddenly dry lips. "What does that mean?"

"Someone hurt you, Ash. Someone broke you and your trust. I want to prove you can trust me. But in order to do that…" He unbuckles his belt and yanks it free from his jeans. The sound of leather sliding against fabric makes me shiver. "You need to give yourself to me. Completely."

Holy fuck. "And how do I do that?"

He takes a step toward me. "If you agree, you're going to do everything I say. If things become too intense, tell me to stop, and I will. Now, do you trust me?"

The rush of excitement outweighs my fear, and I nod.

He smiles. "Take your clothes off."

"What?" I give a nervous laugh, but Lane's expression doesn't waver. He's clearly not joking.

"Take your clothes off," he repeats. He folds his belt in half and snaps the leather, making me gasp.

My pulse jumps in my throat, and I grab the hem of my shirt. I can't deny the need to be with Lane, the ache throbbing low within me. There's something dangerous about the way he's watching at me, like he wants to devour me whole. The look in his eyes sends tremors down my spine.

I twist my hands into the fabric of my shirt, stretching it. "You promise you'll stop if I ask you to?"

"I'm not going to do anything you don't want me to do. I want you to trust me."

And I do, I realize, as I slowly pull my shirt over my head.

Lane has done nothing but protect me since the moment we met, which is more than my own parent has done. I trust him more than anyone in the world.

"Pants." The way Lane says the word, it practically comes out a growl.

I kick my shoes off and unbutton my jeans with trembling fingers. I've never stripped in front of a guy before, and I'm sure I look awkward—all fumbling fingers and shaking limbs. Not to mention my lingerie is a ridiculous combination of plain tan bra and white cotton panties. God, to have the money to buy real lingerie.

"Stop."

Too late. My jeans fall to my ankles. I look up at Lane to ask why he stopped me. Maybe he thinks I look stupid, too. But instead of finding a look of disgust, his eyes sweep over my body and he makes a sound low in his throat.

"God, you're sexy," he says.

I frown. "But you said to stop."

"Yes." He walks toward me and my body practically hums with excitement. "You're so damn readable. Whatever thoughts you're thinking about yourself, I want you to stop. You're beautiful, Ash. In fact, it's killing me not to rip off your underwear and take you right now."

My cheeks burn with a flush, and I look away.

To my surprise, Lane walks by me and grabs the back of a wooden chair. He swings it away from the small kitchen table and gestures to it. "Sit."

"Why?"

"No questions. In fact, unless you're going to tell me to stop, I don't want you to speak at all. You are not going to overanalyze this, Ash. You're mine tonight, remember? That means I don't just want your body, but I want your trust, too. Do you understand?"

I nod. My body's reaction to his demand is unexpected. The thrill of this new game sends my heart ricocheting against my ribs. No man has ever looked at me the way Lane is now, like I'm something desirable, something of worth. And he wants me—I can see the hunger in his eyes. All my life, men have wanted to control and use me. Lane wants me exactly as I am, and has even given me the right to refuse him. No one's ever done that for me before. Even if he's giving the orders, I still hold the power to end it. Having the safety of a way out has made Lane's game even more exciting.

I walk to the chair. My nerves hum liked plucked guitar strings. Slowly, I turn and sit, leaving Lane standing behind me.

"Say it." The warmth of his breath against my neck startles me, and I shiver. "Tell me you're mine."

I arch my neck as a ripple of goose bumps washes across my skin. I try to do what Lane's asked me to do, to clear my head of any thoughts of tomorrow or the future, to just be in this moment and exist in a world where there is only me and Lane. "I'm yours."

He grabs my hands and pulls them behind the chair. Before I realize what he's going to do, he loops his belt around my wrists and fastens them to the wooden rod at my back.

I inhale sharply as my pulse races. I don't know what I was expecting, but it wasn't this. I pull against my restraints but they hold firm. Panic tightens my throat. At the old house, I was locked inside my room for the slightest infraction, forgotten for hours on end. How easy it would be for Lane to leave me tied up like this, alone, in a place where no one would come to look for me.

No sooner does a whimper escape my lips than Lane is in front of me, kneeling. He touches my face with his hand. "Ash, don't panic. We'll stop the second you tell me to. You're in control."

You're in control. His words swirl inside my head, and my pulse returns to a normal rhythm. I nod.

He smiles. "Good. Let me prove it to you. Let go. Just for the night. You can give yourself to me, and I won't hurt you." The smile melts from his lips, and his hands slide up my thighs, igniting sparks beneath my skin. "I'll never hurt you."

He leans forward and kisses the skin above my knee. His lips are like the brush of a feather dusting along my inner thigh, leaving delicious flashes of pleasure in their wake. His kisses build a fire between my legs that grows the farther he climbs, until he's licking the skin along the edge of my panties and I'm squirming from the ache he's built inside me.

He hooks his fingers beneath the band of my panties and slides them off my hips all the way to my ankles. Heat blazes through my cheeks. Despite our already having slept together, a sudden shyness comes over me. I've never had a guy look at me the way Lane is now. I'm not sure what he's used to, or if I measure up. I try to keep things as trim as I can, but it's not like a homeless girl can afford a wax.

As if hearing my thoughts, his eyes flick to mine. "You're gorgeous."

I open my mouth to argue but he silences me with a grunt. "No talking, unless you want me to stop." He arches an eyebrow. "Do you?" He slides his hands back up my legs and digs his fingers into my hips, pulling me, and the chair, toward him, claiming me.

I shake my head. Sure, I'm scared, but stopping is the last thing I want.

He leans forward and every muscle in my body tenses. I've never been kissed *there,* and I have no idea what to expect. The first flick of his tongue rips a gasp from my throat. The second flutters my eyelids as a ripple of pleasure washes out from my center, rolling all the way to the top of my scalp. The next arches my back, making me buck against the chair. Lane only tightens his grips and pulls me closer.

I moan and dip my head back. The sweetness of the pressure building inside me is almost too much to bear. As the heat between us continues to build, I can no longer tell where I end and Lane begins. Every nerve in my body is alive with fire, burning hotter and hotter and hotter, filling every inch beneath my skin with flame. And just when I think the fire will spill out of me, Lane stops and leans back.

"Tell me you want me."

I blink, forcing my swimming vision back into focus. I expect to find Lane watching me with the same hungry expression he wore only seconds ago. But I don't. Instead, there's a softness to his eyes, a vulnerability I hadn't noticed earlier.

"I want to hear you say it," he says.

No. I sit as straight as my restraints allow. It's not want that fills his eyes with desperation, but *need.* I can see the yearning written across his face. He said he tied me to the chair to prove I could trust him, but what if the real reason isn't so simple? What if he's trying to convince himself he can trust me?

Maybe I'm not the only one who's been hurt before.

"I want you, Lane." And I'm not just talking about the building ache between my legs. Sure, he's a little gruff on the outside, but soft as a kitten on the inside. He's fiercely protective of his sister, and compassionate enough to offer help to a homeless girl without expecting anything in return. How could I not fall for him? I want to call him mine and to fall into his arms whenever I've had a bad day. I want to spend mornings in bed lazily tracing circles across his chest with my finger, and I want to spend nights tangled with him in the sheets.

But with me leaving soon and his mysterious relationship with Harper, that'll never happen. That doesn't mean I'm not going to take advantage of the time I have left with him.

He stands suddenly.

A flicker of panic courses through me. "Where are you going?"

"Condom."

Oh, thank God. I settle back into the chair. I'm not sure how much more teasing I could take.

After retrieving a condom from my purse, he steps around the chair and unfastens my arms from the back rungs. But, instead of freeing me, he ties my wrists together in front of me. "You're not getting away from me," he says, smiling. "At least, not tonight." His smile wavers slightly, and I feel a tug in my heart.

"Of course. I'm yours tonight. I promised."

His smile returns. He twists his fingers into the hem of his shirt and whips it over his head. Just like the night before, the sight of him bare chested takes my breath away. He's muscle and ink, a work of art for both my eyes and fingers to enjoy. I reach for him but he snatches my bound wrists and slips them over his head, tying me to him.

The warmth of his skin against mine makes me dizzy with desire. The hardness held back by his jeans presses against my navel, making me wiggle against him, yearning for him to move lower.

He laughs softly, dropping his hands to unbutton his jeans. The anticipation is too much, and I hold my breath. If my hands were free, I'd pull him out myself. He seems to like watching me squirm and takes his sweet time taking off his jeans. Locked this close to him, I can't see what's going on, but I can tell the instant the velvet length of him pushes between my legs, hovering just outside of me.

I whimper. Every cell in my body is on the verge of bursting. If he doesn't take me soon, I'm sure I'll explode. I shift my hips, trying to give him an angle to enter, but he only backs away. "Wait just a sec." He moves his hands behind my back and I hear the crinkle of a cellophane package. A second later, he moves his hands between us and his cock is back, pressing between my legs, only this time it's slick from the lubricated condom.

He thrust his hips forward, the length of him sliding between my folds and pressing against the raw button of nerve that makes me cry out as my legs buckle.

My pulse crashes inside my head like a wave as electricity surges through me. "Lane." My voice is breathless. "I can't hold on much longer. Please. Now."

He smirks and pulls me backward, until his legs meet the back of the chair. He sits so I'm standing between his legs, my arms still locked around his neck. "Show me how bad you want me. Ride me."

I pause for just a second. This will be another first for me, but if it's as fun as the last thing we tried—and it certainly looks to be—I'm game.

I move my legs so I'm straddling his and inch myself forward until the tip of his cock meets the sweet spot just above my opening, and my eyelids flutter. "Holy fuck," I gasp.

He laughs. "We haven't even got to the good part yet." Before I can respond, he grabs my hips and thrusts me down, onto his lap.

I cry out as his dick fills every inch of me, hitting a spot below my navel that's never been touched before, a spot that makes fireworks explode in the darkness behind my closed eyes. A rolling a wave of spasms reaches all the way to my fingers and toes. When I catch my breath I ask, "What the hell was that?"

Lane arches his neck and answers with a groan. "God, Ash, you're killing me."

He pulls harder at my hips, burying himself deeper than I thought possible. I cry out and rock forward, before sliding back down. A sweet pressure builds between my legs, growing each time he pulls me to him. The pleasure comes from everywhere—from my breasts gliding along his chest, to the mass of nerves between my legs grinding against his pelvis, to the soft sweet spot inside me that pulses each time the head of him crashes into it.

Just as I'm on the verge, Lane grabs my bra and pulls it down so my breasts spill over the fabric. He takes a nipple into his mouth and sucks hard, eliciting a gasp from my throat.

"Lane…" I'm so close, and if he keeps it up I won't be able to stop myself. He bites onto my nipple but instead of pain, a flash of pleasure winds all the way down between my legs and pushes me over the edge.

I buck my hips and cry out as the first swell rolls through me in a rush of honey and heat.

Lane grabs my shoulders and slams my body against him, hitting the sweet spot harder and harder, intensifying each spasm. I arch my back and curl my fingers. Every inch of me is electrified as wave after wave of velvety heat rocks through me.

Even as the last ripple rolls through me, I keep riding Lane's hips, until he gasps and I feel him shudder between my legs, the condom suddenly warmer than it was moments before. Lane's grip on my shoulders loosens, but he continues to rock me, over and over, until the heavy pulse of him dies to a soft throb.

Finally, his fingers trail down my arms, and his thrusting stops. He grows soft inside me, but I'm not ready to be free, so I make no move to let him go.

Lane shakes his head, his face flushed. "Holy fuck, that was amazing." His eyes meet mine. "You are incredible."

I can't help but smile. Chris would climb on top of me, grunt, thrust, and then fall asleep directly after, not exactly an ego boost. But Lane is different. He makes me feel sexy, special even.

Carefully, he lifts my hands over his head and unwinds his belt, releasing me. I start to stand when he catches my face and pulls me toward him. He kisses me. Unlike our other kisses, this one is a sweet brush of satin followed by the barest flick of his tongue against my bottom lip. I shudder happily.

Still holding my face in his hands, he pulls back. "Have you eaten, yet?"

I blink, a little taken aback by the question. "I think you're confused. You're supposed to buy the girl dinner *before* having sex."

He frowns. "Have you eaten dinner?"

I have to think for a moment. The last thing I had was the cake pop around lunchtime. "No."

He grabs my hips and gently slides me off his lap. "Get dressed. I'm taking you out. The only places open this time of night are diners, so our options are pretty limited."

"You don't have to do that. I have plenty of food here." *Food you bought me*, I remind myself. "I can make a sandwich."

He narrows his eyes. "Get dressed."

I fold my arms across my chest. "That's silly. We can save money by eating here."

"It's not silly. You deserve to go out."

"Lane."

"Did you or did you not agree to be mine for the night?"

Slowly, I nod.

He picks up my panties off the floor and hands them to me. "Then I'm taking you out." I start to argue and he silences me with the wave of his hand. "Here's one thing you need to know about me, Ash: I *always* take care of what's mine. And for tonight, you're mine. And then maybe, when we get back, I'll take care of you again." He winks at me as he slides his belt through the loops of his jeans.

Immediately, the tightness between my legs returns. "Really?"

He grins. "Well, the night's not over yet."

Chapter Twenty-Four

Ashlyn

Beginnings
Dissolving the things that came before
Leaving old paths for new
Washing stains white
Beginnings, we're told, are where we'll find hope
What they don't tell us is that beginnings are really endings in disguise.

I bite the cap of my pen, already worn with teeth marks, and reread the words of the poem I just finished. A few more and I'll actually have enough for an entire book of poetry. And when that happens I'll…

Try and get published? A lump pushes up my throat at

the prospect of people actually *reading* the words that have been bleeding from my heart these last months. What if they hate them? What if this whole poetry thing is one more failure waiting to happen?

The early fall air is warm, and a breeze rustles through the curtains, tickling the hairs around my neck that have fallen loose from my ponytail. I set my notebook aside and lean my head against the worn couch, and enjoy the wind grazing my face. Despite my protests, Lane replaced the leaking air conditioner that only blew lukewarm air with a brand new unit. The prickly warm nights are nowhere near as uncomfortable as the feeling of being trapped. Besides, the nights have grown cooler in the days I've lived here, hinting at the season change just around the corner.

Normally I'd be excited. Between spiced pumpkin lattes, sweaters, and changing leaves, fall has always been one of my favorite seasons in the Midwest. Only now, I won't be here to experience it.

And fall isn't the only thing I'll miss.

My gaze drifts to the unmade bed in the corner. A shiver jolts down my spine as the memories of last night's lovemaking with Lane rush to the front of my mind. His hands pinning my wrists to the mattress, his teeth on my neck, and his skin salty on my tongue. The images come faster and my temperature spikes. The memories make my head spin and I snatch my notebook before I forget a single detail.

• • •

Lane

"Tell me you want me," he whispers in the dark

Trapped in leather, his touch lighter than silk
He holds me in a cage with the door wide open
"Tell me to stop," he says, "and I will."
But I don't want him to stop
The second he lets go, that's when I'll truly be lost.

The words dig into my heart like Lane's tattoo machine, each letter a hundred stabs with a needle. I toss the notebook aside and stand, even though I have nowhere to go. "Fuck!"

Hank, stops chewing his bone long enough to cock his head at my behavior.

"I didn't ask for this," I tell the puppy. "I can't afford to have feelings for anyone right now. We're leaving in less than a week!"

The day after Lane tied me to the chair, a box showed up on my doorstep with my childhood stuffed panda bear, several yearbooks, and a brochure for an Atlanta community college. To be able to go to school full time, without having to work, is something I never dreamed possible. A month ago an opportunity like this would have been a dream come true. I should be happy.

But I'm not.

With a sigh, I flop on the floor beside Hank and rub his belly. His rolls onto his back to give me easier access, his tail thumping happily against the floor. It's been almost a week since I told Lane I'm leaving for Atlanta, and he's not staying away to make the move easier. He's brought me dinner every night. And while he doesn't always stay, before he leaves he makes certain I'll get a good night's sleep.

I don't ask him to stay even though I desperately want him to. I know there's a girl named Harper in the picture, but I don't know how she fits. Lane's told me their relationship "isn't like that." I want to ask what that means, but at the same time, if I'm leaving, why make things more complicated than they already are?

Laying on the floor, I can hear the muffled sound of Lane's shop radio as well as the buzz from his needle. Over the last week, these sounds have come to represent something I've never had before—*home.* For the first time in my life I have a place that makes me feel safe and protected.

A small voice whispers inside my head. *Is it really the apartment that makes you feel that way? Or Lane?*

I push the thought out of my head. Despite my best attempts to keep him at a distance, Lane's infiltrated my life in more ways than I care to admit. His scent lingers on my sheets, his art decorates my skin, and his touch haunts my dreams.

"What am I supposed to do?" I ask Hank. I've worked so hard to guard the remaining bits of my heart, only to have given them away without realizing it. And now it's too late.

He stretches his neck and licks my nose.

There's a community college here in town, the voice whispers. *Yes, you'd have to work while you attend, because you're not a freeloader, and it won't be easy to juggle school and work, but you can do it. And isn't he worth it?*

I chew on my fingernail as I mull the idea over. It is a possibility—to stay. I'm sure I'd qualify for some kind of financial aid. I wouldn't be the first person in history to work while going to college. And with access to the computers at school, I can pursue publishing options for my poetry.

I can keep the life I've built.

I can have Lane.

That is, if he wants me.

Because he has some chick's name tattooed on his chest. That has to mean something, right? Even if he said it "wasn't like that." What the fuck does that even mean? And if he wants me to stay, wouldn't he just say so?

I groan and roll onto my back. Hank takes this as an invitation to climb on top of me and lick my face again. Laughing, I push him off. "You're not helping the situation."

He grins like he understands me.

Right.

I sit up and pull the puppy onto my lap. "What do we do?" I ask him. "There are a million reasons to go and only one to stay. I risk my entire future if I don't go, but I risk my heart if I do. What if Lane doesn't feel the same way about me as I do about him? What if he can't really be with me because he's already involved? What if I drive myself crazy and end up in a mental ward?"

Hank huffs and rests his head on my leg.

So much for his help.

My phone buzzes and I snatch it off the coffee table.

Lane.

My heart flutters when his name pops up on the screen. His message is a single word.

Dinner?

I can't help but laugh. That silly boy is obsessed with feeding me. I quickly type back, *Sure.*

His reply is immediate. *Great. My last appointment cancelled. I'll see you at six.*

Smiling, I glance at the clock. It's nearly five, which gives me an hour to get ready. I need all the time I can get. Even though a shower and quick makeup application will take a half hour, I need the remaining minutes to psych myself up. With my move date rapidly approaching, I need to know how Lane feels about me—if my staying is something he even wants. Is he falling for me as hard as I've fallen for him? I've been used my entire life, so I won't risk my future or my heart over a maybe. I'm done with the games, vague answers, and guessing.

Lane is worth the sacrifices and the hard work I'd have to do to stay. I'm happy with Lane. I'm home. But in order for this to happen, he's going to have to answer my questions.

I need to know who Harper is, and if there's room in Lane's life, and heart, for me.

And tonight I plan to ask him.

Chapter Twenty-Five

Lane

I'm standing at the counter, double checking the bag I packed for Harper to make sure it includes her allergy meds as well as a toothbrush, when the door chime sounds.

"Hey, Dad!" Before I can walk out from behind the counter, Harper rushes to me, wrapping her slender arms around my waist.

"Hey, kiddo." A pang of guilt shoots through me at how little time I've spent with her this week. Ignoring it, I squeeze her against me until she squeals. Hopefully, if all goes well tonight, I won't have to feel guilty anymore.

Emily breezes through the door with a strand of licorice dangling from her mouth. "Hey, big brother."

"How was the movie?" I ask.

"Great!" Harper answers first. "Aunt Em bought a ton of candy and snuck it in her purse."

I narrow my eyes at my sister. "How much is a ton?"

Smiling, she pulls the licorice from her mouth. "Chill, Laney. There's no such thing as too many gummy bears."

"Yeah. I'll remind you of that when Harper gets a cavity."

"You worry too much." Em reaches out and ruffles my hair. "You got the kiddo's bag all packed? We're anxious to get on with our girl's weekend."

"Yeah." Harper releases my waist and grins. "We're going to go shopping, get some dinner, and then watch movies until we fall asleep."

I frown. "How about until ten o'clock?"

"Yeah, sure." Emily takes the backpack off the counter and slips it over her shoulder. "Until ten o'clock." She winks at Harper, who giggles.

I sigh. I suppose there are worse things for a child than to be spoiled silly by her aunt.

"So… " Emily smirks and arches an eyebrow. "Working *late* again?"

Ignoring her, I turn to Harper. "You know what? I think I forgot to pack your phone charger. It's in the back on the counter. Why don't you get it?"

She shrugs. "Sure."

A second later she disappears behind the curtain, and I turn to Em. "I'm going to tell her."

"What does that mean?"

"Ashlyn. I'm going to tell her about Harper. Tonight. I'm going to tell her everything."

Em's smile dissolves. "What? *Why?* You know she's leaving in less than a week, right?"

"I know. It's just… " Sighing, I jam my hands into my back pockets. "I don't want her to go, Em. Maybe she doesn't have to. Maybe she'll stay."

The remaining licorice falls from Em's mouth onto the floor. "Holy fuck, I didn't think it was possible."

"What?"

She grabs my arm. "You. Lane. Lane Garrett. Man with an iron heart. You like her."

I make a face. "Iron heart?"

Still holding my arm, she starts hopping up and down. "You *like-like* her. Oh my God." She cranes her neck toward the window. "Am I dreaming? Are there zombies outside? Is it the end of the world? *What's happening?*"

I yank my arm from her grip. "Calm down. Just because I like her doesn't mean she'll stay." The memory of walking into an empty apartment and finding Harper's mother gone hits me square in the gut, and I turn away. "I might not be enough. You said she doesn't like kids."

"That's what she told me, but I don't believe it. After all, didn't you tell me how great she was with Harper?"

"Yes. But why would she lie about something like that?" I ask.

Em shrugs and places a hand on my cheek, forcing me to look at her. "I don't know. But I do know this; you're enough. You're more than enough. I bet when she sees what an amazing dad you are, she'll fall even more in love with you."

"What?" I jerk back, startled by this revelation "You think she's in love with me?"

"*Please.*" She drops her hand and smiles. "I'm not blind, Laney. The girl had it bad for you from the minute she saw you."

"Really?" Despite my best effort, a smile tugs at my lips. "You're not just saying that so your brother makes a royal ass of himself tonight?"

She folds her arms across her chest. "Just because you're my annoying, overprotective big brother doesn't mean I don't want you to be happy." Her face softens. "Because I do. That's all I ever want for you."

I pull her to me. She yelps and tries to push away, but I only cuddle her harder until she laughs. It's funny how whenever I look at her, I see the small girl she was, crying beside our dad's fresh grave—the girl I promised Dad's partner I'd protect. "When did you grow up to be such an amazing, strong woman?"

She tilts her head up and smiles. "I had a great older brother to guide me."

I hook an arm around her neck and kiss the top of her head. "And now?"

"Now I'm good."

The words she's not saying swell inside my chest, tightening it. "You don't need your old, big brother anymore?"

She leans her head against my shoulder. "I'll always need my big brother, just not as much. That doesn't mean I'm going anywhere." She wraps her arms around my waist and gives me a squeeze. "You're stuck with me."

I'm glad she's tucked beneath my chin so she can't see the impact her words have. *That doesn't mean I'm going anywhere.* The words echo inside my head, striking a chord that vibrates throughout my entire body. I always told myself I was doing what Dad wanted me to do by following her to parties and monitoring her every move. But what if my overprotectiveness wasn't about fulfilling my obligation to take care of the family, but was more about the fear of losing someone else I love?

I chuckle softly. "I think I may be a little fucked in the head, Em."

She shrugs. "We all are, Laney. At least you're not scared to admit it."

No. I'm not scared to admit it. There's only one thing I'm terrified of. "I'm scared I'm going to lose her, Em."

She pushes off my chest. "Then you have to tell her the truth. You have to tell her *exactly* how you feel. No more holding everything inside."

"I don't hold things inside."

She crosses her arms and makes a face.

I grunt and push my fingers through my hair. "Fine. Maybe I do. It's just… what if I tell her everything, about how I feel, and it's not enough?"

She's quiet a moment, pressing her lips into a tight line. Finally, she touches me lightly on the arm. "Then you have to be strong enough to let go."

Chapter Twenty-Six

Ashlyn

There's a sharp knock at my door. Hank barks, and I grab a hair tie from the small pedestal sink in the bathroom and put my hair in high ponytail. I walk out of the bathroom and glance at the oven clock. Five forty-five. Lane's early.

I'm brimming with a mixture of excitement and dread as I walk to the door. Tonight will determine whether Lane feels the same way about me as I do about him. Tonight will either be the beginning of something amazing or the end of everything.

I give myself a little shake before I unlock the deadbolt. Whatever happens, my future is on the other side. I place a hand on the doorknob. There's no going back now.

I've barely cracked the door open when it flies inward. With a yelp, I stumble out of the way, but I'm not fast enough. The door's edge clips my shoulder, sending waves of fiery pain down my arm.

The sun backs the man in my doorway so he's only a red silhouette. I blink until my eyes focus. Even then I'm not certain I believe what I'm seeing—my biggest nightmare manifested before me.

"No," I whisper, my throat so tight it's on the verge of closing.

"You think you can hide from me? I'd call you stupid, but that would imply you have a brain." My stepdad strides inside my apartment and slams the door hard enough to rattle the walls. His body is rigid, from his arms to the tendons flexing in his jaw. His hands are fists, and his eyes are so wide I can see the red spider web of veins around the edges. Anger radiates off of him in waves so hot they burn against my skin.

I scramble away only to hit the couch's armrest with the back of my knees. I tumble over the edge, landing on a cushion. "W-what are you doing here?"

Growling, Hank darts for Charles' ankle. Before the puppy can sink his teeth in, Charles kicks him in the side. Hank yelps as he tumbles backward.

"Hank!" A flare of anger burns through my fear, giving me the courage to stand. I push myself off the couch and start toward the corner where Hank is cowering, but Charles blocks my path.

He glances around the room, his lips curling in a sneer. "I should have known you'd end up in a dump like this."

The urge to curl into a ball is overwhelming. A whimper pushes up my throat and I swallow it down. If not for the throbbing in my shoulder, I'd be convinced I am having a nightmare. Charles took everything I had—my home, my mother, my belongings. What more can he want? "Why are you here?" I ask again, a slight waver to my voice.

He laughs and crosses his arms. He's not a large man, shorter than Lane by several inches, but his presence fills every inch of the tiny apartment, to the point I can no longer breathe. "Like you don't know."

When I don't say anything, he makes a disgusted sound. "You really are that stupid." Before I can respond, he grabs my arm. His hand is fire hot and slick with sweat. I try to recoil, but he only digs his fingers in tighter, just enough to bring pain, but not enough to bruise. He's a master at knowing the difference.

This time, I can't hold back the whimper, and I cringe at how pathetic I am. He wrenches my arm forward and draws me closer, ducking his head low so our foreheads almost touch. I turn my head away but he squeezes my arm, making me yelp.

"Look at me when I'm talking to you!" The words are a roar, thundering in my head and reverberating through my bones. My knees go weak, and it takes every ounce of strength I have left to remain standing. "You know why I'm here."

His breath is sour, and flecks of his spit speckle my cheek. I grimace.

"You stole from me you stupid, worthless girl! And I'm here to get back what's mine."

I always knew he was slightly unhinged. I mean, what kind of man can charm a perfect stranger one minute and terrorize his own family the next? Surely he must see none of my meager possessions ever belonged to him. I shake my head. "I don't have anything of yours."

"Liar!" With his hand on my arm, he shoves me backward. "You stole money, *my* money, that I worked hard for—something your lazy ass knows nothing about. How did you get this place, anyway? Are you selling drugs? Your body?" He releases me suddenly, a disgusted look on his face.

I scramble away from him, rubbing my burning arm as I do. I don't bother to correct him. Years of him assuming the worst have taught me it's pointless to try to explain. Instead, I steer the conversation back to where it started. "What money do you think I stole? Look around. I don't have *anything.*"

His eyes narrow. "You think *I'm* an idiot? You think I wouldn't find out about the money you conned your mother into giving you?"

Shit. He found out about the money Mom gave me to move. I don't believe she lied to me that she'd saved it from her earnings. To Charles, everything belongs to him.

Somehow, despite the lump of terror wedged in my throat, I find my voice. "You need to leave. This is *my* apartment and you're not welcome here. If you don't… " I glance at the phone sitting on my coffee table only a few feet away. "I'll call the police."

"By all means." He pulls his own phone out of his back pocket. "I'll call them myself to report your theft." He gestures to around the room. "I'd actually be doing you a favor. Spending the night in a jail cell will sure as hell be a step up from this place."

I almost relent. If there's anything Charles knows how to do, it's influence people. Even without proof, he might actually be able to convince the cops I'm a thief. He's a master at keeping his real persona hidden behind the mask of a church-going, white-collared, respectable man. For the first time in my life, anger overpowers my fear. It burns through my veins like acid, curling my fingers into fists. "How dare you come into *my* home, kick my dog, and threaten me!" I take a step toward him.

For just a second, his eyes flutter wide with surprise before they return to their usual expression of contempt. I go on, "You're nothing but a sad, old man who's so pathetic you get off bullying a girl—a girl you were *supposed* to take care of."

His cheeks puff with rage. "You little bitch. How dare you talk that way to me?" He spits the last word through clenched teeth. Even though I flinch on the inside, my anger gives me the courage to stand firm. I spent my entire childhood living in terror of him, but since being kicked out, I've learned there are scarier things than a fat, balding, fifty-something investment banker. In fact, compared to the meth tweakers, perverted truck drivers, and drug dealers I've encountered, he's nothing.

Absolutely nothing.

He bears down on me, his chest bumping mine, only this time I don't back down. "Why would I bother taking care of the useless waste of skin you are? Don't you get it? You're worthless. You're nothing."

"No." I tilt my head, meeting his steely gaze head on. "I'm more than you'll even know. You've just got your head stuck so far up your ass, you can't see anything but your own shit."

A shove catches me off guard. For the ten years I lived with the man, he always used words as his weapon, careful to keep his hands to himself—or when he used them, he knew not to leave a bruise. The time he bumped against me, sending me spiraling down the stairs and breaking my rib, I'd thought had been an accident. Now I'm not so sure.

I cry out as I collide with the coffee table and roll onto the floor. Pain explodes from my hip and knee, sending shockwaves through my body. He's never blatantly struck me before. It's clear I've pushed him past the point of caring about his image.

He stands over me, his face crimson and his fists shaking. "How dare you talk to me that way."

My own anger cracks, and fear rushes through. Without thinking, I'd poked the bear with a stick.

And now I'm going to pay.

Chapter Twenty-Seven

Lane

"Found the charger!" Harper pushes the curtain aside and stops in her tracks. "Why do you and Aunt Em look so serious?"

"C'mere, Harper." I get down on my knee and motion her close. Looking unsure, she takes slow, reluctant steps, stopping when she reaches me.

"Am I in trouble?"

I smile and shake my head. "Of course not, honey. I just need to talk to you about something important before you go off on your girls' night with Aunt Em."

She frowns. "Okay. What is it?"

I open my mouth but the words don't immediately come. God, this is harder than I thought it would be. What if Harper freaks out? It's been just us for so long. What if she hates the idea of having someone else in our life? Work keeps me busy enough—what if adding Ashlyn to our lives gives us even less time together? Would that make me a horrible father?

Emily gives an impatient huff behind me. "Geez Louise, nobody is dying. Your daddy just wants to know how you would feel about him dating."

"I was getting to that." I shoot her an angry look over my shoulder.

Em only shrugs. "Yeah, but by the time you spit it out, *Harper* would be dating."

Ugh. The very idea makes me shudder.

Harper squeals and grabs my shoulders. Her eyes are wide. "Are you serious? Who is she? Are you going to get married? Are you going to have kids? Am I going to be a big sister?"

"Whoa!" I hold my hands up, her barrage of questions making my head swim. "Chill, kiddo. It's not like that. There's a girl I like, but I have to know if she likes me before anything more happens. No weddings. No babies. Just a couple of dates, okay? We need to see if this will work. Besides," I add, "you need to meet her. All women in my life must get your vote of approval or they're out the door. Got it?"

Harper laughs at this. "Got it. So when do I get to meet her? Today?" She hops up on her toes excitedly.

I can't help but grin at her enthusiasm. "Not today. But if all goes well, soon."

Her smile wavers. "Aw!"

"What do you mean, 'aw'?" Em taps her lightly on her arm. "Your dad mentions a new girl and suddenly Aunt Em is old news?"

Harper rolls her eyes. "That's not true."

"Good." Emily hoists Harper's backpack higher on her shoulder. "Because there's fun to be had and more candy to eat."

"No, there isn't." I scowl.

"Of course not. Did I say candy? I meant broccoli." Em winks at Harper. Before I can argue further, she looks at me, her smile gone. "Good luck, big brother. I'll have my fingers crossed. I could get used to seeing you happy. It suits you."

I open my mouth to answer, when I hear a slam overhead, followed by a muffled cry.

"What the hell was that?" Em asks, face pointed toward the ceiling.

Heat surges in my veins. "Ash," I murmur. Had she fallen? Was she hurt? I start for the door when I hear angry shouting—a man's.

Fuck.

My pulse beats so loudly in my ears it's nothing but a crash of sound. I'm at the door in an instant, pausing long enough to glance back at Em and Harper. "Don't go anywhere until I come back. Got it?"

Harper's eyes are glassy with fear. "What's going on?"

I shake my head and turn again to the door. "I have no idea, but I'm going to find out."

Chapter Twenty-Eight

Ashlyn

"Where is my money?" Charles leans over me and screams.

With my heart beating a frantic rhythm against my ribs, I scuttle away until my back meets the front of the couch. Jolts of pain from my hip and knee beat in time with my pulse as white spots speckle my vision.

What did I do? I've always known my stepdad was mentally unstable, but I always figured once I left the house, I'd never have to deal with him. I especially never expected him to barge into my apartment and start throwing me around.

Charles leans down and grabs the front of my shirt, twisting his hand into the fabric. "Did you spend it on fucking drugs, you worthless whore?" He shakes me hard enough my brain rattles against my skull. Still, his words bite more than the bruises blooming on my legs.

I open my mouth to tell him he can have the money,

anything to get him to leave, when a large shadow appears in my doorway.

"What the fuck is going on in here?"

Lane. Part of me rejoices at the sight of him, while another part hates that he has to find me this way, literally cowering in front of the demon from my past.

Still holding my shirt, Charles swivels his head around, a look of surprise on his face. "Who the hell are you?"

"I'd ask you the same thing." Lane, his jaw clenched tight, strides into the room with long, rigid steps. "But I really don't give a fuck." Before Charles can react, Lane grabs his shoulder and pulls him off of me, swinging him back so he stumbles against the recliner in the corner.

"What are you?" Charles pushes to his feet, but his stance in less sure. His eyes dart to the open door. "Her pimp? Her drug pusher?"

A low growl escapes Lane's clenched teeth and his fingers curl into fists. "Don't you dare talk shit about Ashlyn. If you know what's good for you, you'll leave this apartment and never come back. Or else." He tilts his head from side to side, cracking his neck.

Slowly, I push myself to my feet. I want to reach out to Lane, to tell him this isn't his fight, but Charles reacts first.

He shoves his shoulders back, but his attempt to puff out his chest looks more ridiculous than intimidating next to Lane's much larger frame. I don't know if it's my time away from home, or Lane's appearance, but Charles' presence no longer fills the room. It's like he shrinks before my eyes, until I see him for what he truly is—an old, pathetic, overweight bald man. He raises a finger at me and, to my surprise, I don't flinch. "I'm not going anywhere until that bitch gives me my money back."

Lane shakes his head. "Wrong answer." Before I can react, he reaches forward, grabs Charles by the front of the shirt, and hurls him across the room, where he crashes against an end table. My scream is broken by the sound of shattering glass from the lamp that topples onto the floor.

Lane turns to me. "I'll buy you a new one."

"How dare you!" Charles climbs to his feet on wobbling legs. "You're going to pay for that. He makes a fist and raises it over his shoulder.

Before he strikes, Lanes lands a blow square against his jaw. The crack of skin and bone makes my stomach wrench, and I cry out.

I curl my fingers against my lips. "Stop." Surprisingly, seeing Charles in pain brings me no pleasure. He's brought so much misery to my life, I dreamed of this moment, when he would look at me and *his* eyes would be full of fear. But now that the moment is here, it's more bitter than sweet.

All I ever wanted was for Charles to accept me. I tried conforming to his rules—that didn't work. I tried making myself invisible—that didn't work. I even left—that didn't work either. And now, staring at this pitiful man in front of me, I can't figure out why I ever cared. The only thing I want now is for him to get out of my life, once and for all. "Lane…"

But he doesn't respond. There's a wildness in his eyes that shakes me to my core, almost like Lane's checked out, and the man standing in his place is unrecognizable from the one who holds me until I fall asleep.

Charles swings back, but his punch goes wide and whiffs harmlessly past Lane's chin.

Lane retaliates with an uppercut to Charles' nose. Blood explodes from his nostrils, speckling his polo shirt with crimson.

I press a hand to my clenching gut. *No.* This isn't what I want. No more blood. No more pain.

Charles is blinking, his eyes unfocused. He raises a fist.

Lane squares his shoulders and lifts clenched hands in front of his face.

No. I don't know how much fight Charles has left in him, but I can't take any more.

Charles swings, and Lane easily ducks the blow. Lane rears back for another strike when I grab his bicep, halting him. "No!"

Slowly, he turns to me, the muscles in his arm unwinding beneath my fingers. He meets my eyes, his face questioning. "He hurt you," he says, the words like a judge passing a sentence.

My pulse is crashing so loudly inside my head it echoes like thunder. "Yes." I keep pulling on his arm until it falls to his side. "But he can't hurt me anymore. It's all over."

Chest heaving, Lane frowns. Confused lines pinch his forehead.

Charles glares at me from over the bloody hand pressed to his face. Each time he enters my life he leaves it more broken. My furniture is toppled and splintered, my puppy is shivering in a corner, and my beautiful Lane has blood on his split knuckles.

I'm putting an end to it all.

"You want your money?"

Charles' eyes narrow but he says nothing.

I walk to my purse and sort through an inner pocket

until I find the bills my mom gave me. "Here." I hold the wad above my head. "I don't want anything to do with you, do you understand? I don't believe for a second this is yours, but if it will get you out of my life, I'll pay." I take a step toward him, emotion choking my voice. "Just know this is it. I never want to see you again. You're a horrible man and an even worse father. Part of me wants to be the bigger person, but honestly, I hope you take this money and choke on it."

He drops his hand from his face, revealing the swollen, bloody mess Lane made of his nose. "You'll both be lucky if I don't call the police on you for theft and assault."

Lane folds his arms and laughs. "Buddy, my dad was a cop and I've got a lot of friends on the force. You make that call and see what happens. From my end, it looks like forced entry and self-defense. I guess it'll be your word against mine."

Charles' eyes go wide, and his lips pinch in a frown.

I have to clamp a hand over my mouth to fight the urge to laugh.

Charles sees this and snarls, "My money!" He snaps his fingers at me.

I take a step toward Charles and Lane tenses beside me. I glance over my shoulder to let him know I'll be okay. I walk past my stepdad and stand beside the open door. I lift the money above my head and let go. The breeze catches the bills, pulling them from my fingers. They flutter down the steps to the ground below. "Get out."

"You bitch!" Charles rushes to the door, but I step in his path, blocking his exit. "Get out of the way."

"Sure." I shrug. "But first, this is for my dog." Taking a page from Emily's book, I bring my knee up and connect with his groin.

He doubles over, eyes bulging and cheeks puffing out. I give him a push and he tumbles out the door. I slam it shut behind him.

Lane stares at me, openmouthed. "I can't believe you just did that."

A grin pulls at my lips. "Me, either!" A laugh bubbles up my throat. "I'm done with him! I'm really done with him!"

Lane's smile is unsure. "But the money…didn't you need that?"

Just like that, the balloon of happiness swelling inside my chest pops. Why does Lane care about the money? Does he want me to go?

He must sense the change in me because he shakes his head and reaches for me. "Ashlyn, I didn't mean to upset you. I'm just trying to figure out what you want. I want you to be happy, no matter what."

I want to tell him that he makes me happy, but the words get tangled on my tongue. "What do *you* want?"

"You."

The way he answers without hesitation stills my heart.

"You're all I think about, Ashlyn," he continues, "since the day you walked into my life." He grins, tightening things low inside me. "From the moment we kissed, I realized something—you're my moon, Ashlyn. You pull at me like the moon pulls the fucking tides. I can't fight it. I can't resist. I can only go to you. I'll always go to you. But I also know I can't make you stay if you don't want to."

So many words and so many emotions rise within me, churning into a tangled mess. There's no way this can be happening. Even though these are the words I've been craving, the desire to turn and run coils my muscles tight. I'm not good enough, I'm too damaged, and I'm a million other things that make a relationship impossible. My stepdad, while kicked out of my life, is going to be harder to kick out of my head. And doesn't Lane deserve better? My life is so very fucked up and unsure—staying with Lane would only bring my shit into his world.

"Ash," Lane's hand wavers in the air, still reaching for me. "Please, say something."

Slowly, I bring my eyes up to meet his. "Tell me. I want to hear you say it."

He jerks back. "What?"

"I'm scared. I'm a fucked up mess. You saw what my stepdad is like. You know what he's done to me. I'm not going to be fixed overnight. I'm a walking disaster. I cry a lot, and locked doors terrify me. Some days I'm too scared to leave the house, and others I want to drive until I reach an ocean, turn around, and head to the next one. There are a million reasons you should let me go, Lane. I'm a walking disaster. Is that what you want?"

He closes the distance between us in two swift strides and places his hands on either side of my face. When he speaks, his breath is warm against my skin. "I want you, Ash—neurotic mess, walking disaster, *all of you*. My dad passed at an early age, putting me in charge. I'm overprotective of my family to a fault and I'm terrified of not living up to the man my dad expected me to become. I'm moody and ambitious. There are days when all I know how to do is work, and others when I feel so anchored by responsibility I want to get in my truck and drive until I reach an ocean, turn around, and head to the next one. I'm pretty fucked up, myself."

Grinning, I throw my arms around his neck and press my body against his. The warmth of his skin seeps into mine, unwinding the knots buried inside my chest. "If we do this, it's not going to be easy."

He grins and lowers his head to mine. "Who says I like easy?"

Chapter Twenty-Nine

Lane

I curl my fingers around her as a mixture of relief and exhaustion wash over me. The blood on my knuckles has dried and stretches tight across my skin. I nearly lost my mind when I walked in and saw that man standing over Ash. The desire to hurt him, to make him bleed, consumed me, taking over every thought.

Protect your family. Like the ink on my arms, my dad's partner's words are written on my heart, the syllables pulsing in time with each beat. *Protect your family.* Ash is mine. She whispered as much through tangled limbs and shuddered gasps. And nobody hurts what belongs to me.

Walking into the apartment and seeing her eyes so wide, so frightened, flipped a switch inside me. I was filled the urge to destroy the person responsible—and I might have done just that if she hadn't grabbed my arm and pulled me back.

I bury my nose against the top of her head. Her hair's damp and smells like shampoo. I breathe in her scent—apples, without the usual mix of coffee—holding it inside me like I hold her in my arms. I'm scared to let go. I can't be sure she'll stay when she knows everything about me—about the mistake I made at sixteen, about the girl who ripped out a chunk of my heart and the baby who filled the hole. She needs to know how Harper is a part of me, and there's no loving me without loving her.

I know now I should have been upfront with her at the very beginning. Instead, I've been so focused on her keeping her at a distance, by the time I realized she slipped into my heart, it was too late.

So it's now or never.

"Ashlyn?"

"Mmm?" She murmurs the sound against my chest.

God, I almost wonder if I should wait. After the day she's been through, I wonder if it would be cruel to make her endure another surprise. At the same time, I know I can't wait. She's shaken—I can feel the slight tremble of her shoulders—yet I know if I put this off, I'd betray the line of trust that's opened between us.

I grab her shoulders and gently push her away. "We need to talk."

Her brow crinkles in concern. "Is everything okay?"

Hell, I don't know. There's only one way to find out. Her eyes are so intent, so worried, I can no longer hold her gaze. I glance around the room, at the mess left behind. So many broken things—many of which can't be fixed. I can only hope I don't do the same to her. I sweep a hand through my hair. "I wanted to talk about this at dinner, but I guess now's as good a time as any."

Her hands fall from my waist. "Lane, you're scaring me."

I sigh and motion to the couch. "Do you want to sit?"

She folds her arms across her chest and shakes her head. "I don't really feel like sitting."

"Right." I can't sit either. Nervous energy courses through me, prickling my skin and winding through my muscles. I pace a short path across the living room, my boots grinding the broken glass against the floor. "It's not fair of me to ask you to stay without you knowing the truth about me—without you knowing my past."

She nods slowly.

"Ash, when I was sixteen, I went to a party and had too much to drink."

She makes a face. "If underage drinking is your biggest secret, I can handle that."

"It's not. You see, my dad had passed a year before and left me in charge of the family. The responsibility was crushing. I went to the party looking for a good time. I didn't want to think about my mom or my sister, I just wanted to have *fun*—something I could barely remember having. I met this girl and—well, she was unlike any girl I'd ever met before. She was exciting. She made me forget all about school, my family, my dad, my *responsibility*."

Ash frowns at this, her eyes questioning.

"One thing led to another, and I lost my virginity in a fucking coat closet." The words taste sour on my tongue, and my lip curls in disgust. I hate to tell her this story, to blurt out my mistake and let it fill the space between us.

"Lane, we're not children. I know you've been with other women, just like I've been with other guys."

"I know. That's not what I'm getting at." My throat feels like it's on the verge of closing, as if my body is working against me, to keep me from spilling my secret. "Something more happened in that closet—something other than sex."

Slowly, she lowers herself onto the couch. "What?"

God, this is so much harder than I expected. I wish I could just spit the words out, but they bury themselves deep within me. I know once they're out, there will be no pulling them back. They have the power to make Ash leave—*forever.* My body tenses, bracing for the worst. "After the party, I never expected to see the girl again. We were having fun, no strings attached. Even so, about a month later, she showed up on my doorstep."

Ash leans forward, her eyes widening with realization. "Lane, what—"

Before she can finish, the door to her apartment swings open. I spin around, half expecting to find her stepdad. Instead, Emily stands in the doorway, her lips parted as she takes in the toppled end table and broken lamp.

"What the hell happened up here?" she asks. "There were all these loud noises and shouting. You said you'd be right back."

"I know. We had an incident and I was just trying to *explain* a few things to Ash before we left." I make a face, hoping she'll catch the hint.

She doesn't.

"What the fuck is an incident?" She steps inside the apartment and surveys the damage. "Is everyone okay? Harper and I were freaking out."

"Harper?" Ash is on her feet, her gaze accusing. "She's here?"

"Yeah." Em nods to the door. "She's right— "

Before she can finish, Harper appears in the doorway, her eyes wide. "Daddy, is everything okay? Aunt Em and I heard yelling." She looks from me to Em, before her gaze rests on Ash. "Oh. I know you. What are you doing here?"

The silence that follows stills my heart. The flush in Ash's cheeks pales as realization filters through her. Still she says nothing, until the words she's not saying stretch and swell, digging a canyon between us.

Panic rolls down my skin in prickly waves. I'm desperate for her to say something, *anything,* just to fill the void.

Instead, she blinks slowly, as if dazed, and places a hand against her forehead. "Wait. If *you're* Harper, and he's your— " She looks up at me, her face a mixture of horror and understanding. "Oh my God. You have a kid."

Emily places a hand over her mouth. "Shit. I thought you'd already told her." She backs through the doorway and grabs Harper's hand. "We're going to get ice cream."

Harper wrinkles her nose in confusion. "We are?"

"Yup." Emily nods. "Right now. Sundaes. Big ones." She guides Harper to the stairs. "Lane, call me as soon as you can, okay?" Before I can answer, they disappear from view.

"You have a kid," Ash repeats. Even though she's looking at me, her gaze is unfocused, more like she's looking *through* me.

Fuck. This is exactly what I didn't want to happen. "Ash, if you could just give me a second to explain."

She blinks again, this time her eyes focusing on mine. "You have a kid." It's not so much a question, but the answer to one.

"Yes. Harper is my daughter."

"Jesus Christ!"

The volume of her voice startles me, and I stiffen.

"Oh my God. I just… I can't… Fuck!" She spins around, sweeping her fingers through her hair, pulling it from the ponytail until it falls over her face.

"Ash, please." I reach for her, stopping short of actually touching her. "Can we talk about this?"

She spins around, her cheeks flushed and her eyes brimming with tears. "There's nothing to talk about, Lane. This changes everything!"

I yank my hand back. "It doesn't have to."

"You just don't get it, do you?" She half laughs, even as the tears spill down her face. "I'm a walking shit storm. You saw my stepdad, and my mom's not much better. I don't know the first thing about how a family is supposed to operate—I barely managed to survive this long on my own." She juts a finger toward the empty doorway. "I won't be responsible for fucking up the life of a young girl. I won't do it, Lane."

"Ash, you won't fuck it up. If you'd only calm down—"

"How do you know? Do you have psychic powers you haven't told me about?"

"I just know."

She tilts her chin, meeting my gaze square on. "Well, that's one of us. And that's not a gamble I'm willing to take with a kid. You shouldn't either."

She brushes past me, and I snag her arm. "Ash, I know you. You're an amazing person. You're kind, and smart, and—"

"Damaged," she cuts in, pulling free from my grasp. "More than you can possibly know, Lane. A girl like me has no business being in the life of a child. I'm doing you a favor."

Her words stab into my heart like a dagger. "What are you saying?"

She freezes, but doesn't turn around. "It's pretty obvious isn't it?"

Maybe. Still, I need to hear the words out loud. Only then will they become real. "Say it, Ash."

Her shoulders slump. Still she doesn't turn.

"Good-bye, Lane," she chokes.

Chapter Thirty

Ashlyn

"Ashlyn," Lane calls after me as I descend the stairs. "Please don't do this."

I almost stop. *Almost.* Lane is the first shot of happiness I ever had, and now I'm running from it. I hoist the garbage bag of clothes over my shoulder and tighten my grip on Hank's leash. I don't have a plan. I just know I need to go before Lane can convince me to stay. I won't be the distraction in Lane's life. I won't do to his daughter what was done to me for ten years.

Hank whines as we jog to my car. I glance down find him watching me, his ears pinned flat against his head. He obviously knows something isn't right.

Behind me, the thud of heavy footsteps descends the stairs. "Ashlyn." Lane's voice is closer than I expect, and I flinch. "You're not even giving me a chance."

People always talk about heartbreak, but that doesn't come close to describing what I feel. To me, when you break something, the damage is immediate and the cuts clean. My heart, on the other hand, feels like it's being torn to ribbons, shredded to a pulp. The ache is unbearable, making me stagger the last couple of steps to my car.

"I'm giving you every chance." Despite my better judgment, I turn and face him. I instantly regret it. His face is a mixture of pain and desperation. And I'm the one responsible for putting those emotions there. "I'm giving you a shot at a happy life with your kid. She deserves better than me."

He shakes his head, the tendons in his jaw flexing. "There *is* no better than you."

Another rip deep in my chest precedes an agonizing wave of pain. Stupid, silly, boy. He can only see what's on the surface. He has no idea how far my damaged roots run. One of these days, he'll understand. He might even thank me if I ever see him again—which I won't.

I turn away. I know I'm doing the right thing. Kids were never part of my plan. Considering my own parental influences, I'm sure to fuck up royally. I can't, *won't,* risk it.

Especially not when a young girl's life is at stake—a girl who looks exactly the age I was when my mom met Charles, forever changing my life for the worse. If only I knew about his kid before any of this happened, I could have put some distance between us. I could have…

My shoulders slump. Who am I kidding? The only thing that could have kept me away from Lane was never meeting him in the first place. And now that I have, now that I've fallen so completely for him, the only thing that will free me is distance—and lots of it.

I open the door and throw my bag of clothes into the backseat.

"Ashlyn." There's a note of pleading in his voice that hooks into my heart. *Damn it.* I pause long enough to shake my head. I have to go before I change my mind.

I slam the back door shut and wrench open the driver's door. I pick up Hank and place him in the passenger seat, before climbing into the driver's seat.

"Don't go," Lane says.

Invisible hands squeeze my heart. I gasp. After all these years of being unwanted and unloved, I finally found someone who wants me to stay.

But I can't. I'm doing this for me, for the girl I could have been, the childhood I could have had if my stepdad never entered my life. I slam the door, placing a wall of metal and glass between Lane and myself. Only then do the rivets screwed into my muscles loosen. With shaking fingers, I put the key into the ignition and start the car.

Lane takes a step back. He jams his hands into his back pockets resignedly, and presses his lips into a thin line. "Where are you going?"

I can only shake my head and shift my car into gear. I can't speak past the lump knotted inside my throat. Even if I could, I wouldn't have an answer.

I have no idea.

Chapter Thirty-One

Lane

She's gone. Long after she pulls away I stare at the empty spot where her car was parked. Left, like the other girl I opened my heart to, like my father, and even Harper someday when she gets married and starts a family of her own—without me.

A growl pushes through my clenched teeth. I spin on my heels and march up the stairs to the vacated apartment. Inside, I spin around, searching for any sign of Ash, anything she might have forgotten, something I can hold onto—something real.

But aside from the pain swelling inside my chest, the broken table and shattered lamp, there's no trace of her—like she never existed.

Rage explodes inside me. With an angry yell, I upend the coffee table. It crashes on its side with a satisfying crack, one of its legs breaking off in the process. The rush of adrenaline that follows burns away most of the hollow ache inside my chest. Still, a lingering stab of pain remains.

I grab the back of the chair we made love on and fling it against the wall where it smashes to pieces, leaving a gouge in the drywall—ruining the new paint job. *Doesn't matter,* I think. When only seconds ago I was desperate for a piece of Ash, now I want nothing to remind me of her.

I march into the small kitchen and swipe my arm along the short counter, knocking coffee mugs, ceramic canisters, and a vase with a wilted daisy onto the floor. Anywhere the ghost of her might linger, I fling to the floor until broken shards of glass and ceramic litter the linoleum, covering the paint stain from the night Ash and I first slept together.

But it's not enough. The ache she left inside me continues to grow, threatening to swallow me whole.

I continue to topple furniture, pull fixtures from the walls, and upend the mattresses until sweat soaks the front of my shirt and I'm panting with exhaustion. My muscles are loose like noodles and my insides comfortably numb. I pause, looking around the obliterated studio. Every inch has been decimated.

Just like me.

Satisfied, I turn and head for the door. I sweep my eyes over the wreckage one last time and that's when I spot the edge of paper protruding from under the sofa. Kicking debris aside with my foot, I make my way to the couch. The paper has my name written on top in a feminine, loopy script. At first, I think it's a letter, but it only takes me a couple of lines to realize it's a poem.

Lane

"Tell me you want me," he whispers in the dark
Trapped in leather, his touch lighter than silk
He holds me in a cage with the door wide open
"Tell me to stop," he says, "and I will."
But I don't want him to stop
The second he lets go, that's when I will truly be lost.

I reread the words several times, fighting the urge to crumple the paper in my hand. Instead, I fold it into a neat square and tuck it inside my pocket. Even lost from my sight, the words written on the page continue to play through my mind, branded on my brain.

But I don't want him to stop.

The second he lets go, that's when I'll truly be lost.

I guess that's not exactly true. Not only did she want me to let go, she didn't even bother to look back as she ran.

I swallow hard and push the thought away, focusing my attention instead on the demolished room. As bad as it looks, I haven't done anything that can't be repaired or replaced.

Unfortunately, a little paint and spackle won't repair what's broken inside me.

Some things just can't be fixed.

Chapter Thirty-Two

Ashlyn

All the windows are down and a rush of air streams through the car, whipping my hair and drying the tears streaking down my cheeks. I wish it could blow through my head and clear the memory of Lane standing in the road, growing smaller as I drive away, until he disappears all together.

I'm doing the right thing. I remind myself over and over, until the words are a meaningless tangle of letters in my mind. If it's the right thing, why does it feel so wrong?

Because you're selfish, another voice chimes in, my stepdad's voice. *You're a fuckup who'll do irreparable damage to that child if you stay. But you don't care, do you? You only think of yourself.*

No. I shake my head, my lips trembling. I'm not thinking of myself. I'm doing this. I'm leaving.

And because the temptation to see Lane would be too

great if I stayed in the area, I've decided to drive to Atlanta. I'll call my aunt as soon as I can be sure I won't cry into the phone. I'm sure she'll understand—at least I hope so.

The twin smokestacks on the edge of Springfield fade in my review mirror as I travel farther down I-55, leaving the town, and Lane, behind me. I hold my breath as I pass the last exit, the exit that leads to my old house, as if I might accidentally suffocate on the poison it emanates. It's not until I drive another twenty miles that I take my first deep breath and loosen my white-knuckled grip on the steering wheel.

Maybe this is exactly what I need. Distance. Followed by time.

No sooner do I have the thought than an unfamiliar ding sounds from my dash. I glance down to find the gas gauge needle dipping well below the red line.

"Shit!" I left in such a hurry I didn't think to check the gas. Not wanting to get stranded on the side of the highway, I turn on my blinker for the approaching exit. My heart plummets when I read the sign.

REST AREA.

It's further out than the ones I used to sleep at, so I'm not familiar with it. Still, the irony I should end up in one is not lost on me. A sinking feeling washes over me as I pull into a parking spot and turn off my car. "We're not staying," I tell Hank, who watches me intently. For once, we're actual travelers, not homeless vagabonds, making what I hope to be a small pit stop before we move on.

The small, square, brick building is no different from the other rest areas where I've slept—just big enough for bathrooms and vending machines. Sun-faded park benches and rusted barrel trash cans are scattered throughout a grassy field in desperate need of mowing.

My muscles coil and my chest shudders. *Not staying,* I remind myself.

I grab my purse off the floor and open my wallet. A five-dollar bill and some change is all I find.

Fuck. That's barely more than a gallon of gas—nowhere near what I need to get to Atlanta. I had no idea, when I'd thrown the money my mom gave me out the door, I'd be throwing away my gas money. I have a debit card, but with payday a couple days away, I only have fifteen dollars in my account. Panic squeezes my ribs as I zip my wallet closed. *Stay calm, Ashlyn. You can figure this out.* I grab my phone and dial my Aunt's number. Several rings later, the call goes to voicemail.

After I leave a message, I end the call and toss my phone back into my purse. "Shit!" I know better than to call my mom, so I'm out of options.

Fresh tears prick the corners of my eyes and I quickly blink them away. It figures. This is what I get for trying to do the right thing.

Hank whimpers, and I turn to find him staring at me, concern etched in his eyes.

Keep it together, Ash. "It's okay, buddy. We're fine." I scratch the soft fur behind his ears, and his tail thumps against the seat. "We just have to wait for Aunt Karen to call us back. She'll help."

We just have to wait. As the sun lowers and the possibility of spending the night becomes more probable by the second, a hard lump pushes up my throat. "Want to go potty?"

Hank's tail thumps harder.

"Okay." Grabbing the puppy, I open the car door and

set him on the grass outside. After sniffing around for several moments, he finds a spot to relieve himself and I use one of the plastic bags at a nearby dispenser to clean it up. Afterward, I settle onto the brittle bench of a nearby picnic table and watch the travelers and truck drivers drift in and out of the building, as Hank chews on a stick he's found in the grass.

Any minute now Aunt Karen will call, and she'll know what to do. I glance at the clock on my phone. Ten minutes pass, then ten more. The sky darkens to a tangerine orange as the sun begins to sink into the horizon. Anxiety twists ropes around my chest, pulling tighter with each passing minute. I cannot stay here. I won't spend another night in rest stop.

A sick feeling rolls through my stomach as I consider my options. I've been in this situation before, and there's really only one way out. I have to do something I hate doing more than anything.

I have to beg.

A man and a woman, both appearing to be in their sixties, pull up in a nice-looking Buick. They make their way up the walkway toward the bathrooms. I stand, my stomach a knot of anxiety as I approach. "Excuse me."

They stop. The woman looks at me with mild curiosity and the man with annoyance. "I'm so sorry to bother you. You see, I'm on my way to visit my aunt and I'm nearly out of gas. To make matters worse, I forgot my wallet and have no money." I cringe inwardly at the lie, but in my experience, people are more forgiving of forgetfulness than homelessness. "I was wondering if you have change you can spare—"

"No!" The man practically shouts before I can finish. He grabs his wife by the arm and pulls her into the building.

I exhale loudly and wander back to the bench. This is how it goes sometimes—my spirit crushed with each rejection for hours on end, and without a dollar to show for it. Exhaustion sinks through me like lead, weighing me down. I drop onto the bench and wait for the next person to approach.

Funny how, only hours ago, I was happy. For the first time in my life I had a plan, I had a place to call my own, and I had *Lane*. Now I have none of those things and my future is as uncertain as it ever was.

My phone buzzes in my pocket. I snatch it, my chest swelling with hope until I read the caller.

Lane.

For just a second I consider answering it, telling him I made a huge mistake, and begging him to let me come back. I swallow those words deep inside me, where they mix with the pieces of my broken heart. I've come too far to be weak now.

Hank looks up from his pile of splinters—all that remains of his former stick—as if to question my decision.

"We're going to wait for Aunt Karen to call," I tell him. "We'll be fine."

He chuffs and lowers his head between his paws.

What did I think? How can I expect him to believe me when I don't quite believe it myself? With a sigh, I lean back against the table, stare into the darkening sky, and pray for a miracle.

Chapter Thirty-Three

Lane

Muttering a curse under my breath, I hang up the phone and set it in my truck's cup holder. I honestly don't know why I bothered to call—maybe I just needed one final thing to convince myself.

She's really and truly gone.

I stare out the windshield, tightening my grip on the steering wheel. The urge to drive after Ash is overwhelming, but I don't have the first idea where to look. She could be at a friend's house, on her way to Atlanta, or parked on the side of the road like I found her the night I gave her the apartment.

My stomach churns at the idea she could be alone, God knows where. What if something happens to her? What if her car breaks down? What if someone messes with her?

I shake my head, as if I can dislodge the ideas from my

brain. If only Dad's cop blood didn't flow inside my veins. I can't protect everyone, especially when they want neither my protection, nor me. I've been left before. I should know how this works.

You weren't enough, a voice whispers in my head. I turn the key in the ignition and crank up the stereo in the hopes the music will drown out the words circling through my head.

She said she wouldn't leave, but when she learned the truth about you, you weren't enough to make her stay.

Gritting my teeth, I slam my palm against the steering wheel. "Damn it!" The word is a growl, ripping from my throat. A woman walking her poodle several yards away looks up, startled. Hell if I care what she thinks, or what *anyone* thinks for that matter. I'm done.

At the very least, I should be happy things fizzled out between Ash and me before they could get started. Hell, her leaving is probably a blessing. I mean, if my kid is a deal breaker for her, then it's a deal breaker for me. My kid is fucking awesome, and if Ash can't see that, or won't bother to see it, then she doesn't deserve to be in my life.

So that's that.

Putting my truck into gear, I pull out onto the road with my windows down and music blaring. I'm not really sure where I'm headed, but at the corner I turn right, making sure to go the opposite direction Ash went.

Chapter Thirty-Four

Ashlyn

The rest stop's overhead lights flick on as soon as I end my call with Aunt Karen. I exhale, but it does little to alleviate the knots of tension wound into my chest. "She can send us money," I tell Hank, who's too busy biting the top off a dandelion to listen, "but we won't get it until tomorrow. So until I figure out what to do, it looks like we're stuck here."

I hate the idea of spending another night at a rest stop. Unfortunately, without enough money for a hotel, I have no choice but to sleep in my car. Cops will harass you if they catch you sleeping in store parking lots, so it looks like my options for the night are limited.

Hank sneezes, shooting dandelion tuffs across the grass. At least one of us isn't worried.

My head grows heavy, filled to the brim with rushing thoughts. I drop it in my hand and lean against the park bench. I should be happy to have my problem partially solved. In the morning, I'll find the closest Western Union and Aunt Karen will wire me enough gas money to for the drive to Atlanta. With any luck, Hank and I will be there this time tomorrow.

Instead of feeling relieved by this, my stomach churns at the thought. I can't help but mourn all I'll be leaving behind—my apartment, my job, Emily…Lane. Thinking of how things ended between us, and how I'll never see him again, does something to me. I feel the weight of his absence like an anchor deep inside me—or maybe it's a lifeline.

A line to the poem I'd written earlier today pushes to the front of my mind.

The second he lets go, that's when I'll truly be lost.

And now I am just that—so fucking lost. And it's not because he let go, but because I made him.

An ache gnaws inside my heart and I mash the heels of my palms against my eyes even though my tears have long dried.

If leaving is the right thing, why does it feel like I'm being ripped to pieces?

"S'cuz me."

With a startled gasp, I glance up to find a man standing in front of me. His dingy T-shirt is pulled tight over his protruding belly, and his gray hair is pulled back into a greasy ponytail. He smiles, revealing nicotine-stained teeth. "I heard you were in need of some gas money."

A tremor of unease ripples down my spine, putting my hair on end. "Not anymore. I got it taken care of."

"Hmm. You sure about that?" The guy brings a hand to his face and scratches the stubble around his chin. "You're about fifty miles away from the next real city. Say I give you twenty bucks? That should be more than enough for you to make it." He pulls a wadded bill from his pocket and waves it in front of me. "What do you say?"

With a knot in my throat, I cringe away from the dirty bill. "No thanks."

Laughing, he tucks it inside his shirt. "You drive a hard bargain, girly. How about I double that amount and you do something for me. That's my truck over there." He motions to a silver big rig in the semi lot. "You come on over, give me a little attention, and I'll give you forty."

"What?" I recoil, climbing over the top of the table in an attempt to put as much distance between us as possible. Abandoning the dandelions, Hank scrambles to his feet. "Get away from me, you pervert!"

The trucker holds his hands up. "Easy, girly. No use getting all uptight. I'm not talking sex—just a blowjob. What do you say?"

"I say you're a fucking pervert, and if you don't get away from me this second, I'm going to call 911!" I pull my phone out of my pocket and hold it up like a weapon.

He makes a face. "Why do you have to be a bitch like that? I'm just trying to help you out."

He takes a step toward me.

A deep rumble emanates from Hank's chest and his lips curl back, revealing all his teeth.

"Whoa!" The guy staggers back. "Get your dog under control."

"He is," I answer. Snarling, Hank moves forward and I make no move to stop him. "Get the hell away from me."

"Fine. Whatever." The trucker slowly walks backward

until his boots hit the sidewalk. From there, he turns and jogs back to his truck. Only when the perv's locked inside his cab does Hank stop growling. Still, his eyes never leave the truck, and my muscles refuse to unwind.

"Fuck," I whisper.

Hank doesn't move, his body rigid. It's then I notice how much he's grown in the last couple of weeks, how the chubby puppy has become lost to the lean dog before me. I can't help but mourn for the innocent baby he was—the puppy who loved everyone, until he was kicked this afternoon. Now, because of me, he knows the world holds people who will hurt him.

This realization reaffirms my decision to leave. Would the same thing happen to Harper if I stayed? How much pain would I bring to her life just by existing in it? I won't risk her innocence to find out.

No. As much as it feels like I'm ripping my own heart out, the best thing I can do for Lane and Harper's lives is to leave them behind.

I glance down at the phone still clutched in my white-knuckled grip. Thanks to the trucker, I can't stay here. I scroll through my numbers until I find the name I'm searching for. I can only hope she answers, that despite all the things I've lost tonight, I still have a friend.

Chapter Thirty-Five

Lane

My phone's ringtone cuts through the music blasting from my truck speakers, thanks to Bluetooth. A glance at my dash shows my sister's number on the screen. Grinding my teeth together, I hesitate a second before answering. I know Em's going to want all the details of what happened between Ash and me, and that's not really something I feel like rehashing at the moment.

Still, the responsible father in me can't *not* answer if there's a chance my daughter might need me.

"Lane?" Em's worried voice filters through the speakers and fills the cab.

"Yeah?" I check my rearview mirror before switching lanes. I've been driving aimlessly now for more than an hour, circling the city in hopes of finding a fraction of peace between the asphalt and diesel fumes. But the open roadway that usually calms my nerves fills me with growing unease.

"I know where she is," Em says.

My chest pulls tight. "Yeah, me too. She's probably a third of the way to Atlanta by now. And if it's all the same to you, I'd rather not talk about it right now."

Em's quiet a minute before answering. "Yeah. Okay. But she's nowhere near Atlanta. She's stranded at a rest stop about forty minutes south. She ran out of gas and called me for help. I thought maybe you could—"

"No." I grip the steering wheel so tight my knuckles burn. "Whatever you're thinking, just no. I can't get involved. We…I…we're just done. If you need to help her, I'll come get Harper. You at your apartment?"

"Really, Lane? You're just going to let her get away without a fight?"

"She asked me to let her go." The image of Ash naked and tethered surfaces in my mind. *I'm yours.* The memory of her voice swirls like honey inside my head and I shudder. "I promised her if she asked me to let her go, I would."

Emily snorts. "Fine. So you let her go. That doesn't mean you shouldn't tell her how you feel."

I shake my head even though I know she can't see me.

"Honestly, Em. I don't know how the fuck I feel."

"That's bullshit. I'm an outside party and even I can tell that you're crazy about her, and she's crazy about you. She's freaked right now. She told me on the phone about her stepdad showing up and then Harper—"

"Exactly," I cut in. "Harper is my world. If Ashlyn can't handle that, she has no place in my life."

Emily gives an impatient sigh. "That's not fair. You're asking this poor girl to be understanding when you haven't exactly been upfront with the information."

I say nothing, ignoring the gnawing of guilt inside my gut.

"Besides," she continues, "Ash isn't leaving because she can't share you with your daughter, she's leaving because she doesn't want to hurt her."

"What? That doesn't make sense. How would she hurt her?"

"I think she's worried she's not good enough to be a role model or something. I'm not really sure. That's why I think you should go and talk to her."

"Em, that's really not a good idea." Even as I say the words, I can feel my resolve cracking. Every muscle in my body, every nerve, every cell is screaming for me to find her and take her home where she belongs. Because fuck if I don't feel it in my heart—she belongs with me.

"Really, Lane? Because isn't this rescuing shit kinda your thing? Isn't it what you live for?"

I remember Dad's face in the moments before his death, so pale and tired beneath the oxygen mask. For the first time in my life, his iron grip was limp in my own. *Take care of the family.* Even though he didn't have the strength to voice the words himself, they were there, written in his eyes.

Take care of the family.

And Ash is mine. I felt it the second our eyes first locked, and something long asleep inside me finally stirred. I want her like no one else. From the moment I carried her out of the party, I knew I had to protect her. When I grabbed her keys to lure her inside the apartment, I knew I had to take care of her, and when she gave herself to me and we came together, melting beneath the sheets, I knew I had to love her.

Keeping one hand on the steering wheel, I run another through my hair as I search the roadway for an exit. I wish I could snap my fingers and evaporate the distance between us. I was an idiot to let her get this far.

"Where's she at, Em?" I ask.

"*Why?*" she asks, her voice suddenly coy.

"You know why. I'm going to get her and bring her home."

What should have been a forty-minute drive I make in thirty. Risky, because Dad was a city cop, so I don't have any state trooper friends to get me out of a ticket. But fuck if I care. What's a couple hundred dollars when Ash is involved?

I take the exit ramp to the rest stop, my muscles loosening when I catch sight of the blue Jetta parked under the streetlight. Instead of parking next to her, I decide to park at the opposite end of the lot so my diesel's rumble doesn't give me away. I can use the extra moments to think—especially when I haven't figured out what to say to her, or how to convince her to come back with me.

I'm not exactly an expert on getting women to stick around.

The muscles in my neck are sore from clenching my jaw the entire way over here. What if this is all for nothing? What if I'm not enough to make her stay?

As I approach her car, I pass two truckers hanging around outside their cabs, smoking. I catch a snippet of their conversation.

"—sweet little piece of ass," one of them says.

"Yeah," the other agrees. "But rigid as a two-by-four. I bet a good pounding would make her pliable."

They both chuckle.

I freeze. A rush of heat rolls through me. I'm not sure how I know, but I'm certain they're talking about Ash.

Fingers curling into fists, I turn and stride toward the men. They don't notice me until I'm almost upon them. I don't know if they can feel the anger radiating off of me, or if it's because I'm staring at them with murder in my eyes, but both men exchange uneasy glances after I stop in front of them.

"You guys talking about that girl in the blue car over there?" I motion to Ash's car with a jut of my chin.

"Don't bother," the one with the beer belly says, extinguishing his stub on the bottom of his boot. "She's real uptight. I tried to help her out, offered her some money, but apparently she's a stuck up bitch."

Before I realize what I'm doing, I've got the guy's shirt twisted in my hands. I slam him against the side of his truck with a satisfying *thwack*. "Don't you dare talk about her that way. You so much as look at her, or any girl for that matter, and I find out about it? I'll beat you down to within an inch of your life, got that?"

"Easy, man," the guy behind me says. He touches my shoulder and I release my grip before whirling around.

The second guy is quicker. He jumps out of my reach before I can grab for him.

"The same goes for you," I say.

The guy holds his hands up. "All right, man. Whatever you say. We don't want any trouble."

"And you think any girl does? Especially from the likes

of you?" I stalk toward him, my hands knotted into tight fists.

"Jeez, buddy. Just take it easy. What's it to you, anyway?"

I raise my fist. "Not an *it*. A *she*. And she's everything."

My muscles twinge from the strain of holding back, so badly do I want to plow my fist into these guys' faces to keep them from looking at another girl ever again. The thought is so enticing I almost let go.

"Lane?"

Ash's voice is like a cool breeze winding through me. The red flooding my vision only seconds ago fades.

She's standing on the sidewalk across the parking lot, staring at me, a can of Sprite in one hand and Hank's leash in the other. The dog strains against the nylon tether to get to me, his tail waving furiously. "What the hell are you doing here? I talked to Em and she said…" She frowns before a flicker of realization flashes through her eyes. "Oh." She presses her lips into a tight line. "*Em*. I should have known."

"Yes. Em called me and told me you were in trouble." Abandoning my plan to beat the two truckers into bloody mash, I stride across the parking lot toward her, her eyes growing larger the closer I come. "Things happened so quickly between us earlier, I just wanted a chance to talk to you before you—" I can't bring myself to say the word *leave*, as if by just speaking it I might make it happen. "Before you do whatever you need to do."

I stop in front of her, so close I can smell the apple of her perfume, so close I can touch her if I want. But I don't. I won't do anything to hold her back if she really wants to be free. Still, the desire to reach for her, to take her in my arms, encircles me like steel wire.

"Lane…" She doesn't approach, but she doesn't move away, either. "You shouldn't have come. I've already said what I needed to say. My mind's made up."

Her words feel like a slap. I force myself not to flinch. "That's fine. I'm not here to make you do anything you don't want to do, Ash. If you need to go, I get it, even though I'll be miserable every second you're gone."

Her face softens. "Lane, I've given this a lot of thought—"

"I wouldn't expect anything less," I say, cutting her off. "By now I've come to realize you don't jump into anything impulsively. Well, except for tattoos of ex-boyfriends."

She frowns and touches the typewriter on her arm.

"I just want to make sure," I continue, "that before you leave, you're seeing things from every angle. I don't want you to go, Ash. But I'm also not going to make you stay." I reach into my pocket and pull out a hundred-dollar bill. "For you. Should be more than enough to get you where you're going."

Her eyes are transfixed on the money. "It is. Actually, it's too much. I can't take that from you, Lane."

I shake my head. "Oh, I'm not giving it to you, Ash. You have to do something for me, first.

She places a hand on her hip and eyes me skeptically. "What's that?"

"You need to listen."

Chapter Thirty-Six

Ashlyn

A frown pulls tight across my face. I'm so tired of being manipulated. "And if I say no?"

He shrugs. "I'll still give you the money. I was just hoping you could hear me out. After all, you got to say what you needed to, but I never did.

The frown melts from my lips. He's right. I did run out on him pretty quickly. And after what we've been through together, don't I at least owe him this? It's not like he can change my mind or anything. "Fine. I'll listen to you, but it's not for the money. Which, by the way, I'm going to pay back as soon as I get to Atlanta."

"Fair enough." Lane grabs my hand and presses the bill into it. Our skin grazes and it's enough to send a shock of warmth jolting through me. Quickly, I jerk free from his grasp before the heat can travel to my head and melt what little resolve I have left.

If Lane notices, he doesn't say anything. Instead, he jams his hands into his back pocket. "Driving here, I was trying to figure out what to say to you, how I could possibly convince you not to go. I had all these words planned." He laughs softly. "Hundreds and hundreds of words. But now that I'm here with you standing in front of me, only four words come to mind: stay with me, Ash."

I feel as if he's ripped through my chest and dug into my heart. I open my mouth to protest, but he doesn't give me the chance.

"I already know what you're going to say—that your leaving is for the best. Em told me on the phone you don't think you're good enough to be a part of Harper's life. But nothing could be further from the truth."

I make a noise to interrupt, but he keeps going.

"You're absolutely amazing. Having met your stepdad today, I'm starting to understand what life must have been like for you growing up. I think most kids in your situation would have crumbled, but not you. You flourished. You became this amazing, strong, hard-working woman—a girl who doesn't depend on other people to take care of her. You became exactly the kind of role model I always hoped Harper would have."

His words hit me like darts. I don't know why he's saying these things to me—words that can't possibly be true. Staying will only hurt him and his daughter in the long run. Why can't he see that? What do I have to do to show him?

I don't deserve him. The selfish part of me, the part that refuses to give up, refuses to speak the words out loud. Still, I know they're true. I turn away, shame burning through me like a wash of flames. I take a step toward my car, but he grabs my arm, his grip loose around my wrist, making it easy for me to break away if I want—but I don't. I know the right thing is to let him go, but I'm not strong enough. Maybe I'll never be strong enough.

"I'm going to hurt you, Lane. I don't want to hurt you."

He pulls me toward him and I don't resist—can't resist. "The only way you'll hurt me is if you leave."

I feel my resolve crumbling by the second. I turn toward him but keep my gaze locked on the ground. The last thing I need is to look at his face and fall into his eyes and drown in their dark depths.

"Stay," he says, his voice soft.

I can't help myself. I look up and sink into the dark pools of his irises. I never stood a chance. From the moment I first saw him, I knew he was bad news. And he is, because for the first time in ten years, I can feel the wall around my heart crumbling and pain flooding through. Tears well in my eyes, burning as they spill over my lashes.

Lane reaches a hand to brush them away, but I step back before he can. There is so much pain in my tears, so much shame. The last thing I want is for Lane to take that from me. My hurt is mine, and mine alone. Why can't he see that? Why doesn't he understand he's better off without me?

"I-I'm no good for you," I stammer.

His hand falls to his side, and he shakes his head. "Why do you think that?"

"Because I'm broken! You deserve someone better, someone who knows how to love without fear, someone who won't hurt you or your daughter."

His jaw tightens. "Damn it, Ash, you're not broken.

Broken things can't be fixed. I hate that someone hurt you, Ash, that someone lied to you and made you believe you're not worth anything. But that's not true. You're worth *everything* to me. You say you can't love without fear? Join the club. I'm fucking terrified right now, Ash. I'm standing in a truck stop, baring my heart to you, knowing full well you can destroy it. But I don't care. To me, you're worth the risk.

My throat tightens, making it nearly impossible to swallow. "What if—"

"What if it doesn't work?" he asks. "What if a meteor falls from the sky and lands on us? What if the sun burns out? There are a million *what if's,* Ash, but there are only two I care about—only two that matter. *What if* we don't try? *What if* you walk away right now and I lose one of the best things to ever happen to me?"

The tears are falling freely now. I attempt to wipe them away with the back of my hand but more cascade down my cheek. What he's said resonates inside me. I've never felt the way I feel about Lane, and I really can't see myself feeling this way about anyone else. Because there's only one Lane, and he's standing right in front of me, asking me to stay. How am I supposed to walk away? How *can* I walk away?

I choke back a sob. Still, there's his daughter to think about. What is she going to think of me? I'm not a mother, nor do I want to be one—at least not until I get my shit together. "What about Harper?"

"I'm not asking you to be anything," Lane says, as if reading my mind. "Harper is a major part of my life, so being with me also means being with her."

"But what if—?"

"We'll take it one day at a time. I'll get the apartment

fixed up and I'll slowly introduce the two of you. I think you are going to love each other."

Having met his little girl, I already think she's pretty great. I wish I was so sure she would think the same about me. Still, maybe it is worth a shot.

"We can agonize over this forever, Ash," Lane says. "We can dissect every possible outcome and brace for the worst. A million things can go wrong—I know that. But we only need one thing to go right. And we're right, Ash, the two of us together. I can feel it. I'm not perfect, and I know this won't be easy. But I'm willing to take a chance if you are."

I bite my lip, letting his words roll through me. He's right about all the things that can go wrong. Still, I can't deny how much I yearn to be with him. Even now I have to ball my fingers into fists to keep from grabbing him and closing the distance between us.

We only need one thing to go right.

It seems foolish not to try, not when everything I've ever wanted—a man who cares about me, stability, a family—is right in front of me. "Okay." I grin. "I can't promise this will work, but I'm willing to try."

He smiles back, and it electrifies my blood. "That's all I'm asking." He lifts his arm, his fingers stretched toward mine. "Let's get the hell out of here, okay?"

"Okay." I slip my hand into his, and immediately a warmth settles through me. I'm safe. "Where will be go?"

He cocks his head to the side as if the answer should be obvious.

"Home."

Chapter Thirty-Seven

Ashlyn

Six months later

Harper laughs as I squeeze a river of chocolate sauce onto my ice cream. It dribbles over the bowl onto Lane's kitchen table. Despite a few muscle twinges, I leave the chocolate where it is.

Lane's kitchen is roughly the size of my entire apartment. Even so, Lane, Harper, and I have squished our chairs together so we're huddled at the table. I love it—the closeness, the sense of family. For the first time in my life, I feel like I belong.

Even Hank appears blissfully happy, curled at our feet, his eyes fluttering in sleep. He doesn't even mind the large bows and princess bling collars Harper insists on dressing him in. I haven't the heart to tell her Hank's not a girl.

"Hey!" Lane tries to snatch the chocolate syrup but I swing the bottle away before he can grab it. "Save some for the rest of us!"

"It's my celebration party." I quickly squeeze out several more dollops before he can stop me. "That means I can have as much chocolate sauce as I want. Isn't that right, Harper?"

Giggling, she shakes a jar of sprinkles over her sundae. "That's how it works."

Lane folds his arms over his chest. "Jeez, you get one lousy publishing contract and suddenly you're queen of the world." He winks at me, turning my insides to jelly. "Seriously, though, we're so proud of you."

"Thanks." Smiling, I scoop up a large bite of ice cream and shove it into my mouth. The publishing contract still feels like a dream, and maybe it will until I hold the book in my hand. Granted, my book of poems didn't sell for much, but I didn't do it for the money so much as to prove I could. The always-critical voice in my head has grown quieter. For now, that's enough.

Harper places her spoon in her bowl and looks at me, her face suddenly serious. "Now that you're famous, are you going to leave us?"

"What?" I freeze mid-bite and quickly put my own spoon down. "Why would you even think that?"

Her gaze falls to her lap and she shrugs. "Sometimes people leave."

Her words stab at my heart like pinpricks. "Yes. That's true. But I'm not going anywhere. I'm going to stay as long as you want me around." Without thinking, I add, "I love you guys." My eyes flutter wide and I quickly glance at Lane. Even though we're together almost every night, and I can't picture my life without him or Harper, we haven't spoken the *L* word yet. And now that I have, it's too late to take it back. When he came to get me at the rest stop, we both agreed to take things slowly. Now I have to wonder if I just screwed it all up. Terror rips through me and I try to sneak a peek at Lane to gauge his reaction.

He won't meet my eyes. Instead, he stands suddenly, the legs of his chair squealing against the ceramic tile. "Excuse me." Before I can respond, he marches from the room.

Shit. What have I done? My pulse beats a nervous rhythm. No longer hungry, I push my ice cream away.

Harper appears not to notice the change in mood because she finishes her ice cream in several large bites. After licking the spoon clean, she jumps out of her chair. "Can I play with Hank in the backyard?"

"Sure, Honey," I respond absently. Where the hell did Lane go? Did my confession freak him out? If so, should I go back to my apartment above his studio to give him some time? Oh God, what if I just messed everything up?

Harper grabs a tennis ball off the counter and, as if by magic, Hank's eyes pop open and he scrambles to his feet. The two of them charge out the French doors and into the backyard, leaving me alone.

I suck in a long breath, trying to relieve the tightness in my chest. It doesn't work. So I stand, my legs feeling like gelatin, and clear the dishes from the table. It's the least I can do before I leave.

After placing the tub of ice cream back in the freezer, I turn and nearly collide with Lane. I gasp and stumble back against the stainless steel refrigerator. The intensity in Lane's eyes unsettles me, because serious conversations seldom go well for me.

"Don't do that." He grabs my wrist and pulls me away from the fridge. "It's your party. You shouldn't be cleaning up. I got it."

I allow him to lead me into the center of the kitchen, my footsteps slow and unsure. "Where did you go?"

He ignores my question and instead asks, "Do you really love me? Do you really love us?"

Shit. This is exactly what I was afraid of, and I curse my stupid, blathering tongue. Lane and I agreed we'd ease slowly into this relationship for Harper's sake, in case things didn't work out. And what do I do? I open my stupid mouth and declare my love—not exactly slow or subtle.

Still, I won't lie. I do love them—both of them. My time spent with Lane and Harper has been the best in my life and I can't imagine an existence without them. If Lane thinks we're moving too fast, and wants to spend some time apart because of it, I'll understand. His protectiveness of his daughter is just another reason I love him.

I swallow hard before I answer. "I do."

His lips are on mine, hard and fast. His fingers weave into my hair, tying me to him. I give a cry of surprise, which he swallows, before I melt into the hardness of his chest. Heat simmers low inside me, before spilling over, surging through my limbs into my fingers and toes.

His kiss is deep and urgent, with little nips of teeth on my bottom lip, before he floods my mouth with the heat of his tongue. I tilt my head back, twist my arms around his neck, and give in, wanting all of him, wanting him to take all of me.

Lane reaches behind his neck, grabs my wrists, and

gently pries them apart, breaking our kiss in the process.

I blink up at him, my lips tingling and hungry for more. I lean forward and he steps back.

"Wait a sec."

Confused—and slightly hurt—I try to retreat, but he won't let go of my wrists, so I can't escape.

Lane shifts his weight from foot to foot and licks his lips. For the first time since we've met, he looks nervous. "I want to give you something." He releases my wrists, reaches into his back pocket, withdraws a small black box, and holds it out to me.

A lump wedges inside my throat and I wobble on my feet. "Is that…is that—?"

"No." He shakes his head. "It's not an engagement ring. I thought you had enough going on with school and writing. But when you're done with school, and you're ready, we can…" He shrugs. "If you want."

I can't help but smile. I've never seen Lane looks so vulnerable, and damned if he isn't adorable. "It's a promise ring? I thought only teenagers did that?"

"Fuck. I don't know what it is." He sweeps his fingers through his hair. "It's just an 'I love you' ring, okay?"

My breath catches in my throat. "You love me?"

His expression turns serious, the heat from his eyes melting right through me. "From the moment I laid eyes on you. You drive me crazy in a way no one has before. I can't imagine my life without you. I just…wanted you to know that." He pauses. "Now please take the ring. The damn dog has more bling than you, and that embarrasses me as a man. It means I'm not doing my job."

I laugh through the tears welling in my eyes and take the

small box from him. "Lane, you didn't have to do this. You know I'm not that kind of girl, right? I don't need you to buy me anything to prove you care."

"I never said you did. But you deserve it. You deserve this and so much more. I want to give you things, Ash. I want to protect you, take care of you, and make you happy. I want to give you the life you deserve, and I want to love you forever—if you'll have me."

So many emotions rise inside me, swirling and expanding, rendering me unable to speak. With shaking hands, I open the small box. Inside, the most gorgeous ring I've ever seen waits for me. It's a daisy. Somehow he knew about my love of the little flower that grows strong in the face of adversity. White oval diamonds surround a single circular yellow diamond on a thin gold band. My breath stills in my chest. But that's okay. Because in this moment, I don't need to breathe, I don't need air—I don't need anything to stay alive except Lane.

"It's beautiful," I finally whisper.

He smiles. "So you like it?"

"I love it."

He arches an eyebrow. "So now you're just going to throw that word around? And here I was thinking I was special."

I swat him with my free hand. "You're an idiot."

"So this is how it is? I buy you jewelry, and you immediately turn into a prima donna?"

"Hey!" I move to swat him again, but he catches my wrist in midair and pulls me against him.

The scent of him, citrus and warm, fills my lungs. My knees weaken and the familiar ropes of desire ripple through me.

"Do you have homework tonight?" he asks, his voice low. "Do you have any exams you need to study for?"

It takes me several tries before I'm able to speak past the lump in my throat. "No. I took my last final yesterday."

"So there's no reason to go back to your apartment tonight?" He winds an arm around my waist, pulling me tight. My pulse races.

"No."

He lowers his lips to my ear. His breath is hot on my neck and I shiver. "Then don't go home. Stay. Be mine tonight." His fingers press into my skin, claiming me, and a burn ignites deep inside me because I want to be claimed. "Stay." He accentuates his request by grabbing my hips and grinding the swell inside his jeans against me.

My breathing quickens, and my muscles coil with need. "But we agreed Harper—"

"Loves you," he finishes. His lips brush against my ear, sending tingling waves coursing down my body. "And so do I."

His words go straight to my heart where they burn pleasantly, like the lingering ache of a tattoo. God, will I ever tire of hearing him say them?

"It's almost Harper's bedtime," Lane continues. "After I get her to bed I can show you how much."

I grin and reach for his belt. "You really want me to stay that badly?"

His answer is a noise that's half groan, half growl.

With nimble fingers, I quickly unfasten his buckle and slide the leather strap from his belt loops in one fluid motion.

He leans back and arches an eyebrow seductively. Suddenly I have the crazy urge to lick his eyebrow, among other things. “What are you doing?”

“You want me to stay?” I fold the belt and snap the leather together making it crack. I want him to take me like he did before, to claim me as his before driving me to the edge and back again. “You’re going to have to make me.”

“That’s how it’s going to be?” His grin is devilish. He slides his hand into my hair and pulls my head back, forcing me to look up at him.

The thrill of being ensnared shoots through me and I gasp.

“If you want me to make you, I’ll make you.” The low rumble of his chest reverberates into my skin. “Just remember to say *when.*”

About the Author

At seventeen Cole found herself homeless with only a beat-up Volkswagen Jetta and a bag of Goodwill clothing to her name. The only things that got her through the nights she spent parked in truck stops and cornfields were the stacks of books she checked out from the library along with her trusty flashlight. Because of the reprieve these books gave her from her troubles, Cole vowed to become a writer so she could provide the same escape to readers who needed a break the reality of their own lives.

www.colegibsen.com

Also by Cole Gibsen...

LIFE UNAWARE

Made in the USA
Lexington, KY
01 February 2016